MYSTERIOUS PAPERCUTS

A Die-Cut Cozy Mystery Series

JUDITH DICKENSON
ACKARET

JAT Trax Studios

Judith Dickenson Ackaret

Published by JAT Trax Studios
PO Box 230151, Tigard, OR 97281-0151

First printing, May 2021

Cover design by DLR Cover Designs
www.dlrcoverdesigns.com
Etsy.com/shop/DLRCoverDesigns

ISBN-13: 978-1-7328821-4-0

eISBN-13: 978-1-7328821-5-7

This book is dedicated to
Jean Edwards, Founder of Edwards Center, Inc.
www.edwardscenter.org

Acknowledgments

Here we are at Book 3 of the Die-Cut Cozy Mystery series. Time has flown for me since writing Book 1, Scored for Life, in 2018. My next book of this series will be on a Christmas theme. I am already setting up an outline in my head for this fun next chapter in the series.

You will notice that I dedicated this book to Jean Edwards of Edwards Center, Inc. (www.edwardscenter.org) She is the founder of a wonderful family-based organization that provides residential, vocational, educational, and recreational services to adults with developmental disabilities. Even after the 2015 passing of my sister, Donna, who had Down Syndrome and lived in one of the twenty houses for over a decade, the people at Edwards Center still treat me and my other sister as family. So, here I say with great gratitude, a big 'thank you'. Jean, you have a heart of gold.

Mom, how could I have written books without your love and support? You live life your way and have taught us girls to be compassionate and never take 'no' for an answer. Thank you for all the laughter we enjoyed together. I love you so much.

To my dear friend, Sue, who has been pushing me to finish this book so she could be the first to read it...I give a huge thanks! I know this past year has been a challenge, but I cherish our conversations and time together. You were placed on this Earth to be a guiding light. Keep the light lit and never give up. Thanks for your edits.

My sister, Deborah, is another person who never gives up. This last year has been a challenge for her, but she seemed to roll with the punches. You wanted your hair to grow back curly, and look...it did! Thanks for all the support and trying to get me to those marketing classes.

Not every mistake is caught in editing, but if anyone is close to perfection in editing, it is my sister-in-law, Debbie Dodd. This time I worked hard to have few as possible edits by the time this book made its way to you, Debbie. Thank you so much for spending the time between quilting to get the red pen out and mark up my manuscript! You make my books better for it.

Then there is my husband, Jerry, whom people comment is a lot like Donald. Well, that's probably because Donald is written like Jerry in some respects. Jerry makes me laugh, and I love him with all my heart. Thank you, my love, for all the technical corrections.

Thank you to my family and friends whose names I have borrowed (mostly without their permission) to provide my book with colorful characters.

And lastly, thank you to all the people who have encouraged me to keep writing.

Author

Judith has been writing from the moment she learned how to put letters on paper. In grade school she wrote and directed plays, created comic books, and teamed up with her friend to write short stories. Her passion was to work behind the scenes in the police field and after some years in the accounting world, Judith was hired by a police department, spending the majority of her career in the Criminal Investigations Division as a Records Technician. In that position, she became a Composite Artist, transcriber, and a youth peer court advisor. Judith's love of paper-crafting has exploded from a small desk area to a full blown two-room studio. (Some of you can relate!) A line of vintage greeting cards and love of box designing is her current distraction from writing. At some point, she wants to write a sit-com.

Along with their three adorable cats, Judith and Jerry (husband and Systems Reliability Engineer) spend a lot of time watching whales from their home on the Central Oregon Coast in the Pacific Northwest.

Books by Judith Dickenson Ackaret

Scored for Life
Glued to See You
Mysterious Papercuts

Reviews

A BUDDING NEW AUTHOR

"This is the second book for this author and it was as good as the first, if not better. Judith kept my interest throughout the book. Characters were great and it was hard to put down, as I wanted to continually know what was going on. AND, the ending...I turned to the last page and got a surprise. Can't wait until the next book!" ... *Amazon review for Glued to See You*

GREAT READ!

"Loved this book as much as the first one. I loved the way #2 took off where #1 left off! Judith is an excellent story teller!" ... *Amazon review for Glued to See You*

CHAPTER 1

Sunday Early Morning Hours

Annie Weston Harper had spent the last hour listening to her mother try and convince her family to go to bed. Instead, the family continued to talk of venturing into the basement of the house to view the secret vault room inside of Annie and Donald's home. It was shortly after midnight, and the group found themselves still interested in what Annie and Donald had found in their house weeks earlier.

"I've been there millions of times and I never saw a secret room," said Marie, the twenty-four-year old woman with Down Syndrome. "I want to see it."

Four weeks ago, a court granted Annie guardianship of Marie, when Marie's then guardian was found dead in her home. Helen Harper had been Annie and Stella's neighbor across the street who, upon her death, left Annie to inherit her house and business, R&H Enterprises.

Marie yawned and brushed back her long blond hair, which had been up in a bun earlier in the evening during the wedding of Donald and Annie. Marie had not changed out of her pink princess dress and tiara, which she wore as the flower girl.

"Just look," Stella said, pointing toward Marie. "Marie is tired. We should all go to bed now and let the honeymooners have their night."

"I don't know about the others, Mom," Dan started, "but I am a bit curious about this vault Annie and Donald talked about. If Lizzy doesn't mind, I'd love to see it."

Dan turned to look at Lizzy, his bride of mere hours as a result of an impulsive proposal during Annie's wedding. Annie had encouraged Dan to propose to Lizzy at her own wedding. Lizzy was Annie's best friend. In fact, Annie introduced her brother, Dan, to Lizzy weeks ago. They began dating and fell in love. Annie suspected her mother had planned the entire double wedding scenario when Stella just happened to have a wedding certificate in Lizzy and Dan's names.

"I vote we all go downstairs and see this room now," Lizzy said, placing her hand on Dan's shoulder. "We have the rest of the weekend to have a short honeymoon. I believe Mom and Dad are planning to send Dan and me to Italy for a romantic honeymoon later. Annie and Donald are planning a honeymoon at Disneyland. We won't be spoiling our honeymoons."

"We have a 'yes' vote from Marie, Dan, and Lizzy," Donald reported. "Dad? Mom? What do you think?"

Rand Harper looked to his wife, Patty. They had arrived a week ago to attend the wedding. Patty nodded. "We're in."

Rand's brother, Robert Harper, had been killed shortly before, when his car had been forcefully pushed off the highway and over a cliff. His widow, Helen Harper, passed away four weeks ago, leaving a vast fortune to Donald and Annie.

"Sorry, Mom." Annie said to Stella. "It looks like you've been outvoted."

"Alright," Stella said in concession. "I will admit, I am a bit curious myself. Let's go now."

Donald and Annie led the group to the office, where Donald held the door open while everyone filed into the room. When he closed and locked the door, Dan gave Donald a questioning look.

"We want to keep this hidden area of the house a secret from anyone outside of this family," Donald said, addressing the group. "I hope everyone is in agreement."

Everyone nodded their heads in agreement.

"Am I inside this family?" Marie whispered to Annie, taking Annie's hand in hers.

"Of course you are, Marie." Annie said, squeezing Marie's hand.

"I will keep the secret," Marie said softly.

Donald moved to the bookcase on the right-hand wall from where they had entered the office door. With one hand, he moved the shelving unit deftly down the wall, making very little noise. A large office safe appeared first, followed by a doorway, as the unit moved aside easily. A light automatically turned on, illuminating a carpeted stairway leading down. Donald motioned Annie to lead the group down the stairs while he slid the bookcase back over the opening.

When Annie reached the bottom step, she could have sworn it moved. She made a mental note to talk to Donald later about checking the step.

"This is it?" Dan asked, as he descended into the room and looked around. The room was small, with a love seat and two tan overstuffed chairs arranged in a sitting area. Paintings of landscapes were displayed on each wall.

"Just wait," Annie said, as she moved to a large painting that extended from the floor to the ceiling. She located a switch behind the ornate frame and opened the painting like it was a door. Everyone stepped to the side to view what was behind the painting. There stood a large vault door inset into the wall. Annie stood in front of a keypad and secretly entered the code numbers. She stepped back and Donald turned the large wheel until they heard a click.

As Donald opened the heavy door, light flooded a large room. Annie could hear gasps of amazement as she began walking through the doorway. After crossing over the threshold, she stepped aside and allowed the group to enter. It was moments before anyone spoke. Annie watched as Dan and Lizzy took in the spectacular size of the room, as well as the contents before them.

"These painting are of great value," Stella remarked as she walked down the center of the room looking at various paintings on display panels. "Is that a Picasso?"

"Mom," Annie said, as she moved close to her mother. "I believe these are the paintings Helen left for you. I'm sorry I did not mention them to you sooner, but so much has been happening lately."

Tears appeared in Stella's eyes. Helen was her dear friend living across the street for many years. Stella had been a librarian in town, and while Helen never worked outside of the home, she was head of many community charities and events and a beloved member of the Bridgewater Harbor residents.

"They're all yours, Mom." Annie said, putting her arm around her mother.

"I wouldn't begin to know what to do with these paintings," Stella said. "I think it's best to leave them here for now. We can figure this out later."

"Good idea," Donald agreed. "The vault room has a humidity control system which will keep the paintings safe. You're welcome to visit your paintings any time you wish."

Stella laughed and wiped a tear from her face.

Annie noticed Dan looking over the two large safes embedded into the wall in the vault room. One safe was labeled 'R' and the other standing next to it was labeled 'H'.

"I take it Robert and Helen had their own safes?" Dan asked.

"It appears so," Donald answered. "Annie and I have only been through them once." Donald turned to Annie, who was now blushing at the thought of the first time they opened and viewed the contents of the safe, and what had happened between them afterward.

"The safe marked with an 'R' is actually filled with currency and Krugerrands," Annie pointed out.

"Krugerrands?" Lizzy asked, showing unexpected interest. "They could be worth a lot of money."

"Can we take a look inside?" asked Dan. "I've never seen a Krugerrand in person before."

Donald opened the safe. Dan gave a low whistle as he moved forward to view the neatly placed trays of coins. He picked up one coin and turned it over in his hand, staring intently.

Close at Dan's side, Lizzy asked, "How many Krugerrands are there?"

Lizzy worked in Annie's paper crafting shop, Ocean Loads of Paper, for several years, and just became the manager of R&H Enterprises. She divided her work hours between the shop and the management of two buildings which Annie inherited from Helen. These buildings housed the numerous boutique shops in the main part of town.

"We haven't counted everything in the safes yet, but as soon as life slows down, Donald and I plan to take an inventory of the vaults' contents," Annie explained.

Just recently, Annie found out more about her business associate, when Lizzy revealed a wealthy upbringing. Lizzy's father had insisted on an arranged marriage for his daughter, as the merging of families would further build his company. An argument with her father over the issue left Lizzy on her own with no support from her family.

Annie's musings were interrupted as Dan placed the coin back in the tray and stood up. Donald moved to close and lock the safe. Annie heard them talking, but her attention was directed to where Stella and Marie were standing. Marie was pointing out where the names of the artists were displayed on the works of art.

Lizzy and Dan turned their attention to a striking painting among the display of paintings in the center of the room. Annie began to follow, but then looked up to where Patty was standing. She noticed Patty looking at a shadow box displaying a photo of a woman holding a new born baby dressed in a blue knit outfit. The same outfit was displayed next to the photo in the shadow box frame. Patty stood with her back to Annie. Rand approached Patty and put his arm around her. They both stood motionless, viewing the display.

Annie walked up behind the Harpers and stood quietly. Donald joined her, standing behind his father. Annie could tell Donald was uneasy, unsure of whether he should reveal he knew he was adopted. It was newfound information for him.

It became clear he was not comfortable talking to his parents about it when Donald cleared his throat, causing Patty and Rand to suddenly turn and face him. Annie saw tears welling up in Patty's eyes. Their uneasiness prompted Annie to be the first to speak.

"When Donald and I noticed this display box, I couldn't help but think how much his Aunt Helen loved him. I recognized Helen's ring in the photo. You must have all been so close at one time.," Annie said.

Patty, sending a sharp look to Rand, took a deep breath and relaxed. With a forced smile she said, "We owe a lot to Robert and Helen."

"I know that Donald loved his Aunt Helen and Uncle Robert, but his love for his mother and father is so much deeper. Aside from my own folks, I would have to say you both make the top of my list for the best parents ever," Annie said, realizing that tears were beginning to sting her eyes. Donald took Annie's hand and squeezed gently. This was definitely an awkward situation.

"Look what I've found!" exclaimed Stella from across the room.

Jolted from a tense moment, Annie was glad for her mother's outburst. It was the interruption the group needed to stop Rand and Patty admitting something Annie thought Donald did not yet want to discuss.

Everyone moved toward Stella who was holding up a book, which Annie recognized as one of Helen's journals. She had pulled it from the shelf containing rows of such books. Helen had a separate volume for each year.

"Helen's journals," Stella began. "These books may be the source of a lot of unanswered questions."

"We found Helen's journals earlier," commented Donald. "Annie wanted to read them in order. I believe she has read several of the books."

"Yes," Annie said. "I was hoping to read them first, before anyone else. There may be private entries and I want to respect Helen and what she may have wanted to keep to herself."

"Then why would Helen put down her thoughts in a book that someone might read someday?" asked Dan.

"Journalizing is not necessarily written for others to read," Lizzy stated. "I keep a journal, and it is my way of thinking things through without the high cost of a therapist."

"My mom kept a photo album," Marie said. "She has pictures in it of when she was little, and when I was little, and when I grew up. I like to look at the pictures of mom and me."

"Well, Annie," Stella said, as she carefully placed the book back on the shelf in the spot where she found it. "This is your house. Helen left these things to you. I believe she had a reason to share them with you. If you want any of us to read the books, then you will let us know. But for now, I respect my friend's privacy."

"Thank you, Mom."

Annie did not realize what an emotional visit this would be when she and Donald decided to reveal the vault room. She wanted to finish the tour and decided that it was time to show everyone the drawer with the jewels.

Guiding the group to the counter area of the room, Annie gave a short explanation of what she and Donald discovered. She then pressed her finger on the locking mechanism. Hearing a click, Donald helped to open the drawer.

Everyone drew nearer when Donald pulled the cloth tab on one of the velvet-cased displays. A dozen diamonds glittered in the glow of the lights above. At first people were stunned, but it was Rand who broke the silence.

"I know something about these diamonds."

"Dad?"

"Robert was my brother after all. All his life he chased after wealth. It's why he became a doctor. He thought the life of a doctor in a specialized field would bring him the wealth of the world. And in some instances, it did. He loved his work traveling around the world helping those in need, but there was a greedy side to Robert when it came to wealth."

Rand told the group it was a story for another day. Looking at his watch he announced that it was nearing one-thirty in the morning, and he was tired. Everyone agreed and began filing out of the vault room. Annie and Donald were the last to leave. Donald secured the vault door and moved the painting back in place to hide the whereabouts of the room.

Annie's family remained gathered in the room waiting for Donald to ascend the stairs and slide open the bookcase. Donald took the first step up the stairs and stopped.

"Did that step move?" asked Dan, watching Donald move up the stairs.

"That's what I was thinking," Donald replied. He stepped down, turned and stepped up on the bottom step again.

Dan was leaning over inspecting the stair as Donald put his weight on it. "It seems loose."

Donald got down on his knees and ran his fingers along the base of the step where it connected to the floor. Dan knelt down and did the same. They discovered the edge of a carpeted runner tucking under the step. It was cleverly disguised and somewhat buried in the floor carpeting

"Dad?" Donald asked. "I get the feeling that Uncle Robert liked secret rooms. Do you know anything about hidden rooms in this house?"

"Robert was a very secretive person, even as a kid," Rand responded. "Nothing would surprise me about him."

Rand began examining the wall to the left of the stairway. If there was a secret room, there must be a switch somewhere. Rand lifted the box from a thermostat control unit attached to the wall. Inside the unit was a red button.

"Stand aside boys," Rand instructed. No sooner had he pushed the button when the stairway began lifting upwards.

Annie stood by, watching the stairs move to the ceiling. She maneuvered herself next to Donald at the entrance. Lights illuminated the opening. There was a short passageway under the stairs that took a turn to the left.

"Rand, and anyone else in the group," Dan said. "If you want to call it a night and go to bed, we can lower the stairs and let you out of the room. Otherwise, I think Donald and I need to find out what is down here."

"Are you kidding me?" Rand questioned. "I don't know about the rest of the gang, but I am wide awake now."

"You're not leaving me out of this," Lizzy spoke up. "I am just as curious as you."

"I'm with Lizzy," Stella spoke up. "But this is Annie's house, and the decision should be hers."

"And Donald's," Annie added. "We are married now. We will both make this decision. Donald?"

"I will go along with whatever you decide, sweetheart."

Dan rolled his eyes at Annie, "Annie, are you game?"

"Well," Annie paused as she thought for a moment. "This is the first time that you and Donald wanted me to join you on an adventure." She recalled as kids Donny and Danny would never let her go with them on their adventures. They did not want a girl tagging along.

"Let's do this!" Donald said, taking Annie's hand and entering the corridor. The others followed Dan and Lizzy. Rand was the last to enter the walkway.

Walking down the hallway, Donald and Annie made a left turn into a brightly painted pathway, which led to a small vestibule. Vinyl tiles with black and gray speckles on a white background covered the floor.

Looking straight ahead was a gray steel door. Annie made a mental note to find out where that door led at another time. But now, she wanted to venture further down a staircase off to her left.

Annie followed closely as Donald continued to lead the way downward. She kept a hand on his shoulder as he descended into the unknown. What in the world did Robert build below her house? Annie's mind was reeling

As they reached the bottom of the staircase, Annie noticed ornate yard art adorning the walls, which were painted in soft blue. The room expanded into what was designed to mimic a front yard. Murals of lawn, flowering trees, and images of a street with houses in the distance were depicted in the artwork.

Annie's attention was diverted to Donald as he tripped on the step of what appeared to be a porch. Before them was a wide front porch with a wooden swing, potted silk flower plants, and a large stuffed black dog resembling Laddie. Donald looked to Dan for answers. Dan shrugged his shoulders.

"Should we ring the doorbell?" Donald asked.

"Don't be ridiculous," Dan said. "Nobody lives here."

Donald turned the front doorknob and slowly pushed the door inward. For some reason he was expecting an alarm to sound. They entered through a small foyer area and into the living room, stopping abruptly at the scene before them.

Annie gasped. Lizzy let out a scream and buried her head in Dan's chest. Dan put a protective arm around her. Stella, Marie, and Patty bumped into the group which had stopped before them.

"I'm scared," Marie said, grabbing Stella's arm. Stella stood in disbelief. She was unable to speak.

Seated on a sofa with its back to the foyer area sat a skeleton.

Rand pushed through the standing crowd. Once he made his way through, he stopped between Dan and Donald and stared for a moment.

"Oscar?" Rand shouted. "Buddy, I haven't seen you in a long time!"

CHAPTER 2

Sunday Morning

"Oh, no!" Patty Harper groaned. "Not Oscar."

"Oscar?" Annie questioned Patty. Annie and the group moved further into the living room to where the skeleton was sitting on a sofa. The bony guy held a remote control in one hand and an empty beer bottle in the other hand. The skeleton's legs crossed at the ankles on the coffee table. "Who is Oscar?"

"Rand purchased Oscar as a gift for Robert during medical school," Patty explained.

"Hey, buddy," Rand said, as he sat next to Oscar the skeleton and put his arm around his shoulders. "How have you been?"

Oscar seems to have a smile on his face, Annie observed with amusement. He was also wearing a cotton Hawaiian shirt and khaki pants. Oscar's shoes were missing, Annie discovered when she saw his feet up on the coffee table.

Rand began to tell stories of how Robert would dress Oscar up in a shirt, pants, and baseball cap and drive around town. He continued to tell of times when Robert and Rand would take Oscar to bars and set him on a bar stool with a drink in front of him. It got the attention of the ladies, as Rand put it, giving an obvious wink to Dan and Donald, who laughed at Rand's stories. They wanted to find out more about Oscar and his escapades. Dan and Donald sat in comfortable looking cloth-covered chairs flanking the sofa.

While the men listened to stories of Oscar and his escapades, the ladies decided to take a closer look at the underground home.

Annie looked at the magazines on the coffee table. They dated back only a few months. She went to the fireplace, which appeared to be electric, but looked real all the same. It was white wood with trim. Above the fireplace opening was a panel of white tile.

Lizzy's hand on her shoulder caught Annie's attention. Lizzy pointed to the kitchen area, where they joined Stella, Patty, and Marie who appeared to be opening cupboards, drawers, and the refrigerator. Before Annie stood the most beautiful and modern kitchen she had ever seen. Its color palette was light teal and it had every modern convenience imaginable.

"I could live here," expressed Lizzy with a sigh, turning slowly, taking in the custom-made details of the kitchen. She faced toward the living room and stopped. "Except for the skeleton. He would have to go."

Annie laughed and agreed with Lizzy. "This kitchen looks like it jumped out of a magazine of expensive homes," Annie said in a whisper to Lizzy.

The kitchen sported an island with a small sink, marble counter tops, and drawers with very expensive looking hardware. Lighting over the island, which hung from a rod attached to the ceiling, appeared to be made from hand-blown glass. Stainless kitchen appliances dotted the room. The refrigerator had a computer screen embedded into the door, which sprung to life when Annie touched it, displaying a calendar and the local weather information. A kitchen window, over a double sink in the counter running along one wall, appeared to have a view of the side yard of the house above. An outside camera was obviously set up to display a screen in the window. It was currently dark outside, but she recognized the location, all the same, as the yard was lit by an adjacent street lamp. A panel on the wall controlled the camera. Next to the camera control was a panel with options to change the view to different scenes of weather, from sunshine to snow.

"The food in this refrigerator is probably a month old," Stella claimed, picking up a carton of milk and noticing the expiration date. "Marie, did you know about this place? Did Helen ever show it to you?"

"No," Marie answered. "Sometimes when I came over to visit Aunt Helen, she was not here. Her car was here, but she was not. I looked all over the house. I would go back to my apartment and call her. When she answered, she said she would be right home. When I went back in the house, she was there."

"Do you think Helen was living in this place?" Patty asked Stella.

"It would explain a great deal," Stella responded. "After Robert died, Helen did not like being left alone. Which is curious, because she was alone all the time Robert traveled the world as a doctor."

Looking beyond the kitchen, Annie found a large dining room with a table and chairs. The table was large enough to seat at least ten people. Annie saw French doors leading to what appeared to be the back yard.

Annie turned her attention to the excited conversation coming from the guys. She viewed them stand and walk away to rooms on the far side of the living room. Annie could hear their voices as they conversed enthusiastically over what they found. She walked through the living room to see what all the excitement was about.

"It's a theater room!" announced Rand. "I could get used to watching movies in here. Donald, this should be your guest house."

"Hey! You guys are going to like this," Dan called out from another doorway. Annie watched Dan wander into a room a with a full-size bar. Behind the bar stood two sets of fully stocked shelves. Annie listened to Donald and Dan calling out various expensive brands of liquor with delight. Donald pointed out the painting of a scantily clad woman reclining across a mirror attached to the wall between the two sections of shelves.

"I could live here," Dan said, as he picked up a very expensive bottle of brandy and gave a low whistle.

"You would have to contend with a roommate," Donald said, with a sly smile on his face, his thumb pointing in the direction of the living room where Oscar lounged on the sofa.

"I'm sure Lizzy would be okay with that," Dan said.

"Oh, I'm sure," Donald laughed, as he walked over to his father, who had discovered a coin-operated game to play.

Annie and Lizzy slowly walked into the bar room, taking in the scene before them. Tall tables stood around the room with leather and wood chairs. Looking at the bar, Annie spotted an antique brass cash register sitting on the counter near the entrance to the room. Lizzy, noticing what Annie had her eyes on, hastily walked over to the register and began punching keys. The till opened and Annie stood wide-eyed at the amount of cash in the drawer. Further inspection proved the cash to be play money. Annie surmised it was put there for show.

"Dad?" Donald said, tapping Rand on the shoulder, interrupting his play on a pinball machine located in the corner of the room. "Did you have any idea about this underground house?"

"Your uncle and I had not recently been on the best of terms," Rand said, trying not to miss a play on the machine. "If I'd known about this place, I might have made a better effort to mend our differences."

Annie and Lizzy moved from the bar room to the theater room.

"Wow!" exclaimed Lizzy as she walked through the room, turning around to view every aspect of the space. The back wall showcased expensively framed vintage movie posters.

"This may be our new spot for family movie nights," Annie added, amazed by the ornate design of floor to ceiling curtains, gigantic movie screen, and large leather recliners with attached trays.

"Annie...," Lizzy moved to a wall of curtains and paused. "Do you think we should pull the curtains back and see if there is anything behind them?"

Annie thought for a moment. Was there a room behind the curtains? She was not sure she wanted to find out on her own. She had seen enough scary movies to know that there is always something dangerous behind the curtain.

"Let's ask the guys to check behind the curtains," Annie said. "We can wait here by the doorway."

Lizzy laughed and called out to Dan and the others. When the men entered the room, they had drinks in their hands.

"Really, guys?" Annie said. "Drinking at this hour of the morning?"

"What did you want?" Dan asked, taking a sip from his glass containing a golden liquid.

"We want you to look behind the curtains and see if there's another room or a hidden body, or anything dangerous," Lizzy said.

Taking a quick last gulp of the drink, Dan handed the glass to Lizzy and walked up to the curtains. With the help of Rand and Donald, the men pulled sections of curtains aside, not finding anything of interest.

They moved to the other side of the room. Continuing to move the curtains aside, they came across a door.

Dan turned to look at Lizzy and Annie standing in the doorway. "What are you two afraid of?" Dan laughed.

"Well," Lizzy began. "There happens to be a skeleton in the living room!"

"Oscar?" Rand chuckled. "He wouldn't hurt a fly."

While Rand and Donald held the curtain open, Dan reached for the door and pushed it inward. He pretended that someone had pulled him inside, waving his free arm wildly out the door. Rand and Donald laughed and followed Dan inside the room.

Annie and Lizzy rolled their eyes, and made their way through the theater to the doorway behind the curtains. They peeked inside seeing a storage room with thousands of DVDs and music CDs placed on floor to ceiling storage shelves. Not finding this room all that interesting, the two women walked out of the theater room and back toward the kitchen to catch up with the rest of the group.

♦ ♦ ♦

After inspecting the kitchen and its contents, Stella, Marie, and Patty glanced in at a formal dining room with French doors on the far wall. Continuing, they moved to another section of the house to explore the rooms. Annie and Lizzy followed from a distance taking in the area as they walked. Lights filled a hallway as they moved forward. Artwork decorated the light blue walls. The floor was carpeted, and the white molding ornate and stylish.

Patty opened the door of the first room on the right. She switched on a light and stood in shock. The room was decorated for a young boy. Toys were neatly displayed on shelves around the light blue painted room and photographs in various sizes filled its walls. A comfortable looking easy chair sat nearby a twin-sized bed.

Patty put her hand over her mouth and began to softly cry. It was heartbreaking to think that Helen grieved for her child. Patty felt an arm around hers.

"I know," said Stella in a soft, caring voice. "Let's leave this room. We've seen enough."

Marie was standing in the hallway when Stella and Patty backed out of the room, turned off the light, and closed the door. Annie and Lizzy, now joined by the three men, stood by Stella, Patty, and Marie. Stella motioned the group forward to the next room.

They came across a bathroom on the opposite side of the hallway. It was a nice bathroom of average size. Clean towels hung on the racks next to a cupboard. Marie opened the cupboard door and found toiletries for guests and clean towels. A glass walled shower stood next to a tub and a half-wall separated the toilet from the rest of the room. Grayish wood-grained tile adorned the floor. A fluffy white carpet had been placed on the floor under the sink.

Dan moved inside and looked around. He lifted the lid on the toilet and then pressed down on the flush lever. "It works!"

"What if it didn't work and had overflowed?" Annie remarked rather sarcastically.

"Someone has to test it out," Dan said, moving to the sink and turning it on. He waited a moment and then turned the knobs to the off position. "And the water is heated."

"Hurry up you guys," Marie shouted, as she was in the lead heading to the next room, which appeared to be a nicely appointed guest suite. It had its own bathroom and a beautiful sitting area surrounding an electric fireplace. The suite was decorated in various hues of blue, teal, and shades of charcoal. The carpeting was a sandy color. The bedding was luxurious and inviting. Stella had to pull Marie back from plopping down on the bed.

A panel on the wall, found by Donald, controlled ambient light from the windows. The windows were programmed to duplicate the light from outside, several floors above.

"I'm thinking each room may have this feature," Donald said, playing with the controls.

With Stella in the lead, maneuvering Marie out the door, the group moved to the next rooms, each as lovely as the last. The master suite was spectacular in both size and content. The king-sized bed backed up to a partial wall in the center of the room. Behind the wall were dressing rooms, and twin full-sized bathrooms on either side. In the morning one could get up, walk around the wall into a private dressing area and their own bathroom. Not only did Helen favor 'his and hers' closets, but bathrooms as well.

A beautiful sitting area was in the far corner, and like the guest rooms, the furniture was arranged around the electric fireplace. Soft white fluffy throws were tossed across the backs of tan over-stuffed chairs. Two French-style patio doors, positioned in the center of one wall, were draped in sheer curtains. Donald and Dan walked to the doors and pulled them open.

A luxurious patio spread out before them, featuring silk flowers, plants, and trees. Lounge chairs and tables sat on a stone tiled floor, and artificial grass gave the appearance of a small lush lawn. A high ceiling, painted sky blue, enlarged the space and made one truly feel like they were outdoors.

Dan walked out first, followed by Donald. The sight before them was one they would never have imagined.

"Is that a swimming pool?" Donald asked. "Hey, guys! You are not going to believe this!"

Everyone came rushing out of the patio doors from the master suite. Having exited, they each stood and stared.

"This is the type of yard I want," Dan said, as he stood next to Donald. "No work whatsoever."

"What about dusting?" Rand asked, stepping up next to Dan.

The group stared at the pool in silence. A pool cleaning robot swirled aimlessly around the bottom. Ceramic pots containing colorful silk flowering plants lined a seating area with lounge chairs. Tables and brightly colored cushioned chairs were placed in an adjacent grouping.

Annie took a seat on one of the lounge chairs, followed by Lizzy, Patty, and then Stella. The guys pulled up patio chairs near the lounges. Marie was at the shallow end of the pool dipping her hands in to check the temperature.

"Annie, tell us what was in the rooms on the other side of the living room," Stella asked. "We could hear lots of laughing and talking. There must be something exciting there."

"I'll say," started Dan. "There is a room with a full bar, expensive liquor, pinball machines, dart boards, and..."

"And a questionable lady painted on the mirror over the bar," Lizzy interrupted. Everyone laughed.

"I like the antique brass cash register," Annie stated. "I wonder how that would look in my shop?"

"It looks too heavy to move," Donald said.

Annie and Lizzy both spoke excitedly about finding the theater room. They described the concealed room for storing movies, TV shows, and music.

"Would one call that a media room?" asked Patty. "We need a media room, Rand."

"If we had the space, I would build it in a heartbeat."

"At least I would know where you were all the time," Patty laughed.

"The water is warm," Marie said, standing up and walking over to the group. "Let's go swimming."

Stella suggested to Marie they all go swimming another time. The chlorine should be checked first since it had not been done since Helen's death. Marie began to pout, but yawned instead. Rand offered to check the chemicals, after noticing a small structure near the pool which housed the pump and chemicals.

Annie then yawned and, swinging her feet up, she laid back onto the lounge and closed her eyes. She listened while everyone discussed the rooms they saw and the puzzling find of an underground home. Plans were already being made for a movie night and guys night in the bar. Annie heard Lizzy asking when the girls should have their night in the bar. How long would Annie and Donald be able to keep the secret of the underground house, she wondered? She could not imagine how the Silver Sleuths might know, but they did have a knack for collecting secrets. She made up her mind not to ask. If they did not know, she did not want to raise suspicions. She trusted her family to keep this area private.

♦ ♦ ♦

Opening her eyes to look at the watch on her arm, Annie realized they had been up all night and it was now very early in the morning. She closed her eyes again. Just a quick nap is all she needed right now, she told herself.

"I think we should call it a night," Donald said, noticing Annie's actions. Calling out to Annie, he held his hand out in an offer to help her up.

Annie opened her eyes and noticed Donald's gesture. She took his hand and sat up, then groaned as she stood up the rest of the way.

"I agree with Donald," she said.

"Let's get some sleep," Stella said. "Later, in the afternoon Patty, Rand, Marie and I have agreed to finish cleaning up the back yard from the wedding festivities. You honeymooners are on your own. We won't bother you all day."

Making their way through the French doors to the dining room, the party set out for the main floor of Annie and Donald's house. Rand and Patty, Marie and Stella, said their good nights, and exited through the kitchen door then across the back yard to their respective homes.

Dan and Lizzy said good night, and exited through the front door. Donald let Laddie out for a bathroom break in his run. Laddie quickly did his business and returned inside. Donald locked up the house and set the alarm. Laddie yawned and followed the two up to their bedroom. He had been sleeping on the couch earlier, waiting for everyone to come back.

Annie entered the bedroom first, noticing Callie asleep on the bed. Callie opened her eyes to see Annie, then closed them, daring anyone to interrupt her. Laddie walked up to the side of the bed, sniffed toward Callie, then turned and crawled into his bed.

Annie's phone made a chirping sound, and she picked it up to find a text message from Lizzy.

"Someone left me a single rose at the front door," Lizzy wrote. "The note said, *'Lizzy, you finally got what you wanted'*. Should I be concerned?"

"What did Dan say about the rose?" Annie texted back to Lizzy.

"He looked at the rose thoroughly, then suggested leaving it outside for the night."

"That might be best. Do you know of anyone who might be upset that you got married suddenly?"

"It would have to have been a person at the wedding," Lizzy wrote. "But where would they get a red rose this late? All of your roses were pink and white."

"True," Annie replied. "No one knew you were getting married, even you."

"Well, I'm not worried," Lizzy messaged. "I have a big strong police detective to protect me."

"I thought Dan was with you!"

"Good night, Annie."

"Donald," Annie called while looking for Donald in the master suite. "Lizzy just had the strangest thing happen to her when she and Dan got home." Annie was still staring at her phone as she walked into the bathroom.

"What's that?" Donald asked, as he was just about to put a toothbrush in his mouth.

Annie told Donald of the single red rose left at the front door and the note attached.

Donald stared at Annie for a moment and then said, "That note could be taken two different ways."

"Being the suspicious person," Annie began, "I would have to go with it being curious."

"It might have been the Senior Sleuths," Donald said. "It's been a very long day. Let's go to bed. We have some serious honeymooning to catch up on tonight." Donald rinsed his mouth and wiped it with a towel. He then leaned in to Annie and gave her a kiss on the cheek before leaving the bathroom.

Annie brushed her teeth, changed into a slinky nightgown, and turned the light off as she left the bathroom. She fumbled her way in the dark to the bed and slid under the covers. Moving closer to Donald, she stopped short when she heard steady breathing.

"Donald?" Annie whispered. There was no answer. Donald was fast asleep.

CHAPTER 3

Sunday Afternoon

I t was late in the afternoon when Annie and Donald finally awoke. Donald crawled out of bed and went to the kitchen to find a note on the table indicating a Frittata in the refrigerator, and instructions on how to heat it up. He did as Stella instructed and also made coffee. To the tray, he added the fruit filled cups set out on a shelf in the refrigerator, and thinking of Annie's sweet tooth, added a small mound of whipped cream to each. It made a full tray to carry upstairs to the master suite.

Donald handed the tray of food to Annie, who sat up as he entered the bedroom. She held the tray until Donald took off his robe and crawled back into bed. Annie then set the tray between them and picked up her coffee mug.

Wanting to spend several hours lounging around and eating the brunch laid out for them, Annie appreciated that her mother made sure their first day as husband and wife was special.

"Wow!" Annie marveled over the wonderful tray that sat before them. "Mom outdid herself."

"I could get used to this," Donald replied, looking at the food, not quite sure where to begin.

"Don't," Annie said. "You married me, not my mother. It's never going to happen again."

"I'd give up breakfast in place of what happened an hour ago."

Donald handed a dog biscuit to Laddie, who had his sniffing nose pointed toward the breakfast tray. Since Laddie had gone outside for his morning run while Donald was downstairs, he must have figured that it was time to go back to sleep when Donald went back to the bedroom. He took the dog biscuit and climbed into his bed. In several bites, the dog biscuit was gone. He looked at Donald and gave a 'woof', causing Donald to toss the second dog biscuit to Laddie. Annie was amused at how Laddie had Donald trained.

"Donald," Annie said, between bites of the egg dish that sat on the tray. "I am thinking we should try out the underground house and maybe go swimming. What do you think?

"I was thinking the same thing. Let's eat, take a shower, and get dressed."

"I'll need to find my bathing suit," Annie remarked.

"Not on my account," Donald said, looking at Annie with a devilish smile on his face. "We have the whole house to ourselves today. We don't need bathing suits."

Annie blushed a little. She had never been swimming in the buff before. It all seemed so exciting and adventurous. But what if someone saw them? She was determined to brave it and be naked in the pool with Donald. The house was theirs today. No one was going to bother them. She had her mother's word on that.

♦ ♦ ♦

After showering, Annie grabbed a towel and dried herself off. She walked to her closet area and began searching for shorts, a tank top, and her slip-on sneakers. She was deciding on bra/no bra when Donald entered the closet and slid the pocket door closed. He made a grand gesture to turn the lock on the door. Annie gave Donald a flirty smile.

Donald dropped the towel, which was wrapped around his waist, and made a John Wayne, movie star swagger, toward Annie. He reached for her towel and in a slow gesture, removed it from Annie's body, and dropped it to the floor.

A bank of drawers jutted out into the room. The cabinet was tall enough to lean on and tie one's shoes, but low enough to sit on if needed. Annie sat on the cabinet while watching Donald's swaggering walk toward her.

"Donald?" Annie said, attempting to look around. "Something moved."

"The earth always moves when I am with you," said Donald, doing his best to imitate John Wayne.

"I'm serious," Annie said, scrambling to sit up. "This dresser unit made a funny sound and moved."

Turning serious, Donald motioned for Annie to move away from the storage unit. He placed his hands on the side and pushed. It slid sideways about six inches. He gave Annie a puzzled look. He pushed a bit more. It continued to move away from him.

"Now do you believe me that the dresser moved?" Annie asked.

"And to think I thought I was the one who moved you," Donald replied, grinning from ear to ear.

"Me and now evidently the dresser unit."

Their flirtation ended when Donald moved the unit all the way over to reveal a stairway going down.

"We'd better get dressed before checking this out," Donald said. "No one mentioned finding a dark hole in the floor when I had this bathroom remodeled. Then again, they only painted the closet," he said as he walked toward the doorway to his own walk-in closet in the bathroom.

"Wait!" Annie rang out. "Don't leave me here with this wide open. She was pointing to the cavernous opening in the floor of her closet.

"Okay," Donald relented, leaning against the wall with his arms folded. "I really hate to do this, but I'll stay here and watch you get dressed. Keep in mind, I would prefer watching you undress."

"Very funny, Donald. Would you close it for now? I can't get dressed in front of a dark hole in the floor."

Donald gave in and moved the dresser unit back in place. He exited Annie's closet and went to his dressing area. When he returned, Annie was slipping on her sneakers.

"Ready?" Donald asked.

"Ready, and I have a flashlight."

Sliding the dresser unit back to reveal the dark hole in the middle of Annie's walk-in closet, Donald moved forward, leading the way down the stairway. "Careful," he said, turning back to Annie. "The stairs are steep."

Annie slowly descended the stairs, all the while clutching the back of Donald's shirt. As they reached the bottom step, Donald located a light switch and flipped it on. Light illuminated the landing of a stairwell. Another set of stairs went further down. Next to the light switch was a door. Donald pulled on the door and it slid back and opened inward, revealing itself to be a bookcase and exposing the sitting area off the dining room.

"I was curious why Helen and Robert had a row of bookcases in this particular spot." Annie turned and pointed to the stairway going down. "I bet I know where that comes out."

"Shall we investigate?"

"After you Holmes," Annie said, gesturing Donald to lead the way.

"Holmes?" Donald said, teasing, as he came back through the bookcase opening. "I shall have the pleasure of interrogating you in my bed chamber later, my dear," speaking in his best British accent.

Annie laughed. Once Donald closed the bookcase door, she followed him down the stairs.

Reaching the bottom of the stairs, they came upon another door. It was a steel door, just like the one Annie saw earlier when they first found the underground house. Donald opened the door out to a landing. Annie was correct. This was the door she saw earlier. They walked out and into the brightly colored hallway with the speckled tile floor. To their right was the stairway descending to the underground house. They closed the door behind them, and headed downstairs.

Annie and Donald entered through the front door of the underground house.

"Where's Oscar?" Annie whispered to Donald, stopping short just inside the front entrance. She pointed to the sofa.

"I believe he's in the kitchen making fried chicken," Donald replied, sniffing the air. He took Annie's hand and walked through the foyer to the kitchen area. Annie half expected to see Oscar in an apron at the stove frying chicken. Instead, she found Stella tossing a Caesar salad.

"Good afternoon, sleepy heads," Stella said. She wiped her hands on her apron and walked to the refrigerator. Opening the door, she reached in and pulled out a container of parmesan cheese.

"Mom, I thought you promised Donald and I would have the house to ourselves today," Annie said, walking closer to the kitchen counter. Annie pulled up a stool and sat down. Donald stood behind her, eyeing the fried chicken and salad.

"You didn't have to make dinner for us," Donald spoke up. He noticed the enormous plate of food before him.

Stella looked up at Donald, "I wasn't expecting either of you today, but you are welcome to join us. I set up the patio table outside."

"Outside upstairs, or out on the patio underground?" Donald asked.

"Us?" Annie asked. "Who is all here?"

"Rand is watching a movie in the theater, Dan and Lizzy showed up, and are playing on the game machines in the bar. Marie is swimming in the pool. Patty is reading a book on the patio. Rand checked the chlorine levels for the pool earlier." Stella answered to Annie. "And Donald, we are eating here, outside on the patio. It's beautiful here."

"You do realize the so-called 'outside on the patio' never changes," Donald stated. "Well, except for controlled lighting, the scenery never changes."

"Of course I do, Donald. That is what makes it perfect for days when the weather up above is terrible. We can still come down here and enjoy the day."

Donald and Annie looked at each other in dismay. The underground had now become a popular family center.

Donald took a carrot from the vegetable plate and followed Annie to the theater. Munching on the carrot, he stopped chewing long enough to open the door. Peering inside, they noticed two figures in the center of the seating area watching a movie. A thin bony arm was draped across the shoulders of Donald's father. Donald laughed, shook his head, and moved inside the room. Annie waited at the door.

"Oscar and I found a selection of The Three Stooges movies," Rand said, as Donald settled in next to Oscar.

"Oscar seems to be enjoying the movie." Donald noticed the smiling face of Oscar, whose head was looking directly at the movie screen.

"He's a big fan."

Annie relayed a message from her mother that dinner was ready and everyone should meet on the patio.

"Does she mean the patio upstairs or down here?" Rand asked Donald.

"I asked the same question," Donald laughed. "She means down here."

Rand picked up a remote-control unit and paused the movie. The two men stood and moved to the theater door, leaving Oscar to stare at the frozen screen. Annie walked just outside the door, next to the bar entrance and announced dinner was ready to Dan and Lizzy.

"So, how's married life so far?" Rand asked, as he lightly slapped Donald's shoulder.

Donald placed his hand on the doorknob, signaling for his father to walk out ahead of him. He turned and said, "Dad, Annie is the best thing that has ever happened to me."

"Of course, you'll miss your parents," Rand said.

"I'm hoping my parents will consider long visits in the future."

"I wouldn't mind spending summers here. We have always loved Bridgewater Harbor."

"Thanks for being here, Dad. It means a lot to me." Donald closed the door and the two made their way to the patio area. Joining in behind the men came Annie, Dan, and Lizzy.

"Hey, Mom said you and Annie are to be left alone in the house," Dan stated to Donald.

"There must be another entrance to this place, other than going through the office in the house?" Donald questioned Dan with a smile.

"I warned her that you and Annie would be suspicious about us sneaking inside."

"We should have a family meeting and talk about this place," Rand suggested.

"I would like to further investigate a door we found in the bar that was locked," Donald said, "But right now I want a piece of the fried chicken before it's all gone."

♦ ♦ ♦

A large table had been set up by pushing two patio tables together. Stella had covered the tables in colorful tablecloths and placed the food in the center. Battery operated candles gave off a soft yellow glow. Music was softly playing in the background. The light was dimmed, as if the sun was setting. A slight breeze swirled around the area. Annie felt as if she were in the tropics. Her mother found a control box and was experimenting with the switches. Finding the right ambiance, she closed the panel door and smiled at her endeavors.

After the platters were passed around and plates filled with food, Annie began the discussion of the recently discovered underground house.

"Anyone have an idea or thought on why Robert and Helen built this enormous home underneath the beautiful home above?" Annie looked around the table as she spoke. "I understand their vast wealth and desire to be secretive, but how could we live across the street and not notice this being built?" Annie was directing her question to her mother.

"Well," Stella began, pausing for a moment to think, "Your father had passed away and I was working at the library full-time. You were in college and working, Dan was in Portland..."

"Donald, Patty, and I were living in California at the time." Rand added to Stella's statement.

"This house was the first house built in the neighborhood," Patty answered. "It is possible that Robert and Helen had the underground before anyone else moved into the area."

Everyone looked to Marie. Marie's eyes got wide, and she remained quiet, looking back at the people staring at her.

"I am not supposed to tell," Marie said quietly, talking to Annie, who was seated next to her.

"Marie," Annie whispered back to Marie, "I think it would be okay to tell now that Robert and Helen are gone. Besides, I am really curious and want to know."

Marie nodded to Annie.

"I knew about all the workers here, but the only room I went to was the one behind the bookcase in the office. I didn't know about the rest of the house." Marie ate a few scoopfuls of potato salad and then took a sip of her lemonade.

Realizing everyone was still watching her, Marie continued, "Aunt Helen and I went on some vacations, and when we came back the workers had gone. Then they would show up again and Aunt Helen would take me on more vacations. We had fun. One time when we came back there was a house in the back yard."

"The cottage?" Annie asked.

"Yes," Marie answered. "It was green on the outside and Aunt Helen did not like it, so the next time we went on vacation and came back, the little house was yellow."

"I wonder if the workmen were building the house in the underground during that time?" Donald asked. "He could have had the underground basics built before the house above, and then slowly add to the house below as he had time and money."

Annie realized that Robert must have had the entire underground house remodeled while Helen took Marie on various trips to hide the fact that a covert operation was taking place. Robert somehow hid the worker vehicles from the street. No wonder her mother had no idea what was going on.

"He wasn't building the house. Robert was remodeling the house," Annie remarked.

"The question remains...why?" Dan asked.

There was a long silence. The noise of clinking utensils was heard above the gentle sounds of music in the air.

Lizzy was the first to break the silence, "Could it be a bomb or fall-out shelter?"

"Not likely," Dan answered, reaching for his glass of lemonade. "We are out of tsunami range at this elevation, and we have no major hurricanes or tornadoes around here. So, that also rules out storm shelter. Could Helen and Robert have been living apart?"

"Oh, no. Not at all," Patty answered. "Helen and I kept in touch often. We mostly talked about Donald though. But I do know that she and Robert loved each other very much."

"What does that leave us with?" Stella asked.

"A hobby?" Lizzy asked.

"A secret laboratory?" Annie added.

"A secret laboratory, Annie?" Dan said, using his best sarcastic tone of voice.

"It's a possibility. There are still areas we have not explored," Annie replied.

There was another long pause as the group contemplated what was said.

"Let's do some exploring after dinner," Dan suggested.

"May I say something?" Stella began, "This is Annie and Donald's property. They should be the ones to decide what to do next." Turning to Annie and Donald, Stella continued, "Annie, I am sorry I suggested the rest of us come down here today. I did promise that we would leave you honeymooners alone. It is already six o'clock in the evening and once I finish cleaning up, I suggest we all leave these two alone with their newly found dream home."

With that said, dishes were cleared, cleaned, the leftover food put into containers and placed in the refrigerator. Annie suspected her mother wanted to have a reason to return to the solitude of the house later.

The first to head back upstairs were Stella and Marie. Rand went to the theater room to retrieve the DVD of The Three Stooges movie, so he could finish watching it in the motor home. Patty stood talking with Dan, Lizzy, and Donald when she turned and noticed Rand carrying Oscar from the theater room.

"Please put him back," Patty said in a firm, no-nonsense voice. "Oscar is not going with us."

Rand, dejected looking, turned and entered the theater with his skeletal buddy. Once inside, a bony hand appeared from the doorway and sadly waved goodbye to Patty.

Attempting to conceal her laughter, she turned to Donald and said, "I really don't know what I see in that man."

Rand returned and followed Patty from the underground house. Before Dan and Lizzy left, Annie motioned Lizzy aside.

"I'll meet you upstairs in a minute," Lizzy said to Dan, watching him exit the house through the front door.

"I can go up with you," Donald called out to Dan. "Laddie is probably wondering where I am. I think I will bring him down here. He might like to explore."

As Dan and Donald made their way upstairs, Annie walked Lizzy to the patio area and, they sat down.

"Tomorrow is Monday," Annie began, "And Donald has to work. I was thinking of spending time in the cottage working on R&H Enterprises business."

"Good," Lizzy responded. "Let's keep the shop closed and spend our time on business. I will call Daisy and let her know. Leases are coming up and everyone is eager to discuss the upcoming plans for maintenance on both buildings."

Annie and Lizzy had spent the next fifteen minutes discussing their plans when Laddie appeared and ran to Annie. She placed her hands on each side of his head and gave him a playful scratch. Then she stroked her hand down his back as he sat next to her. Donald and Dan appeared on the patio.

"I thought you were right behind me fifteen minutes ago," Dan stated to Lizzy.

"Annie needed to talk to me about business," Lizzy informed Dan. "We are going to work in the cottage tomorrow. We have a lot to get straightened out before our big tenant meeting."

"You said you were going to move your things into the house while I was at work on Monday," Dan said.

"You can help me after work. I really don't have that much."

Both Dan and Annie laughed at Lizzy's statement.

"Your clothes alone will take a full truckload," Annie said, still laughing.

"I gave a bunch of clothes to Daisy, if you must know."

"What about me?" Annie asked, feeling a bit left out of the designer-brand clothing giveaway.

"You can buy your own clothes," Lizzy answered. "Besides, she can't even afford clothes from Costco right now. She is saving all of her money for tuition. It's the least I could do to help her out."

"That's right," Dan added. "After she sells your expensive clothes online, she can afford tuition through her Master's degree at Stanford University."

Both Annie and Lizzy gave Dan a look that said they were not happy with his comment. Dan sheepishly sat down next to Lizzy.

Donald saw Laddie run off to what appeared to be a garden shed. Laddie jumped up on one of the wide double doors and it opened. Donald called after Laddie as he neared the structure, and soon the two disappeared inside the building. Dan watched with concern, wondering what they might have found inside the small building. Donald and Laddie had not come out.

Dan, Lizzy, and Annie stood up and cautiously approached the garden shed. Annie was a bit apprehensive about going into the building, and was glad when Dan took the lead. Dan opened the other door and stood to the side. Laddie came bounding out with a big smile on his face. Donald followed.

"I think I know how they got all the large items down here," Donald said. "There's a freight elevator inside this shed."

Dan moved past Donald and entered the shed. Donald turned and followed him inside with Laddie close at his heels. Annie looked at Lizzy, shrugged, and followed the guys.

With the light on, the shed looked well organized with tools hanging on the wall. Most of the tools were for pool maintenance. On the opposite wall, stood large elevator doors. Donald looked back at the group.

"Anyone game to see where this leads us?" Donald asked.

"Push the button, Donald," Dan instructed.

Donald pushed the button and the doors of the elevator slid open. Facing them stood a large elevator inviting them inside.

"Well?" Donald said, looking at Dan.

"Let's do this," Dan responded with the gusto of meeting trouble head-on. Annie grimaced and looked at Lizzy. Lizzy followed Dan inside. Annie stood for a moment facing the three, hesitating. She had no idea where this elevator was going to take them. Laddie gave Annie a soft woof, which she took to mean 'hurry up'. She quickly walked in and stood next to Donald. Donald pushed the button marked 'UP' and the doors slid closed.

As the elevator moved slowly upward, Annie took Donald's hand. Donald turned and smiled. He squeezed Annie's hand to let her know everything was fine. Laddie positioned his head under Annie's other hand, and she began petting him.

The elevator stopped with a bounce, and the doors slid open. Dan made a move toward the open door and poked his head out. Donald did the same. They exited the elevator with Laddie close at Donald's heels. Dan located a light switch, while Annie and Lizzy stood still, trying to figure out where they were. The elevator doors began to close. Lizzy let out a short gasp, and Annie swiftly hit a button on the panel. Apparently, it was not the correct button. The elevator began to make a slow decent.

"Why did you do that?" Lizzy shouted at Annie.

"I hit the wrong button by mistake," Annie shouted back.

The elevator stopped and the doors once again slid open. They were back where they started. Lizzy leaned past Annie and pushed the button to take the elevator back up. Once on the upper level, the doors opened to find Dan with his hands on his hips.

"Nice move, Annie," Dan said. "Would you mind getting off the elevator?"

The two women exited and stood inside what seemed to be a small room. There did not appear to be a doorway out.

"Another secret room?" Annie asked.

"Yes, but to where?" Donald replied.

The group began searching for a lever or button to push to expose a doorway. Donald searched the floor, getting down on his hands and knees. Laddie got down on his front legs with his tail up in the air, attempting to find out what was so interesting on the floor. His head was close to Donald's, as if he were teaching Donald how to properly sniff the ground. After a moment, Laddie began scratching at a spot on the wall. He gave a soft woof and scratched the wall again.

"Hello?" Came a voice from the other side of the wall.

"Mom?" Annie shouted. "Is that you?"

"Annie? What are you doing behind the wall in the garage? Are you okay?"

"We're fine, Mom," Annie replied. "Do you see a doorway from your side?"

"No, just a wall."

Dan walked over to where Donald and Annie stood. He began pulling on objects and hooks hanging on the wall.

Annie pushed on a section of wall and suddenly it popped open. It had a magnetic spring closure. Donald helped her pull the wide door open, and the group exited the elevator room.

"Good heavens," Stella exclaimed. "I heard a motor noise and thought someone was in the garage, so I came down from my apartment to check. Then I heard voices and scratching sounds on this wall."

"Laddie found a freight elevator in the garden shed downstairs," Donald said, proudly acknowledging his smart dog with a generous scratch under the dog's chin.

"We took the elevator to the upper level and realized we were in a room without a visible door. Good thing you were on the other side, and we heard your voice," Annie said.

After spending a few minutes discussing what they found, the group dispersed to their homes, leaving Annie and Donald standing in the garage.

"Should we go back downstairs and make sure everything's turned off?" Annie asked Donald.

"The lights are on motion sensors from what I have been able to tell," Donald answered. "But...since everyone has gone home, we can check out the swimming pool."

CHAPTER 4

Monday Morning

Annie was up with the light of daybreak. She showered and dressed as quiet as possible, to avoid waking Donald. Laddie kept an eye on Annie as she opened the bedroom door to exit into the hallway. She paused and turned to look at Laddie and thought that he might want to follow her to the kitchen. She waited a moment and sure enough, Laddie slowly rose from his bed, stretched, and walked to the door.

Once in the hall, Laddie stood still listening, and then moved past Annie to the top of the stairs. He stopped, ears perked, and raised his nose in the air. Annie, still walking forward, nearly bumped into Laddie, and had to catch herself before flying over the top of him.

"What did you hear, Laddie?" Annie whispered to the giant black dog. Laddie made a low growl and lowered his head as he walked down the stairs. Annie froze, and wondered if she should wake Donald. She decided she should, and ran back down the hall to the bedroom to wake Donald.

Annie followed Donald down the stairs to find Laddie at the front door. He sniffed at the base of the door. Annie looked out the front window. She observed a dark figure leave the front gate area of Dan and Lizzy's house. She signaled to Donald, pointing out the person closing the gate. They kept their eyes on the figure, who got on a bicycle and rode down the street toward town.

Annie reached into her pocket, pulled out her cell phone, and called Dan.

"This better be good," Dan snarled as he answered the phone.

"Good morning to you too, Shirley."

"Annie, what do you want now? Do you have any idea what time it is?"

"I guess I could wait until later to tell you that Laddie sensed someone at your house."

"What? When?" Dan demanded.

"Donald and I spotted someone leave through your front gate, jump on a bicycle, and head toward town."

The line disconnected.

Annie turned to find Donald running down the stairs. Annie was on the phone when Donald had gone upstairs to dress. He was now making an attempt to put on tennis shoes and a sweatshirt. He pulled Laddie's leash from the hook on the wall by the front door. Laddie was overjoyed to go outside and barely stood still for Donald to hook up the leash. Donald paused to punch numbers into the alarm keypad, and then moved out the front door. Annie followed.

Across the street, swear words were ringing through the early morning air as Dan ran out the front door and down the front walk to the gate. He opened the gate and paused, and looked down the street. The bicyclist was long gone by then. Dan turned his attention Annie and Donald standing outside.

"Could you tell who it was?" Dan asked Annie.

"I witnessed a medium height person with a dark hoodie and dark jeans. His shoes were black. He got on a black bike. Actually, I can't be sure it was a male."

"Oh, my goodness!" came a shout from the front porch area. There, stood Lizzy gaping at a blue bag sitting on a chair next to the front door.

"Don't touch that!" cautioned Dan. He raced up the front walk to the porch. Annie ran across the street to Dan and Lizzy's house, while Laddie decided he needed a potty break. Donald accommodated Laddie's urge to sniff around the gate area.

"But the bag is from Tiffany's," Lizzy exclaimed excitedly to Dan. "It looks like a bracelet box."

"Stand back," Dan commanded. He peered inside the bag at what was definitely a bracelet box. "Let me find some gloves and check this out first. Dan went to retrieve gloves, which left Annie and Lizzy to stare inside the blue bag.

Donald and Laddie approached the front porch. Laddie immediately began sniff at the bag. Donald pulled back on his leash.

"What's in the bag?" Donald inquired, as he attempted to keep Laddie from sniffing the bag. Laddie continued to tug on his leash.

"It looks like a gift for Lizzy," Annie said.

"It does seem strange that someone would leave a gift from Tiffany's on our front porch," Lizzy said. "I mean Tiffany's? I would expect a licensed courier and a knock on the door."

Annie gave Donald a look. He smiled as if he knew what Lizzy was talking about. Annie realized that Lizzy would be familiar with Tiffany's, recently discovering that Lizzy grew up in a wealthy environment.

"Who would be sending you expensive jewelry?" Annie asked Lizzy.

"Certainly not my parents," Lizzy declared. "They would hire armed courier to deliver the package during normal waking hours." Lizzy stopped and stared at the package, then asked, "Should I be concerned?"

"Someone is wooing you, Lizzy," Donald said with a big grin on his face.

Annie knew Donald was joking, but Lizzy looked at him with a serious expression.

"I was just joking, Lizzy," Donald said, pulling Laddie back, away from the bag.

"No one realizes I am here," Lizzy said, "Except my parents."

"Now that you got married to Dan, everyone knows you live here. I'm assuming your mother announced your wedding in the society pages, if there still is such a thing," Donald suggested.

Dan returned with thick leather gloves and asked everyone to step aside as he grabbed the bag and walked to the street. He set the bag down on the sidewalk. Next, he kicked the bag down the walkway. Nothing happened.

"Dan!" Lizzy shouted. "It's not a bomb. It's jewelry!"

Dan retrieved the bag and carried it back to Lizzy. He pulled out the bracelet box and carefully opened it. Inside was a stunning bracelet with three rows of diamonds connected by bars of smaller diamonds, all of which wrapped around the wrist. Everyone just stared at the diamonds sparkling in the case.

"Are those diamonds real?" Annie questioned, moving to have a closer look.

Lizzy pulled the glittering jewelry out of the case and held it up. She examined the front and back of the bracelet. "Yes," said Lizzy.

Lizzy reached in and pulled it out an envelope from the bag. She easily opened the envelope containing a card since the flap was not sealed. Lizzy read the message out loud to the people near her.

"Lizzy, I realize now that I should never have let you go. I know we had our differences, but we could have worked them out. Please know how much I love you."

"What?" Dan shouted, seizing the card from Lizzy and reading it to himself. He stuffed the card into the envelope and dropped it into the bag. "Do you know who this person is?" Dan asked Lizzy, now taking his gloves off and tossing them on the chair next to the front door.

"It could be one of several men I dated in the past," Lizzy stated. "Given that my parents were wealthy, I had many men interested in me. Their interest ended though when I said I did not want my parent's money."

"Are you going to keep that bracelet?" Annie inquired.

"No," Lizzy said. She handed the bracelet to Annie and asking her to lock it up in the vault room in her house. Annie looked to Donald, and they both agreed to do so.

"I need to go to work," Dan said. He picked up the gloves, handed the bag and the bracelet box to Annie. Annie placed the diamond jewelry in the box and put it in the blue bag.

Annie made plans to meet Lizzy at the cottage in a couple of hours. First, she wanted to walk to Ione's Bakery & Coffee Shop to pick up donuts for everyone.

♦ ♦ ♦

The sun was out, but the air was cool as a breeze drifted off the ocean. Annie sat outside on the patio with her mother and Marie. Stella had made omelets with ham and cheese with a side of fresh cut fruit. Annie had earlier taken a plate of food to Donald in his office since he began work early. Neatly arranged on a plate in the center of the table was a stack of croissants and donuts. Marie eyed them closely as she ate the last bite of her omelet.

A warmly dressed Patty and Rand exited their motorhome and joined the ladies at the table outside. Even though the sun shined, it was cool outside especially for native Californians. To Annie, it was warm and the sun inviting.

"Good morning," Patty said to everyone sitting at the table. She pulled a chair out and sat down next to Annie.

"Would you two like some breakfast?" Stella asked and then offered, "I can whip up an omelet or scramble some eggs. How about coffee?"

"Just coffee for me, Stella," Rand said. "Those donuts for anyone?"

"Help yourself," Stella said, sliding a carafe of coffee in front of Rand.

Both Rand and Patty selected a pastry. Rand filled Patty's cup with the dark liquid, then did the same with his own.

"What's on the agenda today?" Annie asked Rand and Patty.

"We were thinking of heading to Portland to do the sight-seeing we had planned to do yesterday," Patty said, taking another bite from the donut. "We apologize for interfering with your brief honeymoon and taking over the underground house."

Donald walked out to the patio and pulled up a chair.

"Son," asked Rand, "I was hoping we could borrow your truck today to drive into Portland." Rand lifted the plate of donuts toward Donald. Donald took a chocolate croissant.

"Sure, Dad," Donald said, taking a napkin from the holder on the table. "I think the gas tank is full."

Although she heard Donald and his father talking, Annie's attention turned to the house on the hill. It appeared dark and quiet, looking out over the ocean beyond her.

Annie was determined to find out who owned the house and why it had been abandoned all these years. Annie decided to ask her mom to help locate the owner's information at the county records office once everyone finished breakfast and went on their way for the day.

Stella loved researching records, and had a knack for knowing how to track down information. Dan was interested in that house now, and he would appreciate any information she found.

"Annie?" Donald asked, as he tapped Annie on the shoulder to get her attention. "What are your plans today?"

Annie snapped out of her thoughts when she had heard her name called and felt Donald's light touch.

"Lizzy and I want to work on R&H Enterprises today," Annie said. "We have a meeting tomorrow night with the shop owners."

"Well..." Donald said as he stood up, "I need to go back to work. Mom, Dad, hope you have fun in Portland."

"Would you like us to pick up anything from the big city?" Rand asked Donald.

"Nothing I can think of right now," Donald said, as he handed the keys to his truck to his Dad, gave Annie a kiss on the cheek, and went back into the house.

Rand and Patty stood and went back to the motorhome to get ready for a day in Portland. Annie waited until they were out of earshot before she asked her mother if she had time to do some research for her on the house on the hill. Stella was all too excited to help out and questioned Annie about the information she was needed. After some detailed discussion, Annie helped clear the table before heading over to the cottage.

Unlocking the door to the cottage, Annie stood at the entrance in thought for a moment. For a business with so many leases, there seemed to be very little paperwork. Annie moved to Lizzy's desk area and began to search the files. There had to be more than what was currently in the file drawers.

Lizzy entered the cottage with a small plate of donuts and a cup of coffee. She had a messenger bag slung over her shoulder. Annie's associate was dressed in black slacks, a silky light gray blouse, with her curly hair up in a stylish twist on her head. Her diamond stud earrings glinted in the light of the room.

"Now that I am married, your mother seems determined to make me fat," Lizzy said, setting the plate of donuts on Annie's crafting table near the front door.

Annie laughed, agreeing with Lizzy as she looked at her own waistline.

"What do you want to tackle first?" Lizzy asked, placing her black leather bag on the floor near her desk.

"Should we be concerned that the only information we have about R&H Enterprises rests right here in these few boxes that we unloaded?" Annie asked Lizzy.

"Yes, that bothered me as well," Lizzy said. "Had you thought about the number of hidden rooms around here? Does Robert have a secret office we have yet to discover? There were a few doors we never opened downstairs."

"You might be on to something," Annie said. "Maybe we should begin downstairs. It feels like we are missing something big."

"You should ask Charles Conklin, Robert's attorney in Newport," Lizzy said.

"I could do that," Annie started, "But we might want to check downstairs first. I have a strange feeling about the underground house being larger than we already know."

Annie heard tapping on the door and turned to see Patty standing outside. She moved to the door and opened it

"Oh," Patty said, as she stepped inside and stopped when she saw Lizzy at her desk. "I thought you were alone."

"I need another cup of coffee," Lizzy said, walking around the corner of her desk. She started for the door, then stopped when she realized she did not have her coffee cup in hand. Slightly embarrassed, she returned to her desk to retrieve her mug. "Can I get you two coffee?"

"No, thank you," Patty said, looking a bit nervous.

"I'm fine for now," Annie answered.

Lizzy left with her coffee cup and closed the door behind her.

"Please come in and sit down," Annie motioned to the comfortable chairs in the sitting area of the cottage office.

"Annie," Patty said, while she was sitting down. "I thought this would be a good time. Rand went to re-check on the pool downstairs before we left in case Marie wanted to swim later today. I wanted to talk with you alone, without Donald, to explain something."

Patty told Annie about her reaction to the framed baby clothes in the vault room and admitted that it was Helen holding Donald on his day of birth. She said that she feared the truth would come out after Annie read Helen's journals. Patty wanted Annie to hear her side of the story first. She wanted to be the one, along with Rand, to tell

Donald the truth. She was hoping Annie would understand and keep the information to herself until they had a chance to talk with Donald.

"Patty," Annie said. "Whatever you need to discuss with Donald, he should hear it from you and Rand. You don't need to tell me anything. I can stop reading Helen's journals until you to talk to Donald. Please keep in mind, you remain his only parents, and he trusts you more than anything."

Patty stared at Annie for a moment, then said, "He knows, doesn't he?" Tears welled in her eyes. She reached for a tissue from the box on the coffee table.

"He found out when Dan discovered the truth while questioning a suspect, Ronnie, the brother-in-law of Eddie. Dan arrested Eddie for blackmailing Helen, the stress of which caused the heart attack that killed her," Annie replied. "Ronnie admitted Eddie had been extorting money from Robert to keep secret the birth of Donald. Robert refused to pay any more money. During a fit of anger, Eddie ran Robert off the road and over a cliff, causing Robert's death."

"Oh, dear," Patty said with a shudder. "I had no idea. They did not deserve to die. Helen was a wonderful and kind woman. Robert was a brilliant man, although strange at times." Patty dabbed the tissue on her eyes. She took a deep breath and stood. "I'd better get going. I see Rand waiting for me outside. I would appreciate our conversation be kept between us for now."

Annie agreed and stood. She gave Patty a hug, and Patty left the cottage. Annie watched as her mother-in-law walked down the pathway to the RV. Annie contemplated whether she should tell Donald of the conversation. She took a deep slow breath and exhaled. No, she thought, Patty and Rand should be the ones to discuss this with Donald.

Annie left the cottage and went to the house to talk to Lizzy about going to the underground house and attempting to locate an office that Robert and Helen used for R&H Enterprises.

Entering through the kitchen doorway, Annie found Lizzy at the table browsing through a magazine.

"I didn't want to disturb you and Patty, so I stayed here," Lizzy said, as she looked up when she heard Annie enter the room. Lizzy closed the magazine and set it aside. "Is everything okay?"

"Fine," Annie responded. "I came in to ask you what your thoughts were about searching downstairs right now to see if we can find an office or storage room for files and information on R&H Enterprises."

"Ready when you are," Lizzy said, standing to rinse her coffee cup in the sink and place it in the dishwasher. "First, I need to get my phone. I left it on the desk in the cottage."

"I'll go with you. I want to get my notebook."

The two women chatted as they walked up to the cottage. Annie stopped suddenly and grabbed Lizzy's arm to stop her. They both stared at the open door of the converted office for a moment.

"I was sure I closed the door behind me when I left," Annie whispered to Lizzy.

"Should we call Donald to check inside?" Lizzy asked Annie, clutching her arm with a tight grip.

"Don't be silly," Annie said, as she moved forward to the cottage. She peered into the window and not seeing anyone inside, she entered through the door.

Nothing seemed out of place at first glance, but when Lizzy walked to her desk, a red rose was resting on a stack of files. Attached was a note folded in half. She opened the note and read aloud to Annie, "We should talk."

"Get your phone," Annie began. "Let's talk to Donald. He can check the cameras to see who came in here while we were in the house." Annie and Lizzy left the cottage, closing and locking the door behind them.

After knocking on the office door, Annie and Lizzy entered to find Donald finishing a phone call. Annie told Donald of the rose left in the cottage and asked if he happened to be watching the cameras and had seen anyone sneaking around the yard. Donald said he was in a meeting for the last hour.

Donald began checking the footage of the time period Annie had given to him. They watched Patty leave the cottage and walk back to the RV. Patty entered through the RV door, as Annie was leaving the cottage and heading to the main house. After she entered the house, a dark figure could be seen moving out from the backside of the garage and through the shrubbery along the back fence.

Donald pointed out that the person, dressed in black, was carrying a rose. Annie and Lizzy watched as the figure entered the cottage and a moment later exited, leaving along the same path as he had entered.

"Come to think of it," Donald said, "Laddie growled at some point during my meeting. I quieted him down, but he kept his attention on the back yard. I was too busy at the time to take a look."

"Donald, someone may be stalking Lizzy," Annie said with concern in her voice. "Is there some way to trap this person?"

"I can set up a camera inside the cottage," Donald said. "First, I want to check out behind the garage after work. Maybe we can find something that will tell us a direction where this person comes from. The cameras do not show a person walking up the driveway." Donald continued to view different cameras, not finding any further movement.

"Lizzy and I will be downstairs in search of an office that Robert might have used," Annie explained to Donald, as she began moving the bookcase to reveal the hidden stairway.

"Would you ask your Mom and Dad if they may have seen or heard anything?" Lizzy asked Donald, as she pushed a button on her phone and lifted the phone to her ear. "I am calling Dan. This is getting too creepy."

CHAPTER 5

Monday Afternoon

A nnie descended the stairs from the office, followed by Lizzy. Reaching for the thermostat box, Annie opened it and pushed the button to raise the stairs. Watching the stairs slowly rise up and click into place, Annie moved forward into the now lit hallway. As she turned the corner, her mind wandered, trying to figure out where Robert would hide an office. She pondered about how he must have spent a great deal of time thinking about hidden mechanisms, locking devices, and areas to place unexpected rooms.

Before she realized it, Annie was standing at the top of the stairs going down to the underground house. She paused and gazed around. Taking slow steps down the stairs, she examined the area, studying the layout of the house and surrounding areas. How was the underground house positioned below the house above?

Lights illuminated areas ahead as Annie and Lizzy walked up to the front porch. When they took a step up on the porch, lights turned on inside the house. In a way, Annie thought to herself, it was a bit eerie. Almost as if someone sees them coming and lights the way.

Once inside the house, Annie and Lizzy walked into the living room and glanced at the empty sofa where they first discovered Oscar. They looked at each other.

"Rand moved Oscar to the theater room," Annie said.

"I wish we had waited for Dan and Donald to come down here with us," Lizzy said, shivering slightly.

"You are being silly, Lizzy," Annie admonished. "We are perfectly fine by ourselves." She walked to the French doors off the dining room which led to the back yard and swimming pool area. "Oh!" Annie stopped short.

Lizzy ran into the back of Annie, almost knocking her down. "How...how did Oscar get outside?" Lizzy asked, staring at the lazing skeleton by the pool.

"Obviously, someone put him there. He did not walk to the pool chair by himself," Annie said, stiffening her stance, determined not to let this unnerving display deter her from her mission of finding an office where Robert kept his records. Annie then remembered Patty mentioning Rand checking the pool chemicals, and she relaxed.

"He does seem happy by the pool," Lizzy said, as they walked past the lounging skeleton with a plastic wine glass in one hand and sunglasses on his face.

"I bet Donald's father did this," Annie suggested. "He came down here to check the chemicals in the pool before they left for Portland."

"It sounds like something he would do with Oscar," Lizzy commented. "Let's find that room, so we can get back to work."

After an hour of searching, Annie and Lizzy walked to the kitchen. Looking in the refrigerator, they found a pitcher of lemonade from the previous day's gathering. Annie found a couple of glasses, and Lizzy searched the cupboards for some snacks. Annie filled the glasses with ice, and then set them on a tray.

With snacks and refreshing drinks, the two women walked out to the pool area. They stopped and stared at Oscar. Shrugging her shoulders, Annie continued on to comfortable chairs on the other side of the pool from their boney companion. She set the tray on a table between the chairs, kicked off her shoes, and made herself at home.

Annie and Lizzy discussed the meeting of the shop owners coming up the following evening. They talked about the needed maintenance and how soon they could get it finished. Annie suggested having a white board at the meeting to list what the shop owners wanted in maintenance and to use it to make a schedule of what and when repairs would be made.

The sound of a doorbell interrupted their talk. Both Annie and Lizzy stared at the opened French doors leading into the dining room of the house.

"Who is here ringing the doorbell?" Lizzy questioned.

"Oscar?" Annie asked. "Would you go find out who is at the front door?"

"Wouldn't it be freaky if he got up and answered the door?" Lizzy said.

Donald appeared through the doors, paused when he noticed the women sitting in chairs. He walked to the patio by the pool and stopped. "This is how you work...sitting around the pool with Oscar? How do I find a job like this?" He walked up to the table, picked up Annie's lemonade and took a long drink.

"We're taking a break," Annie said. "Donald, we have searched through this entire downstairs area for the last hour. I cannot find where Robert hid his office."

"He seemed to have liked bookcases," Donald said. "Have you tried all the bookcases?"

"Yes, and cabinets, the fireplace, closets...you name it, and we have tried to find a secret room behind it."

"I came at the request of your mother. It's lunchtime," Donald said. He stared at Oscar who was now dressed in khaki shorts, a Hawaiian shirt, flip-flops, sunglasses, and a wine glass in his hand. He shook his head and said, "I can't help but notice that Dad was here earlier. And he's added footwear to Oscar's wardrobe!"

◆ ◆ ◆

After lunch on the patio in the back yard, Annie and Lizzy once again went downstairs to continue searching for a hidden office. As they approached the kitchen, Annie set her pad of paper down on the breakfast bar and pulled out a chair to sit down. Lizzy joined her.

"Let's map out what we know about this underground house. How does it fit with the house above? This house isn't that big, even with the small pool."

"We need graph paper," Lizzy remarked. "I'm going upstairs to Donald's office and ask if he has any. Don't solve the mystery until I return!" Lizzy dashed out the front door, her footsteps sounding loud on the stairs heading upwards.

The house was disturbingly quiet after Lizzy left the underground house. Annie stood and walked over to the open French doors in the dining room. She peered at the chair where Oscar sat. He had not moved and seemed to be enjoying the poolside relaxation. Annie backed into the dining room, closing both doors and locking them.

She walked to the master bedroom and made sure those French doors closed and locked as well. Walking down the hall and glancing in each room as she passed by, Annie made sure she was alone.

"Oh, this is silly," Annie said aloud. She sat down at the breakfast bar in the kitchen and drew several sketches of the floor plan for the upper and lower houses. The counter was now displaying scattered papers, each with drawings of rooms, patio areas, stairways, and the shed housing the elevator in the underground patio.

Hearing footsteps coming down the stairs, Annie turned and saw Lizzy, followed by Donald, hurrying along a few steps behind her. Lizzy pulled up a chair next to Annie and handed her a pad of graphing paper, a ruler, several sharpened pencils, and an eraser.

"Thanks!" Annie said, taking the pencils and setting them down after pulling out the pencil with the sharpest point. Donald and Lizzy watched Annie draw out the rooms of the underground house on graph paper.

About fifteen minutes later, Donald got up to rummage through the refrigerator for a snack. Not finding anything that interested him, he closed the refrigerator and began systematically going through the cupboards.

"I think I like the junk food in our kitchen upstairs better," Donald announced. He pulled out a bag of potato chips and set them on the counter next to Lizzy. "Hey, I think the theater has a candy counter. Would you ladies like a candy bar?"

"Something chocolate," Annie said over her shoulder to Donald.

"Licorice," Lizzy said.

"Oh!" Annie exclaimed after Donald left the room. "I think I might know where another room is hidden." Annie stood and hurried to the front door. Lizzy followed as Annie shouted out to Donald that they were going upstairs.

Donald, hearing Annie call out, walked out of the theater room with a handful of candy, looking bewildered as to where Annie and Lizzy went. As he approached the front door, he heard the fast footsteps of Annie and Lizzy running up the stairs.

"Should I follow you?" Donald asked Annie, trying to decide what to do with his arm load of treats.

"Yes," said Lizzy. "And bring the candy."

Donald reached the top of the stairs and stood trying to catch his breath. Attempting to determine which direction Annie and Lizzy had gone, he heard knocking noises and headed toward the sounds. He followed the hallway to the elevating stairs. There he found Annie moving along the hallway knocking on the wood planks that were designed to look like a tall fence.

Annie continued down the wall, pressing against it with both hands, when surprisingly a section of the paneling popped open. Annie looked at Donald and Lizzy and gave them a smile. She had found another secret door.

"You're getting good at locating hidden rooms," Donald said, as he swung the doorway open.

Lizzy, Donald, and Annie now stood in front of an inset door which appeared to be made of metal. Annie stepped forward and placed her hand on the doorknob. She knew the door would probably be locked, but she just had to try. She attempted to turn the knob. Annie stepped back and stared at the door, willing it to unlock. Trying the knob again, she discovered that it remained locked.

"Do you have a key to this door by any chance?" Lizzy asked.

"You do have a set of keys that Aunt Helen left you," Donald remembered. "Where are they? I'll go get them for you." Donald heaved his load of candy into Lizzy's arms.

Annie gave Donald instructions on where to find the keys she had hidden in one of her bags. She thought about how it might be best to store them from now on in the office safe. She may be tempting fate by leaving them in her closet.

Annie and Lizzy paid attention as Donald went back down the hallway. Lizzy looked questioningly at Annie. Annie could tell Lizzy was curious why Donald would go back toward the underground house.

"There are other ways to move between the floors," Annie explained to Lizzy. "Remember the metal door as you approach the stairs going down to the house? Through that door are stairs leading up to the main floor, with a doorway opening the bookcase into the small sitting area next to the dining room. It appears that Robert likes to hide doors in bookcases. Another set of stairs goes up and ends in my closet, hidden by a movable dresser. Donald and I accidentally discovered it."

"Annie, you inherited a very mysterious house," Lizzy said in a low whisper, as if she thought someone might be listening in on their conversation. Annie laughed.

Moving down the hallway, Annie continued pressing her hands against the wood plank fencing. Near the end of the hall, just as the walkway took a turn to the left, Annie found yet another hidden door. She swung the door open wide and again tried to turn the knob on the inset door behind it. The handle did not budge. Lizzy stepped up balancing the sweets in one arm, and placed her hand on the doorknob, giving it a firm turn. Nothing.

"I had to try," Lizzy said, shrugging.

"I think I hear Donald coming back," Annie said. "I hope he has the keys. This is getting more exciting now."

Donald walked through the gray metal door in the vestibule with a smile on his face and handed a large envelope to Annie. She opened the flap and dug around inside until she felt keys. Pulling out a handful of the metal objects, she walked over to the first hidden door and inserted a key. It would not turn the lock.

"You found another secret door?" Donald asked, noticing the opened fence section down the hallway. He was truly amazed of Annie's ability to find hidden doors.

"Can you believe it?" Lizzy asked. "Two hidden doors on this wall. There are two rooms here."

"Or one big room with two doors," Donald said.

"None of these keys are working to unlock the door," Annie said with annoyance in her voice. "Donald, do you think Robert put the keys in his safe in the vault room?"

"If he did, I never saw any," Donald replied.

"Where would he hide the keys?" Annie pondered aloud.

♦ ♦ ♦

Annie was setting the table for dinner, still thinking about the locked doors and trying her best to figure out where Robert would hide the keys. Dan, bounding through the front door, shook Annie from her thoughts.

Dan set bags of Chinese food on the dining room table, turned to kiss Lizzy and walked off to wash his hands.

Stella, Marie, and Lizzy began to dish the food out on the serving plates. Annie went to the kitchen for napkins and chopsticks. Donald filled the water pitcher and added ice. He brought the water to the table and began filling glasses.

Annie finished what she was doing, and she saw her family all taking part in dinner preparations. She smiled as she thought about how wonderful it was that Lizzy had become part of her family, and how Marie fit comfortably with this group. It was all Annie could ask for. Moments like this made her realize what a fortunate person she was at this point in her life.

"Annie?" Stella said. "Are you going to sit down and eat?"

Annie had been daydreaming again. She quickly sat down between Marie and Donald. Dishes were passed and plates filled as the conversations began around the table.

"I have exciting news for you, Annie," Stella said, as she placed beef and broccoli on her plate and passed the serving dish to Marie.

Marie passed it along to Annie without placing any of the food on her plate. Everyone stopped to listen for the bit of exciting news. Stella continued to spoon out food onto her plate without speaking another word.

"Well, Mom?" Dan asked.

Stella looked up at Dan. "I went to the courthouse today to look up the information Annie had asked me to research."

"And...?" Dan asked impatiently.

"What did you find out, Mom?" Annie inquired, leaning forward with anticipation.

"I found out who owns the house on the hill," Stella said coolly. "Pass me the rice, please."

"Mom!" both Annie and Dan cried in unison.

"Okay, okay," Stella said, laughing at how anxious her kids were to hear the news.

"Well...," Stella said. "The house on the hill is, or was, owned by Robert Harper."

The group froze for a moment, letting the information sink in.

"Robert Harper?" Annie questioned.

"Yes, and when he passed, Helen Harper inherited the house. Which means, you now own the house," Stella reported. "I contacted Charles Conklin and asked him to verify the information for me. He is doing some research and will get back to either you or me. Probably you, since I told him you would be paying his fee."

"That's no problem," Donald said. "We'll take care of any fees."

"Then someone is trespassing on OUR property," Annie said, looking straight at Donald and then to Dan.

"I told you before, I had patrol check out the house. There is no one inside...at least from what they could see through the windows."

This news certainly surprised Annie. She decided she would go to the house and check it out. She wondered if behind one of the locked doors she would find a room which had the keys to the house on the hill. There was no way she could hire a locksmith without letting the entire town find out about the underground house. She needed to figure out another way to get inside. Annie knew attempting to chop through the doors with an ax would be useless, as the doors were made of metal.

Annie suddenly realized that the only food on her plate was the beef and broccoli. She had been absentmindedly passing all the dishes on to Donald while listening to the news from her mother. Donald noticed Annie looking at her plate, and began picking up dishes from the center of the table and holding them for Annie to serve herself more food.

"On another subject," Donald spoke up, waiting for everyone's attention. "Annie, Lizzy, and I made a search downstairs for Robert's office. Annie may have found it, but it's locked, and we have no idea where Robert hid the keys."

Donald began to tell the story of Annie and Lizzy locating the locked doors. He explained that the doors had been constructed of metal, so he figured they must be rooms of some importance. He did not want to call a locksmith, as that would cause gossip around town.

Donald asked if anyone had suggestions for getting inside the rooms. Discussion continued during dinner around both the house on the hill and the hidden rooms downstairs. Both Annie and Dan told the story of seeing flashes of lights and possibly someone in the window in the house on the hill on the afternoon of the weddings.

The family was listening as Donald explained about the dark figure sneaking around the back of the garage, which made Stella shiver. Both Donald and Dan said they would check out behind the garage as soon as they finished dinner.

Once the dinner dishes had been cleared from the table, Dan and Donald made their way out the kitchen door, followed by Annie and Lizzy. Stella and Marie stood at the opened kitchen door and watched the four young people walk through the yard to the back side of the garage. Stella looked at Marie in question.

"I want to go," Marie said, and began walking through the back yard. Stella shrugged and reluctantly followed.

When they were all gathered, Annie suggested that Stella and Lizzy go left to the side of the garage and wait for Dan and Donald. Annie and Marie would move to the right side of the garage, and stand near the cottage. Annie was able to see Lizzy and her mother from her vantage point.

"We don't see Donald or Dan," Stella called out.

"Marie and I will check this side," Annie responded. "Stay there, Mom, and we'll circle around to you."

"We're going there without Donald?" Marie asked, sounding a bit unsure of the situation.

"Sure," Annie said. "You like a mystery, right?"

"I like Nancy Drew."

"Okay, then," Annie stated. "I'll be Nancy and you be Bess or George."

"I want to be Bess. She's pretty and gets scared like me."

"Let's do this, Bess," Annie said, moving forward, hugging the fence line behind a tall shrub.

Marie giggled and followed closely behind Annie, at times hanging onto the back of Annie's shirt for security.

As Annie and Marie reached the back of the garage, they spotted Lizzy standing on the other side, waving to them.

"Have you seen Dan and Donald?" Annie called out to Lizzy.

"No. Just you and Marie."

Annie walked the length of the back of the garage with Marie close behind her. They reached Lizzy, wondering where the guys were. As they were looking around, a door opened up nearly knocking into

Annie. She jumped back just in time to see Dan emerging from a hidden door at the corner on the back side of the building.

"Another hidden door?" Annie asked Donald.

"Neat, huh?" Donald smiled. "I tripped over a rock and fell into the door, which popped it open."

"Donald and I found stairs, which lead down to a small room under the RV pad." Dan said. "It seems to be a sump pump room. It may be draining water coming off the hill to the street. I bet the pump had been installed to keep water out of the underground house."

"It also looks like the pump needs some maintenance before winter rains begin," Donald added. "I can take a closer look later."

"That doesn't explain the creepy guy sneaking through the back yard," Lizzy pointed out.

"True," Dan said. "Well, maybe we should go back down to the room with flashlights and check the place out further."

"I'll check the garage and see if I can find a couple of lights," Donald offered, heading around the corner of the garage and out of sight.

Stella walked up to the group standing in the back of the garage. "I locked up the house. I didn't want any surprise visitors."

"Dan and Donald found another secret room," Marie spoke up.

"Oh, dear," Stella said. "Annie, if I knew this house had so many secrets, I would have suggested you sell it immediately."

"Mom! Donald and I love this house. And I bet you love it, too."

Stella did not say a word, but the expression on her face told Annie that her mother would not have it any other way. This property had now become the home she, too, cherished. Annie knew that her mother shared her love of their newly enlarged family gathering here.

Donald returned with the flashlights. As Dan and Donald descended into the dark stairway, Annie and Lizzy could not resist finding out what was down in the sump pump room...if anything of interest. Stella and Marie remained at the top of the stairway with the door open. Stella instructed Annie to give details as they went, so she would know they were okay.

"Hey!" shouted Donald. "We found another door. It's locked."

CHAPTER 6

Tuesday Morning

Annie woke early, dressed, and was sitting in her cozy sitting area when Donald joined her with a cup of coffee. Laddie followed Donald and made himself at home on the cloth-covered chair next to Donald.

"You tossed and turned all night," Donald told Annie. "What's troubling you?"

"How many secrets does this house hold? Are they good secrets, or are we going to find out something sinister about this house?"

"My aunt and uncle were not sinister-type people," Donald stated. "My uncle may have been a secretive man, I'll admit, but think of how exciting it will be discovering the mysteries here."

Annie squeezed Donald's hand, and took a sip from her coffee cup. "I think I will head out early to the shop this morning. I have a lot of catching up to do."

"I have no meetings scheduled today, so I might be able to catch up on some work as well. Your mom mentioned something about grocery shopping and a list on the kitchen counter. Do you want me to add anything to the list?

"Potato chips and chocolate," Annie told Donald as she kissed him, and stood to leave. Laddie followed her out and down the stairs. She opened the door in the laundry room, which led to Laddie's enclosed run. He rushed through the doorway and began sniffing for the perfect spot to relieve himself.

When she finished filling Callie's food and water dishes, she entered the kitchen to find Donald adding to the list on the counter. Annie saw such things as beer, cookies, chips, summer sausage, crackers, and sparkling water written on the paper.

"There is nothing healthy on this list," Annie commented. "And before you comment, I know I'm contributing to the snacks list as well. Maybe we should add some vegetables to make it look like we made an effort to eat right."

Donald kissed Annie and picked up the cup of freshly brewed coffee from the machine before walking to his office. The light of day was shining brightly at six-thirty in the morning, and Annie felt ready to tackle much-needed shop work. She looked forward to getting back to a normal life and schedule.

♦ ♦ ♦

Entering the long line at Ione's Bakery & Coffee Shop, Annie spotted LaVerne and Lorraine in line a few people ahead of her. Once they got their coffee and donut, they settled at a small table near the street-side window. Annie soon joined them with her usual coffee and chocolate croissant, and a bag full of pastries for Lizzy, Marie, and Daisy when they arrived at work later.

"Ladies, may I join you?" Annie requested, as she walked up to the table.

"Oh, Annie Weston Harper," LaVerne said. "Please, grab a chair, sit down, and tell us all about married life to that hunky man of yours." LaVerne looked around the somewhat crowded room and then spoke, "Young man? Yes, you. Would you be a gentleman and bring that chair over here?" She pointed across the room at an occupied table of two. An empty third chair was at the table.

The baffled young man rose from his chair, went to the table where two young women sat, and asked to take the chair. The young girls coyly smiled him and offered the chair. He set the chair down for Annie to sit on.

"Now, go ask one of those girls out while they are still looking at you," Lorraine said in a soft voice to the lad. She raised her voice for all to hear, "Oh, what a gentleman you are, sir. Thank you kindly." The young man, red-faced, walked to his table and sat down, too embarrassed to look at the girls, who were now giggling.

"Young people today don't know how to mingle," LaVerne declared. "They think meeting someone should only be online. You miss so much trying to find that right person on the internet. In my day..."

"Your day was a hundred years ago," Lorraine broke in. "Things are done differently these days. These young people have no self-esteem. They like to hide behind a computer." She directed her attention toward Annie, "So, Annie, are you happy to be back to work?"

"I love my shop," Annie replied. "I noticed you two are out and about early. Are you on a case?" Annie asked almost in a teasing gesture.

Lorraine leaned in toward the center of the table and lowered her voice, "As a matter of fact, we are,"

"We're on a case for Detective Surely," LaVerne said.

"Dan?"

"He's Detective Weston now, LaVerne," Lorraine corrected.

"Oh, that's right," LaVerne said. "Yes, Detective Weston asked us to help him with some surveillance of the house above your house."

"Really?" Annie said. "Detective Dan Weston asked you for help?" This was a surprise to Annie. Was Dan getting soft? Why would he ask the Silver Sleuths, unless he was finally admitting that they knew everything happening in town? Annie smiled inwardly. She was definitely going to ask Dan about this. "Have you discovered anything yet?"

"Today is our first day," Lorraine said quietly.

"If there is anything going on at that house," LaVerne proclaimed, "the Silver Sleuths will uncover the mystery."

"If you get into a bind, you can count on me," Annie added lightheartedly, remembering the last time she had to rescue the ladies from an investigation.

"We'll keep that in mind, Annie." LaVerne returned, clearing her throat.

It was then that Annie got an idea. Lorraine once mentioned that her late husband was a locksmith, and she herself had learned the lock picking trade. Could Lorraine teach her how to pick locks? Annie decided it was worth it to ask.

"Lorraine? Would you be able to teach me how to pick locks?" To Annie, the words coming from her lips seemed like someone else asking. Lock picking was something a criminal would do, right?

Annie waited for an answer. Lorraine looked at LaVerne and then responded to Annie.

"Whatever for?"

"I just wanted to learn in case I lock myself out some day," Annie said, trying to choose her words wisely. She did not think they were buying it.

"What's the real reason, Annie?" LaVerne asked.

"Okay, I have a locked door in the house I want to open. The keys were not in the group of keys that Helen left me."

Lorraine leaned in to whisper to Annie, "In the underground?"

"What?" Annie tried to hide her surprise and not appear like she knew of an underground house. She was not very good at lying.

"We know about the secret underground, but Elsie and Millie don't." LaVerne said, leaning in and whispering as well. "Robert made Lorraine's husband sign a paper saying he would take the information to his grave...which he did. We only know there was some type of construction going on."

"Really?" Annie said in mock surprise.

"I would be happy to help you out," Lorraine said. "Especially, when you were there for us at Eddie's house. When would you like to begin?"

"Today, if possible," Annie said. She was trying to contain in her excitement. She was going to be a lock picker! "Can I come over after four o'clock today?"

"I'll be home," Lorraine said. "I expect you want to keep this quiet from everyone?"

"Oh, yes," Annie said. "Please don't tell anyone. More importantly, don't tell Dan."

♦ ♦ ♦

Back at the shop, Annie was having a difficult time keeping her mind on business. Just the thought of learning this new skill, although a bit criminal in design, was exciting to her. She wondered what her law enforcement father would have thought.

Maybe she should just show Lorraine and LaVerne the underground. They already knew there was something being built underground, just not what was there at the moment. They may have suspected a house, but were not sure. Then again, if she let Lorraine pick the lock, it would ruin the fun of learning a new skill. She was just learning for fun, she reminded herself. She would never use it for any illegal purpose.

Annie's thoughts were interrupted by the door chime with Lizzy, followed by Marie and Stella, entering the shop.

"Good morning, everyone!" Annie said, realizing she was a bit too cheery.

Lizzy eyed Annie suspiciously, "What have you done?"

"Nothing," Annie said. She stood from her crafting desk and walked to the office. Realizing she had walked into the office for no good reason and feeling a bit embarrassed, Annie walked right back out and stood at the counter.

"I am waiting for a call from Mr. Conklin," Stella announced, pulling her cell phone from her purse and looking at the screen. "Then I am going back to the county records office and do some more research. I think I am on to something important."

"Can you tell us what it is?" Lizzy asked, leaning on the counter toward Stella.

"Not just yet. I have some bartering to do with Mr. Conklin for information."

"Mom," Annie said, "I will pay Mr. Conklin whatever he charges. Just continue the research. I am assuming it is about the house on the hill?"

"Oh, I know you are willing to help pay for Mr. Conklin's services, but I want to be able to entice him with one of my paintings to get the help with the information I am looking for. He is a very good researcher. Much better than me."

"What exactly are you trying to find?" Lizzy asked.

"I don't want to say at this time." With that said, Stella bid good bye and left the shop.

"Boy," Lizzy said. "You Weston women can be very secretive at times."

"Don't forget, you are a Weston woman now."

"So, that gives me license to be secretive?" Lizzy questioned.

Annie laughed.

Daisy entered the shop, and noticing the closed sign was still displayed, she closed the door and turned the sign to 'open'. Then she entered the office and hung her purse and sweatshirt on a hook.

"Good morning," Annie said. We have a full day of work ahead of us today. Marie is in the storage room getting supplies out for the first class.

"I'll go help."

After Daisy entered the storage room, Annie turned toward Lizzy and whispered, "I am going to learn how to pick locks!"

"What? Why? How?"

"Just don't tell Dan," Annie warned. "He doesn't need to know."

"I guess now that I am a Weston woman, I can keep this secret."

"Remember when I rescued LaVerne and Lorraine from Eddie's garage?" Annie asked.

"Yes. And then you got stuck in the doorway."

"That was an accident...as I was saying, Lorraine told me that her husband had been the locksmith in town, and he taught her how to pick locks. She is going to teach me tonight."

"And you are going to try to pick the locks on the doors of the rooms downstairs?"

"Yes!" Annie said, almost shouting. She realized she had raised her voice. She looked at the door of the storage room and waited to see if Daisy or Marie might have heard her and would come out to check. There was no movement at the door. She turned back to Lizzy and continued speaking in a lowered voice. "Anyway, Lorraine is going to teach me, and I will try to get the door locks open without having to show her the underground house. If I told her, then others might find out. We agreed the information would stay with family for now."

"Can I go with you?" Lizzy asked.

"I should go alone." Annie said. "I don't want to make Dan suspicious. You know how he gets."

"True," Lizzy said, thinking about Dan's usual reaction to news of Annie's activities. "Does Donald know?"

"Not yet," Annie said. "I need to call him and let him know that Lorraine agreed to teach me the art of lock picking this afternoon."

Annie pulled her cell phone from her pocket to make the call to Donald.

Lizzy told Annie that she was going next door to confirm the meeting at Ione's Bakery & Coffee Shop for tonight at seven o'clock. All the shop owners had been contacted and agreed to be in attendance. Ione normally closed the shop at five or six.

Lizzy had previously sent new contracts out to the owners with the adjusted lease agreement and an agenda for the meeting. She factored in current maintenance and repairs needed in the following year, along with taxes and insurance, and was able to reduce the lease amounts. After conferring with Annie, they agreed it was a fair asking price for the leases.

Even though Annie owned the buildings now, she still contributed the amount that was in her lease agreement. Her store was profiting, and she wanted to raise her lease rate in line with the others, but Lizzy convinced her otherwise, reminding her it was set at what Helen wanted, and Annie relented at that point.

Late afternoon came slowly for Annie. Daisy and Marie took care of the shop while Annie taught a class making a decorative box for small gifts or candy. Lizzy kept to herself in the office, ordering supplies and preparing for the meeting tonight. At one point, Annie heard Lizzy in the office practicing her speech out loud. She was relieved that Lizzy was taking over the management of R&H Enterprises. Managing a paper craft shop was all Annie could handle right now.

"It's three-thirty, Annie," Lizzy said. She was clearly excited for Annie.

"Thanks for reminding me, Lizzy." Annie gathered her purse and tote bag filled with crafting paper, scissors, double-sided tape, glue, ruler, small cutting board, small scoring board, and decorative bits she had made earlier. She was hoping to have an hour or so this evening to come up with a new box idea.

"Annie, you need a crafting room at the house," Lizzy remarked, noticing the bulging tote bag. "It must be tiring to carry all that stuff back and forth."

"You're right, Lizzy," Annie said. "I think I will set up the area around the crafting table in the cottage. I could use the bookshelves to store supplies in decorative boxes. It would be a perfect place for my crafts, if you don't mind my being there."

"After the incident with the rose," Lizzy said, "I would love the company while I work out there."

"Speaking of the rose...have you any idea who might be sending you the gifts?"

"I have no idea. There is nothing specific about any of the notes, just the possessive comments."

"Didn't one of the notes say something about not letting you go?" Annie looked at her watch. She had twenty minutes to get to Millie's house, where Lorraine was currently living, for her first lesson in lock picking.

"That's right," Lizzy said. "I will gather all the notes together and ask Dan what he thinks."

"Good luck asking Dan for his opinion," Annie laughed, as she turned and left the shop. Walking back to the shop, Annie poked her head through the doorway and called out to Marie, who was standing at the counter.

"Would you like to walk home with me, Marie?"

"No thanks," Marie said. "Mom wants me to get dessert at Ione's. I can walk home by myself."

Annie turned toward Daisy and asked, "Is William working today?"

Daisy nodded.

Marie blushed and said, "He's just a friend."

CHAPTER 7

Tuesday Evening

Annie had ten minutes before she was to meet Lorraine at Millie's house. Because her walk home was short, and Millie lived across the street, she would just have time to drop off her purse and bag, say hello to Donald, and give Laddie a hug.

Laddie bounded out of the office, almost pushing Donald over. Annie laughed at seeing how excited Laddie was to see her. Annie gave Laddie a big hug and rubbed his back. Donald stood by watching the scene before him.

"I was wondering if you were going to get home in time," Donald said, moving around Laddie to give Annie a kiss. He walked to the kitchen sink and rinsed out his coffee cup before setting it in the dishwasher.

"I have been so excited all day," Annie stated. "I feel like I am learning something daring, and at the same time, I can't help but feel like I am infiltrating the Silver Sleuth world. I may even find out how they know everything before anyone else."

"Annie, my spy," Donald laughed. "You need a code name."

"You are teasing me, Donald. Seriously, this lock picking skill could come in handy around here. Think of all the locks we've encountered so far."

"True," Donald said. He leaned against the counter with his arms folded in thought. "Do you think Lorraine would teach me how to change the tumblers in a lock? I could re-key just about every lock on this property. It might also be beneficial to re-key your shop doors every year or so."

"Donald, that's brilliant. I don't think Lorraine would turn you down. The ladies all like you. Come with me and we can ask."

Donald let Laddie out for a quick potty break and locked the house. He turned on the alarm before they left the house. Annie sent a text to

Marie that the house alarm was on, and both she and Donald would be at Millie's house.

At exactly four o'clock in the afternoon, Annie and Donald rang Millie's doorbell. LaVerne answered the door and invited them inside.

"We were not expecting you, Donald," LaVerne stated.

"I have a request for Lorraine," Donald said.

Lorraine walked into the living room from the kitchen area. "I suppose you want to learn how to re-key locks?"

Annie and Donald looked at each other in surprise.

"Ah, yes," Donald said hesitantly.

How did Lorraine know that Donald wanted to learn to re-key locks? Donald had not thought about it until about ten minutes ago. With only a look, they decided not to even ask.

"Let's get started then," Lorraine stated.

Lorraine led Annie and Donald to a shop behind the garage. She unlocked a series of locks, then opened the door and switched on the lights. She motioned for Annie and Donald to enter.

Once inside, Annie found herself looking at what could be a commercial locksmith shop. Various displays featured door locks, deadbolts, padlocks, and other types of locking devices that Annie had not seen before. Displays of key blanks were on a center island, the counter of which took up most of the center of the shop. Standing on the island counter top were several upright displays of miniature doors with varying types of locks. One had a regular locking doorknob, another had a deadbolt, and still another had a lock Annie had seen before, but not used on a regular basis.

"When my husband passed away," Lorraine began, "I closed his store and put the inventory in storage. When Millie offered us a home here, she insisted I clear out the storage locker and put it in this room, in the back of the garage. We now call it the shop."

"What's behind these doors?" Donald asked, pointing to the floor to ceiling cabinet doors.

"Oh, dear," Lorraine said, moving between Donald and the cabinets. "Just inventory from my husband's store. Nothing more. Now, let's get started. Annie has a meeting to go to tonight, and I am sure you will want time to eat dinner before the meeting."

Lorraine moved to the counter in the center of the room and pulled forward one of the displays with a miniature door. She turned the knob to show it was locked.

"The first thing about learning to pick locks is that you must never use your skills for illegal purposes. Only pick a lock you have legal authority to enter. With that said, let's move on to tools of the trade."

Donald looked at Annie and smiled, both recalling LaVerne and Lorraine getting caught in Eddie's garage about a month ago.

For the next hour, Annie began learning to pick a common household lock. The more she worked at it, the easier it became to open.

"Donald," Annie said in a loud whisper. "I'm actually doing it. I am able to pick a lock."

Lorraine gave Donald a look and said, "That's nice, dear. But this happens to be one of the easiest locks to pick. I would not recommend having this brand of lock on any door. I just started you out on this one for practice."

Not discouraged, Annie decided she would check the locks in her house and see what she could pick. Lorraine loaned her a few picks and told her how to purchase them online. Lorraine advised Donald that she had some time tomorrow after four o'clock to begin his lessons on re-keying locks. He made a notation in his phone calendar. Annie and Donald then thanked Lorraine and left for home.

Once home, Annie immediately went to the office door and inspected the lock. Standing inside the office, Donald decided to go sit in his desk chair and watch as Annie worked the lock. When the door kept moving while she worked, she decided to go to the living room side of the doorway and close the door. Periodically, Annie checked to see if the lock was open by testing the knob. Donald waited patiently while Annie fumbled with the lock picking tools, dropping them every so often, and making various noises of frustration.

"Donald?"

"Yes."

"The door is locked."

Grinning widely, Donald rose from his chair and walked over to open the office door. He was trying desperately not to laugh.

"Don't mock me. I just need practice."

Annie's phone chimed, and she noticed a text from her mother. "Mom is running late. I need to get dinner started."

Annie took one last look at the door lock and pouted. She was not going to let this deter her one bit. Being the determined person she was, she would practice every chance she got. Relax and let the feeling of the pick guide you, Annie kept reminding herself. After another failed attempt, Annie stood and walked to the kitchen to start dinner.

"Want some help?" Donald said, checking the lock on the office door before closing it. He followed Annie to the kitchen.

♦ ♦ ♦

Annie and Lizzy sat at a small, two-person table, watching the shop owners slowly file inside the coffee shop. Lizzy seemed calm, prepared, and organized. She dressed in what Annie could only describe as a business suit purchased from Rodeo Drive. Her hair, styled up off her shoulders, stayed in place with a pearl studded curved comb. Her make-up was impeccable. If Annie had never met Lizzy, she would have thought Lizzy was a high-priced lawyer.

On the other hand, Annie looked down at her own outfit to discover she wore black slacks littered with cat fur and a white blouse that now had a coffee stain on the front. Her hair was in a pony tail. She was definitely nervous.

How were the vendors going to handle Annie as the owner the buildings? She really had not heard any discouraging words in the last month, but she feared they would turn on her, and she would not know what to say. Thank goodness Donald agreed to be at the meeting.

Speaking of Donald, Annie thought to herself as she looked up to see Donald and Dan walk into the coffee shop. Donald went directly to Annie, and Dan went to purchase a donut and coffee. Lizzy stood and walked gracefully over to greet Dan.

"You look a bit unraveled, Annie," Donald said, sitting down in the chair that Lizzy had just left. He took a sip from Annie's coffee cup and a bite from her not-yet-touched chocolate pastry.

"What? Why would you say that?"

Donald made obvious his gesture of looking down at Annie's feet.

Annie looked down at her shoes and grimaced. How in the world had she not notice two different shoes on her feet? She then took notice of her blouse. Some how she had managed to get a fresh coffee stain on it.

"Oh, good grief!" Annie exclaimed while trying to fold the material of her blouse to hide the dark brown colored stain on the front. She looked up at Donald, "I just don't want anyone in town to hate me for owning the buildings they are renting. That's why I put Lizzy in charge. She's a tough business woman."

"So, they would hate her?" Donald teased.

"Certainly not, Donald," Annie said in surprise. She sat back in her seat. "They love her. She looks like she knows what she's doing all the time. How can you not love that? I'm a mess!"

Lizzy walked back to the table carrying a bouquet of mixed flowers and a box of Moonstruck Chocolates. She set them on the table and stared dryly at Annie. Donald stood to offer the seat back to her, but she shook her head no, choosing to stand instead.

"Another anonymous gift?" Annie asked.

"I'm afraid so. Ione said that they just appeared out of nowhere on her counter. There was a note to give them to me at the meeting."

"But we've been here for at least thirty minutes," Annie remarked. "How could we not see flowers this size being delivered after we arrived?"

"Dan wanted to fingerprint the vase, but Ione and the staff have been handling it," Lizzy said in a soft tone of voice. She did not want anyone to hear her talking about the flowers. "Do you think it's a shop owner sending me these gifts?"

"I would have been suspicious about the flowers, but not when there is a diamond bracelet involved. That bracelet costs more than what these people can afford."

Lizzy nodded in agreement. She looked at her watch and then turned to look at the audience, who were talking among themselves. "Time to begin, Annie," Lizzy whispered.

After introducing herself and Annie, and explaining the direction R&H Enterprises was taking, Lizzy finished her speech in twenty minutes. She opened up the floor for questions or discussion.

The group seemed quite pleased with the information regarding reduced monthly payments and the scheduled maintenance already occurring. They now understood where the money was being directed. Lizzy was being paid a salary, but Annie chose not to take compensation as the owner. That left the majority of lease payment going to maintenance, taxes, and insurance. A small amount would be allocated to hire a CPA.

Several shop owners reported that Sheryl Doxie did the majority of the Bridgewater Harbor taxes each year. Lizzy told the group that she would keep Sheryl in mind. In the end, everyone was in agreement, things would continue as it did before Robert and Helen Harper had passed away.

Lizzy asked if there were any further questions before ending the meeting. Fred, from Fred's Hardware Store stood and asked, "Robert made us display a frame with a cut paper design on it above our door. Now that he's gone, can we toss it?"

The room rumbled with comments of similar framed art in the other shops.

"Since the pieces were put there by Robert Harper, I will stop by each of your businesses and retrieve them. Please don't discard the pieces. They belong to Annie now. She will decide what to do with them," Lizzy addressed the owners. "I can stop by tomorrow."

Ione walked up to Lizzy, holding a piece of framed paper cut art for the audience to view. "Is this what you are talking about, Fred?"

"That's it, but mine looks a little different," said Fred.

The audience nodded in agreement. They each had a similar framed piece of paper. Lizzy repeated that she would collect them all tomorrow morning and forward them to Annie. Ione handed the frame to Lizzy, who in turn gave it to Annie.

Annie briefly scanned the paper inside the frame. It was a curious piece of art. She could see no purpose for the way the paper was cut and framed. She set the frame down on the table and continued to listen to the questions from the shop owners.

Lizzy kept her promise that the meeting would only be one hour long and promptly ended the session. She announced she would notify every one soon of the next scheduled meeting.

♦ ♦ ♦

It was eight-thirty in the evening, and just about dark outside due to the clouds moving in off the ocean, when Annie and Donald walked through the front door of their house. Annie set her framed art on the floor near the front door. She was planning to take it to the cottage in the morning.

Marie was watching a romantic comedy on the television and finishing a last bite of ice cream. She stood and took her empty dish to the kitchen. Rinsing out the bowl, she placed it in the dishwasher.

"Should I start the dishwasher?" Marie asked.

"If it's full. Thank you, Marie," Annie responded. "I'm going downstairs to work on that lock."

"Want some company?" Donald asked.

"Can I come?" Marie asked.

"Sure," Annie responded.

"Is Oscar there?" Marie asked, with a look of concern on her face.

"I believe he is still on the patio," Donald said.

"I think I will stay here."

"He doesn't bite," Donald said trying not to laugh.

"He's scary."

"We'll leave Laddie up here with you to watch television," Donald said, while walking to the office door.

Annie was planning to work the lock on the door closest to the entry under the stairs, but Donald suggested they look around the underground house. First, he wanted to check on Oscar and make sure he had not moved from the last time they saw him. Sure enough, Oscar was enjoying his seat near the pool and still sporting sunglasses.

Annie followed Donald into the house and down the hallway to the first bedroom on the right. He turned the doorknob, but discovered it was locked.

"Why is this door locked?" Donald asked Annie.

"I believe your mother locked it," Annie replied.

"Why? What's in there?"

"It's a room with a young boy theme and photos on the wall of you growing up," Annie said, placing her hand on Donald's shoulder, showing her support.

"Do you have a key for this lock?"

"No, but I can use the practice trying to pick the lock," Annie said, as she pulled out the set of picks from the case in her pocket.

"Practice away," Donald said, making a grand sweeping gesture with his hand as if to give permission to unlock the door.

Annie knelt down by the door lock and stopped to take a deep breath. She focused on what Lorraine taught her only hours ago. "Feel the lock," Annie told herself.

Within five minutes, Annie felt the knob move and realized she had successfully opened the door. She stopped to take in the moment of her first lock picking experience. She turned to Donald, who was equally surprised by Annie mastering the lock so soon.

With the door slightly ajar, Annie asked, "Are you sure you want to see this?"

To answer Annie's question, Donald moved forward and pushed open the door. He reached for a light switch on the wall and flipped it on. He stood for a moment, taking in the room.

Photos of Donald in various ages were grouped decoratively on the wall. Donald walked up to the photos to get a closer look at each framed picture. The majority of the photos were of Donald and his aunt and uncle in happy poses.

"I remember my aunt taking these photos," Donald said, moving to the next photo. "I realize now why my aunt was so happy to spend time with me. I just don't know why they had to keep such a secret."

"Maybe it's time to talk to your parents and find out the story behind it all,"

Annie stated.

"Not yet," Donald said, turning to answer Annie. "I'm not ready."

"I feel confident now about trying the lock on the door upstairs," Annie said, attempting to change the subject.

"You go ahead. I want to stay here for a little while and check out the room. Give me a shout if you get the lock open."

Annie stood before the metal door in the hallway, attempting to convince herself she could open the lock. She knelt down by the lock and pulled out her set of picks. As she did before, she took a deep breath and told herself to 'feel the lock'.

For the next twenty minutes, Annie continued to work the lock. This was a high-end lock Lorraine discussed in Annie's first lesson. Annie was getting frustrated, but remained determined to succeed. She sat down on the floor to rest for a moment, trying not to get discouraged. Lorraine did say it would take much practice. Annie was the type of person who could do anything she put her mind to, and this was not going to defeat her. Annie worked the lock for a period of time, and was just about to start over when she felt the doorknob move.

"Donald!" Annie shouted. "Donald! I did it! I did it!"

Donald, hearing Annie's shouts, raced out of the room and up the stairs to find Annie jumping up and down in the hallway. He noticed the door was open and standing ajar.

"Annie, you did it!" Donald said, hugging Annie and twirling her around. "Did you look inside the room?"

"No. I was waiting for you."

"Don't be disappointed if it's only a storage room or closet," Donald stated.

"At least now I know I can open these locks. Nothing is stopping us from exploring the rest of the house."

Annie motioned she was ready for Donald to open the door. He stepped in front of the door, pushed it wide open, and reached for a switch on the wall. Light illuminated the room.

CHAPTER 8

Wednesday

Annie and Donald stood speechless at the doorway of a sizable office area. Across the room stood a stylish wooden desk with a matching credenza standing against the wall under what appeared to be a window with closed drapes.

A dark green leather desk chair sat pulled away from the desk. Robert had the usual desk supplies and features, such as a desk mat, telephone, desk lamp, a framed photo of Helen, and a pair of reading glasses left abandoned as if Robert had just risen and walked away.

Annie turned to the left to view a well-built fireplace with an ornate wood mantel. Arranged in front of the fireplace sat two brown leather chairs positioned next to a small round table with a reading lamp. A book, with a bookmark inserted in the middle, lay on the table next to the chair on the left. A small crystal bowl of wrapped hard candies rested next to the book. Sconce lighting surrounded the sitting area. Bookcases stood on both sides of the fireplace and filled the wall space with neatly stored books and knick-knacks occupying the shelves.

To the right of the desk, Annie viewed what appeared to be a work zone. An island stood in the center of the area with a work station at a height comfortable which one could stand and work on projects. Engineering type drawers filled the space below the counter top area of the station. Attached to the wall behind the island were white boards which seemed to be filled with various notations and drawings. Built-in file cabinets lined the back wall.

Annie moved behind the desk, with the intention of making a thorough search. The place belonged to her and Donald, so she did not feel like she was intruding by trying to find out information about Robert or R&H Enterprises. Annie pulled up the desk chair and sat down.

Annie perused the stack of papers on the desk: Invitations to various medical events, cards from colleagues, and a receipt from Charles Conklin dated several months ago. The typed receipt referenced a conditional contract drawn up for the senior apartment complex owned by Felix Bankford.

Annie searched the drawers in the desk. There appeared to be nothing of further interest nor anything else pertaining to the document. She viewed a key in the top drawer and picked the metal object up. She put the key in the lock of the credenza behind her and turned. The drawer opened and when Annie peered inside, she gave a shout of joy.

"I take it, you found something interesting," Donald spoke, as he focused on the papers he had been studying.

"As a matter of fact," Annie declared, "I just found all the documents regarding R&H Enterprises. These are the current records we had been hoping to find."

"When you get a chance, come over here and take a look at these architectural drawings for a shared-wall housing development. From the paperwork I have been reading, this gives the impression of someone wanting to tear down the senior apartments and build a housing complex...not necessarily for seniors. These places would have had lots of stairs."

"I found a receipt from Charles Conklin regarding a conditional contract pertaining to the senior apartments and its owner."

Annie began searching the labels of the files in the drawer. "Here's a file on the senior apartments." She pulled the file out and set the papers down on the desk. Donald walked up behind her and read over her shoulder as she opened the file and tried to gain some knowledge of its contents. What they discovered inside was not what Annie or Donald would expect. Instead, what they found looked like notations about the senior apartments' owner and various comments about money, which seemed difficult to read due to Robert's terrible handwriting.

"I wonder if my dad would be able to decipher Uncle Robert's handwriting?" Donald speculated to Annie.

"It might be worth a try to figure out what is written on this paper," Annie said.

"Now come over here and take a look at what I found," Donald said. "It might relate to the document you found."

Annie listened attentively as Donald explained the drawings and documents regarding the senior apartments. He pointed out the prints of the proposed housing development.

"Donald, you don't suppose Robert was going to buy the property and kick those poor seniors out of their homes?" Annie felt her stomach do a flip-flop at the suggestion.

"That is what it looks like on the surface, Annie."

"It's time to talk to the Silver Sleuths tomorrow," Annie announced. "Do you think that is why LaVerne, Lorraine, and Elsie moved in with Millie? Did they know something was going to happen?"

"With those ladies, I think they probably knew before Robert did."

Annie looked at the time piece on her wrist. It was nearing ten o'clock, and she began to feel tired. She suggested to Donald that they call it a night and go to bed. Donald agreed. Annie closed the credenza and placed the senior file on the desk. She was planning to have Lizzy come to the office and help her search for more information the next day.

Donald walked to the door with Annie close behind. He was about to reach for the light switch, when he noticed Annie eyeing the coat rack next to the door.

"I didn't notice this when we came into the office," Annie said. She pointed out a gray, tailored, suit jacket hanging on the coat rack. She reached up and pulled it off the hook, and instinctively began searching the pockets. Inside the right pocket were a set of keys. Annie pulled them out, gave Donald a knowing look, and tried the keys on the office door. The third key was able to unlock it.

"Good catch, Annie," Donald praised Annie, taking the jacket from Annie and hanging it back up on the hook. As an afterthought, he reached into the inside pocket. "Nothing."

"Do you find it strange that Robert would leave his keys and lock his office door?" Annie questioned Donald.

"I can imagine that happening if he were in a hurry to leave his office," Donald acknowledged. Then suggested, "Maybe he got a call, or someone was at the front door upstairs."

"Why would he lock his office?"

"Could be he closed it without checking the lock first."

"You are full of answers, aren't you?" Annie remarked, yawning through her statement.

"Let's call it a night." Donald said, checking to make sure the door locked, and Annie was still holding the keys. He turned the light off and closed the door.

◆ ◆ ◆

The next morning, Annie pushed open the door to Ione's Bakery & Coffee Shop. It was seven o'clock and the line consisted of early rising tourists. Most of the shop owners would come later, an hour or so before their shops scheduled to open at nine or ten in the morning.

"I think the meeting went very well last night," Ione said, as Annie stepped up to the counter.

"I couldn't agree more," Annie said. "We work alongside a great group of shop owners. Everyone gets along like an extended family. Thank you for letting us meet here."

"You are certainly welcome," Ione said, placing Annie's usual order in a bag.

Annie paid for her order and picked up the bag. William, Daisy's brother, was helping by pouring the drink orders. He handed Annie a cup of coffee. As she turned to leave the counter, she nearly ran into Janette Parker who had entered the shop and was heading to the end of the line.

"Oh, Annie," Janette said, jumping out of the way. "I am sorry. Are you okay?"

"I'm fine," Annie replied, looking down to make sure she had not spilled coffee on her shirt.

"Here are the framed paper art pieces from Spencer's Gallery and Bridgewater Inn for you," Janette said, handing a canvas bag to Annie. "I don't know if you heard yet, but I am the new manager of Spencer's Gallery."

"Janette, that's wonderful," Annie said. Annie had suspected that Jacquie, the gallery's owner, would hire Janette, who was an honest person, talented artist, and knew the art world. It was a perfect match for Jacquie.

"I have so much to tell you," Janette said. "Do you have a minute?"

"Would you mind coming to the shop?" Annie asked. "We can talk in private there. The store doesn't open for a couple of hours."

"I'll be there in a minute," Janette said, as she turned to pick up the slack in line to order.

Annie struggled to place her arm through the handles of the art bag while holding her coffee, donut bag, and purse. She managed to get out the door of the bakery shop with no mishaps. Unlocking her shop, she maneuvered inside safely and set down the bag before spilling coffee everywhere.

By the time Annie had turned on the shop and display lights, Janette was knocking on the ocean-side door of Ocean Loads of Paper. Stepping to the door, she unlocked and opened it for Janette to enter. Annie dragged a stool from behind the counter for Janette to sit down. She sat down across from her.

"Today's my second day as manager of the gallery," Janette began, taking her bear claw from a bag with the familiar Ione's Bakery & Coffee Shop logo on the side. "Yesterday, Jacquie had me contact Dan to pick up the art pieces Lawrence had left in the shop storage room. Dan said that he had already been in contact with a friend of his in Portland who referred him to someone in Seattle. The FBI contacted Dan, because they have an interest in both Walter and Lawrence. Apparently, the art works had been stolen from Seattle. A few are from private collections."

"That doesn't surprise me at all," Annie said. She picked up a napkin to wipe her mouth, then took a drink of coffee. "I am just happy you were able to retrieve your own painting."

Walter and Lawrence were a father and son team of art thieves who recently had stolen a painting from Janette's grandmother. Janette's grandmother died as a result of the dastardly actions performed by Walter.

"If you hadn't purchased the painting, it would be long gone by now," Janette said. "And, we never would have found my grandmother's jewels and learned the truth about Walter. I owe you so much!"

"Nonsense," Annie said. "It was just fortunate that you came to Bridgewater Harbor. And now you're staying, working, and painting. I am very happy for you."

"Thank you, Annie," Janette said. "On another note, Suzette met someone. I think she's in love. She's been acting all giddy lately." Suzette was Janette's cousin who owned the Bridgewater Inn across the street from Annie's shop.

"What? Really? Who is he?"

"He's the new chiropractor in town. His name is Chuck Kirkland. The office is right next to Bonnie's Bell Flower Florist. Chuck seems smitten with Suzette."

Annie was thinking about Suzette and how she came to Bridgewater Harbor after a terrible divorce. Suzette was able to purchase the inn and make it the success it was today.

Janette continued to explain how Suzette and Chuck met, all the while checking her watch to make sure she was not late for her second day as manager.

After finishing her pastry, Janette stood to leave. Annie walked her to the door and unlocked the deadbolt, thanked Janette for bringing the framed papercuts to her, and promised to return the canvas bag soon.

While Annie was cleaning up her mess from the counter, she remembered a shipment of boxes she had placed in the storage room to deal with later. She walked to the storeroom, stopped just inside the door, switched on the lights, and glanced at the ceiling remembering a previous unsettling incident. Nothing seemed out of place. She picked up one medium-sized box and stacked two smaller boxes on top. Walking back out to the main area of the shop, she stopped suddenly and froze.

There on the counter was a beautiful bouquet of fresh flowers and a fancy wrapped gift. Annie dropped the boxes on her counter and went to the shop door. She found the door unlocked! Annie's heart was racing as she made haste to lock the door. She picked up a pair of scissors for protection, and walked through the shop to make sure no one else was inside.

After determining she was alone, Annie grabbed her cell phone and called Donald. She told him about the delivery of the flowers and gift.

Donald said he would check the camera feed and call her back shortly. Annie told Donald she would call Dan to report the incident.

"Annie," Dan said, after Annie explained the situation. "I don't know that we have an actual burglary since your door had been unlocked and you were inside working. Someone might have thought you were open for business. Lizzy's with me now. We will be there in a minute." Dan hung up.

None the less, she felt compelled to check her office, desk, and safe. Annie was secure in the feeling that whoever left the flowers and gift did not disturb anything else. After all, she was not sure how a person would have even had time to deliver the flowers and leave unnoticed, much less enter her office.

Donald called back moments later with a report on the delivery person. He told Annie that a medium height, skinny person dressed in dark clothing and a hoodie over his head had entered, delivered the items to the counter and immediately left the shop.

"As I watched the feed beyond that point," Donald said. "I could see your delivery person through the shop windows. He met someone on the boardwalk and it looked like that person was paying the delivery guy. They left in separate directions."

"Could you tell who it was?" Annie asked.

"No," Donald stated, sounding as if he was being distracted by watching the video feed again. "You have signage on the shop door and I can't see their heads."

Donald told Annie that he would make a copy of the video feed for Dan and email it to him. Having to end the call for an upcoming meeting, Donald said good bye.

Annie stood, staring at the flowers and the attractively wrapped gift sitting on the counter next to the cash register. A small envelope, tucked among the flowers, showed Lizzy's name carefully printed in block letters. She could imagine any number of men wanting to get the attention of Lizzy, but why be so secretive? Who was stalking Lizzy? Could it be the person she saw in the house on the hill?

The sharp sound of a lock turning jolted Annie from her thoughts. Lizzy and Dan entered the store from the street-side door. Lizzy stopped short and stared at the large bouquet of flowers on display in front of her.

"Donald sent me a video of the flowers being delivered," Dan said, as he too stood and stared at the flowers.

"There's a gift for you too," Annie said to Lizzy, moving to the counter and pointing to where the package sat next to the flowers.

Lizzy looked to Dan, questioning if she should open the gift.

"Do you want me to open it?" Dan asked.

"No, I guess it will be okay. The other gift was expensive jewelry. And this is wrapped nicely. I guess it will be safe enough," Lizzy said, turning the package over and over in her hand.

After unwrapping a small jewelry box, Lizzy revealed it contained earrings. "These match the bracelet," Lizzy said, holding the earrings up in front of Annie.

Dan shook his head in disapproval of someone giving his wife expensive jewelry.

"Annie," Dan said, moving to the office. "I want to view this video on your computer."

After making the transfer of the file to Annie's computer, Dan, Lizzy, and she viewed the brief video. Dan requested Annie to replay the video several times.

"I think I know this guy," Dan said, moving closer to the screen. "I am sure I've seen him around town before."

CHAPTER 9

Wednesday Afternoon

Annie cleaned up after the last class of the day, disinfected the tables, and stored the supplies away in the cupboards. She swept the floor and surveyed the area one last time before heading toward the office.

Daisy had taught Marie how to ring up purchases earlier in the day. Annie watched from a distance as Marie counted out change to the customer, and placed the product in a bag. Marie shyly chatted with the woman at the counter. Daisy stood quietly to the side, making sure Marie completed the task at hand.

Annie entered her office and sat down at the desk. Glancing at her cell phone, she was disappointed not to find a message from either Dan or Donald, Annie set the instrument down, and began opening the mail.

Lizzy came crashing through the door trying to balance numerous framed art pieces. Annie made a dash for the door to help Lizzy, as the awkward bundle began escaping Lizzy's grip.

"This is only half of one side of the street," Lizzy said, attempting to place the pieces on the floor. "Have you figured out what to do with all these frames?"

"Yes, the office we talked about earlier this morning has a big island work space, perfect for removing the papers from the frames. The frames are beautiful. I know we can reuse them for artwork produced by customers."

Annie continued to tell Lizzy that Daisy had mastered quilling techniques and wanted to teach a class. Lizzy suggested using the frames for the quilling crafters to display their work. Annie agreed.

"I'll help get all the frames to your house," Lizzy said. "Then we can go through the office. How exciting to think we might uncover the secrets of Robert Harper."

"Lizzy, I wouldn't put it that way when Donald's around," Annie warned Lizzy. "Robert was his uncle, and I am not sure how he feels about some of the dealings Robert had with people." Annie thought about the plans Donald found about tearing down the senior apartments and building shared-wall houses.

After finding some cording, Annie wrapped the frames in brown paper, and tied the package with a handle to carry the frames home. The frames did not seem heavy, just bulky.

"I'm off to pick up the rest of the frames," Lizzy shouted out to Annie as she stood at the door, about to leave the shop.

"Do you want some help?" Annie offered halfheartedly.

"Sure," Lizzy stood at the opened door and answered Annie. "I could use extra hands to carry these things."

The clock on the wall read six-fifteen when Lizzy, Marie, and Annie walked through the front door of Annie's home, each carrying an armload of frames with papercut artwork inside.

"Let's take these down to the office," Annie directed, as she led the way through the dining room.

Lizzy and Marie followed Annie to the small sitting area adjacent to the dining room. After a short while, Annie located the switch which opened the hidden door in the bookcase.

"Robert loved his bookcase doorways," Annie commented. She motioned for the women to follow her.

They descended the stairs and made their way through the metal door. Once reaching the bottom of the staircase and exiting through the door, Lizzy and Marie both recognized the familiar area as they followed Annie down the hallway. Annie set her package of frames on the floor and dug into her tote bag for the keys to the office. She opened the door and turned on the lights. The office appeared as she and Donald had left it the night before.

From the doorway, Lizzy just stood and stared. She moved inside, mouth gaping wide open, and took in the sight before her.

Marie walked in next to Lizzy and stopped. "Wow," Marie said, looking around the room. "I never knew this was here. Is this Uncle Robert's room?" Marie set her package down by the door and stepped further into the office.

"Yes," Annie said. "I believe the office upstairs to be Helen's and this office to be Robert's. You can set the frames over there." Annie said, pointing to the huge island workstation in the room.

Lizzy and Marie moved their packages to the workspace and then wandered about the room, exploring the area. Annie went to the hallway to retrieve her tote bag when she spied Dan and Donald walking down the hallway.

"We thought you might be here," Donald said, giving Annie an affectionate kiss on the cheek. "You left the bookcase open in the sitting room."

"Oh, sorry about that," Annie said. "We had all these frames in our hands. I guess I got too excited to show Lizzy and Marie the office and wasn't paying attention."

"Wow!" uttered Dan, as he entered Robert's office. "So, this is how the super -rich live!" Dan walked over to the fireplace and sat down in one of the leather chairs. He ran his hand across the soft leather arm of the chair. "I could live like this."

Lizzy glared at Annie with a frown, remembering why she left the life of luxury. Annie laughed, as she watched Marie attempting to pull a book off the shelf of a bookcase in the corner of the wall housing the fireplace.

"Marie," Annie shouted in alarm. "Be careful. The bookcase moved. It might not be stable."

"The book is stuck," Marie cried out.

Dan stood and joined Marie. He tilted the book down, and the bookcase move back into the wall and swung away from them, exposing another room. Dan turned to the group, who's mouths gaped open. Everyone watched Dan as he walked through the opening in the wall.

Annie saw a light immediately illuminate a room beyond the bookcase. Marie leaned over, trying to get a glimpse inside the room by peeking around the doorway. Donald walked all the way across the office in seconds. He disappeared through the opening.

"Come on in," Donald invited the hesitant group. "Annie, you are going to love this room."

Marie ventured in first, followed by Annie and Lizzy. There stood a long room with two islands set up for crafting. Windows across the long side of the room shined bright as if the light of day shone through them.

On the opposite wall stood banks of shelving, lined with decorative storage boxes; each box being labeled with the contents. On the far wall and under the windows, a counter spread out in an L-shape. The counter appeared to house different stations for crafting. Annie saw a stamping station, a paper crafting station, a painting station, and to her surprise...a quilling station.

"I knew Aunt Helen had a craft room somewhere," Marie said. "She always had the stuff we needed to make things."

"Well, Annie," Donald said. "This must be the room of your dreams."

"This is a nightmare," expressed Dan, still looking around in bewilderment.

Annie's hand had clasped over her mouth. She stood still, shocked at how stunning the craft room appeared, and well organized!

"I hate to say this, but I have never seen such a wonderful room," Annie spoke up, still turning around and taking in the scene. "Am I imagining it or is this room larger than my shop?"

Lizzy laughed, "I do think it has more product than Ocean Loads of Paper."

Marie went to a door and turned the knob. The door opened into the hallway. Annie walked up next to Marie and removed a set of keys from her pocket. She tried a key in the lock and turned the knob. She gazed up at Donald and smiled.

"Hello?" called out the familiar voice of Stella. "Where is everybody?"

"Would you look at this!" called out Rand. "This must be Robert's office."

Annie, Marie, and Lizzy walked through the door to the hallway, where they noticed Stella and Patty standing by the office entrance. Rand stood inside the office. Dan and Donald walked through the bookcase doorway and met Rand.

The three men stood in front of the fireplace, while Donald pointed out the features of the office to Rand. Their attention turned to the fireplace, whereby Rand determined the unit to be electric. That made sense to Donald, as he could not figure out where a chimney stood in the house above.

Annie guided her mother and Patty through the bookcase doorway and into the craft room. Lizzy and Marie followed. Even though Annie was in the room moments ago, she was just as surprised the second time through.

An hour later, Annie, Lizzy, and Marie walked back into Robert's office. Stella and Patty followed, finding Donald and Dan sitting in the leather chairs sipping on glasses of bourbon. The fireplace was on, creating ambiance in the room. Rand sat at Robert's desk with a glass of the same liquor in one hand and a pen in another, jotting notes on a notepad.

"Well, I see you made yourselves at home," Patty stated.

"We found the refreshments over there," Donald announced, as he pointed to a small liquor cabinet which was earlier concealed. He turned to Annie and said, "I asked Dad if he could decipher Uncle Robert's handwriting." He stood and walked over to Robert's desk where Rand was concentrating on the document. Annie followed and stood next to Rand.

"Any luck, Rand?" Annie asked.

"I think you might find this interesting," Rand began. "Donald told me that he thought Robert was trying to buy the senior apartments with a plan to build apartment housing, not necessarily for the seniors."

"That's what we thought, Dad," Donald said. "Have you found something to the contrary?"

"The notes are pretty cryptic, but from what I can read, Robert was stopping the sale of the senior apartments to a developer. He refers to a contract drawn up by Charles Conklin which prevents the sale of the property under certain restrictions. It mentions the name of Felix Bankford."

"He's the owner and manager of the senior apartments," Stella said, as she joined the group at the desk.

"What you found may be the notes Robert jotted down while creating a formal document," asserted Rand. "Would you mind if I made a copy and studied it overnight?"

Donald turned on the copy machine that was in the work area. They waited for the machine to begin its printing process. Afterwards, Annie suggested they stop for dinner. She was planning on making pizza from the prepared pizza shells she had in the freezer. Marie offered to help. The two headed upstairs, and shortly after the others followed.

With the smell of fresh-baked pizza permeating the kitchen, Donald commented on how hungry he suddenly felt. The others agreed with him. Annie made four small pizzas with different toppings. She and Donald liked the sausage, pepperoni, hamburger meat, and cheese pizza. Dan and Lizzy preferred just pepperoni and cheese. Stella and Marie loved a Canadian bacon and pineapple. Patty and Rand enjoyed everything on their pizza. Marie made a salad, and soon the group was sitting around the table discussing, once again, the notes that Robert left about the owner of the senior apartment complex.

"From what I can make out in these notes," Rand began, taking a bite of pizza before he continued. "Robert was paying a debt of the owner of the property. It seems that the owner was collecting the rent money and gambling it away. The taxes were not being paid, nor was the mortgage payment. The seniors were about to be evicted from their homes."

"Suppose I get a copy of that contract from Charles Conklin?" Annie suggested. "I bet we would find the answers to our questions."

"Or we could search the office some more and find a copy there," Lizzy proposed.

"I have a question," Dan said. "Suppose you find this contract, and find the reason why Robert bailed out the owner, Bankford...what then? What will this information provide to you?"

Everyone stared at Dan for a moment. Annie thought about what Dan had said. Why was this so important? Was it to show that Robert was a kind person inside after all? Maybe he did help people with his wealth. How many others did he help that went unnoticed? Helen, after all, was on many charity boards. The money they acquired could have been used to help others on an as-needed basis. So, if Bankford was embezzling the money and gambling it away, was Robert helping him or the seniors?

"Just curious," Annie said. "I want to know what Robert and Helen did with their money. Maybe Donald and I should do the same."

"You could go broke doing that," Dan said.

"How about ice cream for dessert?" Stella offered. She felt the tension building between Dan and Annie. She saw this happening many times in the past; Dan was being logical and Annie was following her feelings, which often led to friction between the two.

After dinner, the group dispersed to various areas of the underground house. Donald and Dan went to the bar and began playing video games. Rand decided to further study the documents and followed the men to the bar with papers in hand. Marie, Stella, and Patty migrated to the craft room and began exploring what they could create. That left Annie and Lizzy to search the office once more.

Lizzy sat in the soft leather desk chair and leaned over the opened credenza drawer. She pulled out file after file, painstakingly searching through each one. Annie could hear the flipping of pages and the sounds of files being pulled in and out of the sections in the drawer.

While Lizzy continued her search, Annie began pulling drawers out on the work island. She gasped when she discovered the plans for the underground house. Annie pulled out the section of blueprints and discovered various secret rooms she had not discovered yet. A few pages down, the rooms had been crossed out, while other rooms had been drawn in on the blueprints. Apparently, these were not the final plans for the underground house. Annie made a mental note to show the plans to Donald later. She put the papers back into the drawer and went on to the next.

Not finding anything else of interest, Annie moved to the file cabinets along the wall. Seeing that the lock was pushed in, she pulled the keys out of her pocket and tried one that looked like it might fit a file. Sure enough, the lock popped open and Annie pulled the drawer toward her.

"Lizzy, there are lots of files here too," Annie said. "Would you help me go through these drawers?"

"Sure," Lizzy said, standing up and stretching. "I'm not finding anything here. Would Robert have had a briefcase?"

"Check the bottom credenza drawer," Annie replied.

Lizzy pulled open the bottom drawer and discovered Robert's briefcase. She set the Italian leather case on the desk. She pushed the buttons, but they did not move.

"Do you have a key for his briefcase, Annie?"

Annie pulled the keys from the lock of the file cabinet, and tossed them to Lizzy. Lizzy tried the keys and found one to open the case. "It's always the last key tried," Lizzy said. Annie laughed, as she walked around the island work station to Robert's desk.

Lizzy lifted the lid of the case. Annie was now standing next to her looking inside. On top of the stack of papers was the document they were searching for...the conditional contract between Robert Harper and Felix Bankford.

"Here," Lizzy said, excitedly thrusting the paper into Annie's hands. "You read it first."

Annie read the text out loud in a quiet voice. They discovered that Robert had provided Felix Bankford a sum of money to pay back mortgage and taxes. In lieu of re-payment, should Felix Bankford or his heirs decide to sell the senior apartment complex, the seniors would be given first right to purchase the property. The document further stated that the seniors would be given two weeks to come up with a marked four hundred troy ounce gold ingot, the instructions of which are spelled out in a treasure hunt document.

Annie slowly sank down into the leather upholstered desk chair. She looked up at Lizzy, whose mouth had dropped open. The silence had been broken by the sound of multiple hurried footfalls in the hallway. Donald and Rand, followed by Dan burst through the office doorway.

"Dad found something interesting, Annie," Donald exclaimed. "There's a date here on this paper of about four and a half months ago." Donald pointed to a scribble in the upper right corner of the paper. "I think that is when Robert discovered Felix Bankford was embezzling the money from the rent payments and gambling it away. He had not paid the mortgage or taxes on the property. The senior complex was entering the first stages of foreclosure. Robert bailed him out with a condition."

"We found the conditional contract," Lizzy revealed, now reading the document she had taken from Annie's hands. "The condition was to allow the seniors to buy the apartment complex, and set up a board of officers to manage the apartments."

"Before that could happen, the seniors had to pay with a particular four hundred troy ounce gold ingot," Annie added.

Rand looked again at the notes he was deciphering. "I can almost make that out in these scribbled notes. Now it makes sense. There is a notation with an asterisk at the bottom. I still haven't made out what it says. Give me a bit more time. I'll have it for you." Rand held the paper up to the ceiling, as if that was going to reveal a big secret or watermark of information. He brought the paper down and held it in his hands, shaking his head back and forth.

Stella entered the room yawning, "It's eight o'clock. How about we call it a night?" Everyone nodded in agreement. Stella turned to Marie and Patty, who were standing out in the hallway chatting. "We're all agreed. Let's go."

Donald was about to follow Dan out the door, when Annie grabbed his arm and indicated that she wanted to talk to him before leaving.

"You guys go ahead. Annie and I want to check out the house and make sure everything is closed up. We'll see you tomorrow. Dad, would you mind taking Laddie to the dog run for a break?"

"Patty and I are going to take a walk around the neighborhood. Can Laddie go with us?" Rand asked.

"Sure," Donald said. "His leash is hanging by the back door."

"Lizzy and I were talking about walking up to the house on the street above," Dan said to Rand. "Would you like to join us? We can check it out."

"Let's go," said Rand, as they were out the door.

Donald turned to Annie and asked what she wanted to talk about. She walked to the office door and closed it, then motioned Donald over to the work island. She pulled open the drawer where she had earlier found the underground house designs, and placed a stack of blueprints on top of the table. Annie pointed out the notations of the underground house.

Donald gave a low whistle as he perused the papers. Finally, stopping at one set of prints, he pulled the large paper to the top of the stack and pointed to the room they were currently occupying.

"See that room there?" Donald asked Annie still pointing to the room.

"Yes," Annie said, moving in closer to try to figure out what it was that Donald was pointing out.

"We are standing right here," Donald said, again pointing to a spot on the paper.

"It looks like there is a room on the other side of this wall," Annie said, turning her head to assess what she was seeing.

"Exactly!" Donald said with excitement in his voice.

CHAPTER 10

Wednesday Evening

Donald moved to the wall and began examining areas for a switch of some type. Annie observed the entire wall covered with a bulletin board material. Attached to the wall were several dry-erase boards that she had spied earlier. She also detected seams running vertically every four feet, except in the corner where a section appeared to be only three feet wide.

Annie walked to that corner of the room and inspected the area for a switch of some sort. She felt along a vertical strip covering the seam and discovered it seemed loose. She lifted the wooden strip and there stood a lever seated within the wall. Annie pulled on the lever and the wall section opened.

"I knew you would find the door," Donald said, walking to Annie's side and looking through the opening. "From now on, you hold the title of secret door-whisperer." He put his arms around her waist and gave her a kiss.

Annie laughed, "After you Holmes." Annie gave a slight bow, gesturing Donald to go before her into the secret room.

As with the many other rooms in the underground house, this room lit up as Donald walked through the doorway. To the left of the small room stood a bank of monitors filling the entire wall. A control desk with two chairs sat below the monitors. All the monitors were active and displayed scenes of various places around the outside of the house. Annie viewed what appeared to be cameras located in town and around the senior center. A label below the screen on each monitor identified the location of the camera. The cameras were on the buildings once owned by Robert and Helen Harper.

Donald moved to the console area and began examining the controls. A computer sat on a table below the bank of monitors, with a large notepad next to the keyboard. Positioned on top of the blank pad rested a pen.

While Donald kept busy with the monitors, Annie decided to look around the room. The wall opposite the monitors stood blank and lacked anything of interest, but she did notice a door with a keypad to the right of the monitor wall. The keypad had large numbers and small letters, such as that found on a telephone keypad.

Annie thought for a moment and then typed in a five-digit code. A light flashed red. She thought a moment more and then tried another code, this time six digits long. The light on the key pad turned green and clicked. Taken by surprise that she had guessed the correct combination, Annie paused a moment, and then pushed the door ajar.

"Donald?" Annie said, turning to Donald and pointing to the door now standing open to the entrance of another room.

"How in the world did you manage to open that door?" Donald said in surprise as he stood and followed Annie through the doorway, being careful to prop the door open.

"I think Robert really did love you in his own way," Annie whispered, as she walked through a short pathway. "The code spells out Donald...3-6-6-2-5-3." Donald kept quiet as they ventured ahead.

It was dark inside this little space. Annie's head touched something hard. She reached up and discovered the type of pole used in a closet for hanging clothes. Annie's hands began exploring the walls and soon came across a closet door that opened into the vault room. As she pushed through the door, lights illuminated the vault room.

"An emergency exit," Donald acknowledged. "Very clever of my uncle."

Donald and Annie looked briefly around the room, which was untouched from the last time they were present in the vault room.

"Let's get back to the monitor room," Donald said. "I want to find out why my uncle needed cameras in town. If I find a playback log, I might be able to find out who left Lizzy flowers earlier."

"While you do that, I'll go upstairs," Annie said. "I am a bit tired and have some cleaning up to do yet." She kissed Donald and managed her way through the monitor room and the office, then to the metal door that led to the little sitting room next to the dining room. Walking into the kitchen, she found Marie folding a dish towel and placing it on the handle of the oven to dry.

"I finished cleaning up for you," Marie reported to Annie. "Would you like an ice cream bar?"

"Thank you, Marie," Annie said. "Didn't we eat ice cream for dessert earlier?"

"I can never eat too much ice cream," Marie giggled.

"Okay, but only if it's all chocolate. No vanilla."

Marie reached into the freezer and pulled out two ice cream bars. She handed a chocolate ice cream to Annie. Annie suggested they take one to Stella. Marie grabbed another bar and the two exited the kitchen door, locking it behind them. They climbed the stairs of the apartment over the garage and knocked on the door. A few moments later, Stella answered with a surprised look on her face.

"I was not expecting you two tonight," Stella remarked, standing in the doorway with her robe wrapped around her body.

"We brought you an ice cream bar," Marie said, as she handed Stella the treat.

"Oh, you girls," Stella complained. "I have gained five pounds being around you two so much. All we do is eat." Stella invited the two women inside for a visit, accepting the ice cream bar, and began opening the wrapper.

Entering the living room area of the apartment, Annie noticed her mother was watching the evening news. Stella gestured to the two women to sit down on the sofa as she sat in a white soft cloth-covered chair.

The sun was moments from setting, and the sky was a bright parade of colors cascading over the sparkling ocean water. From where Annie was seated in her mother's living room, she viewed Rand and Patty walking up the driveway with Laddie in the lead. Annie stood and walked to the window. She wondered to herself if they found anything of interest at the house on the hill behind her house. Annie excused herself, saying goodnight to her mother, and quickly made her way down the stairs with Marie following close behind.

Annie walked up to Rand and Patty, bent down to give Laddie a hug, and asked him if he had a good walk.

"He was a very good boy," Rand announced.

"Did you walk past the house?" Annie asked, trying not to sound too anxious for information. She was hoping they had seen evidence of someone breaking into the house or worse yet, living in the house.

"Dan and I walked completely around the house," Rand explained. "We checked windows, doors, and even looked in the crawl space. We found the house locked up tight."

"Lizzy and I even tried to peek through windows," Patty added. "We either could not see through the curtains, or what we could make out looked like empty rooms."

Rand further explained that, although Laddie was happy to search around the front and back yards, he did not focus on any one area. He told Annie that Dan had moved the deck chairs to specific positions, so he could tell if anyone used them in the near future. Rand said that Dan was planning on checking the house often.

Annie asked Rand if he thought Dan suspected someone was using the house. Rand told Annie that Dan was thinking something was suspicious, but he would not tell Rand what it was.

"I know I saw something in the windows on Saturday," Annie said. "Someone must be entering the house with a key."

Feeling disappointed, Annie took Laddie by his leash and bid good night to Rand and Patty. After watching them enter their RV, Annie turned and walked into the house with Marie following. Marie closed and locked the kitchen door while Annie disconnected Laddie's leash.

"I thought you were tired and went to bed?" Donald said to Annie, as he came down the stairs, pausing to say goodnight to Marie, who was heading upstairs to bed.

"I was waiting for your folks to return with Laddie," Annie stated. "They didn't find anything suspicious at the house behind us."

Annie told Donald about Rand and Dan checking all around the house and finding it locked up. She mentioned Patty and Lizzy attempting to peek through the windows and not finding anything out of place. There was nothing outside that would indicate someone lived inside the house.

"Did you find anything on your camera feed search?" Annie asked Donald.

"I have a fairly good idea who the gift-giver is, but I need Dan to take a look at the video feed to verify my idea."

"Who is it?" Annie asked, hanging up Laddie's leash on the hook by the kitchen door. Laddie was drinking water from his bowl by the kitchen door.

"I've seen him around town on the various camera feeds," Donald said. He opened the refrigerator door and pulled out a bottle of water. "It looks like a teenager. Hard to tell though. The guy is wearing a dark hoodie and dark pants. He appears in and out of the businesses, and up and down the street. Almost like a delivery person." Donald twisted the top off the water bottle and took a long drink.

"I can ask the shop owners if they know of a teenager making deliveries," Annie said, thinking she would start with Ione. Maybe Ione has someone making deliveries for her. But first thing tomorrow morning she would check with the Silver Sleuths. If anyone knew anything about this delivery kid, the senior ladies would. "Donald, is it possible to get a photo of this delivery person? I can show it around and see if anyone recognizes him."

"I sent it to your email earlier," Donald said, giving Annie a kiss on the cheek. "It's my bed time. The front door is locked. Would you set the alarm before you head upstairs?"

Annie watched Laddie as he led the way up the stairs, followed by Donald. She walked to the kitchen window looking out into the back yard. It was after ten o'clock in the evening now and lights were off in the apartment above the garage. The RV had a dim light on in its back section of the vehicle where the bedroom was located. The cottage was dark.

Annie looked up at the house on the hill and jumped back when she thought she saw someone move on the deck facing the ocean. She reached over and turned off the kitchen lights. Now crouching down under the window, Annie raised up slightly to look out upon the back yard, and up at the house. Whoever was there just moments ago had now disappeared. Was she just imagining this?

Annie remembered that Dan, too, saw something up there. She watched the house hoping to see some movement, lights, or anything indicating someone was there. After fifteen minutes, she gave up, set the alarm, and headed to bed.

CHAPTER 11

Thursday Morning

Annie bolted upright in bed, waking from a disturbing dream. Callie, who was sleeping next to Annie's feet, opened her eyes, and then turned her head to fall back asleep. Laddie snored softly on his big doggy bed. Annie turned to find Donald missing from their bed. She smelled coffee. Suddenly, her troubling nightmare vanished from her thoughts. She was not sure what the vision was about at this point. The images disappeared that quickly.

Getting out of bed, Annie walked into the sitting area to find Donald seated on the sofa with a book. Donald held a cup of coffee in his right hand.

"Good morning," Annie mumbled as she yawned. She stretched her arms out wide.

"Good morning to you," Donald said, watching Annie yawn. "I think your early morning routine is having an effect on me. I find it relaxing to be up before anyone else to sit here in quiet and think."

"Good thoughts, I hope," Annie said with a smile.

"I was deliberating about the young character leaving presents for Lizzy."

Annie sat next to Donald, "Are you considering that he is just a delivery person, and we are no closer in finding out who Lizzy's stalker is?"

"Actually, once we find the man or woman making these deliveries, we can ask who hired him to leave the gifts." Donald said. He took a sip of coffee.

"If we find out that the errand person doesn't know who the gift-giver is by name," Annie admitted. "Maybe Dan could set up some way to catch the stalker the next time a run is ordered."

After forty-five minutes of relaxing conversation and watching the sun splash across the ocean, both Annie and Donald dressed for work and made their way downstairs to the kitchen. The aroma of pancakes and bacon permeated the air in the kitchen. Annie found Marie pouring pancake batter onto the skillet and Stella flipping bacon in a frying pan.

Laddie excitedly followed Donald down the stairs and ran to the back door, waiting for Donald to let him outside.

"I was hoping you would get up early for breakfast," Stella said. "I sent a text to Dan and Lizzy to come over."

Annie made her way to the coffee maker. She waited patiently for the hot liquid to finish brewing. She pulled the cup from the machine and handed it to Donald. Then she made herself coffee. She picked up the cup and inhaled deeply before taking her first sip.

Rand and Patty knocked twice and then opened the kitchen door. At the same time, Dan walked through the front door with Lizzy close at his heels. Stella began issuing tasks to be completed by the group to prepare the table in the dining room for breakfast. It only took moments before everyone sat down and ready to eat.

"Dan," Annie began to say as she paused to pass around a plate of bacon and scrambled eggs. "Rand and Patty said you did not see anyone in the house behind us."

"Not a living soul." Dan said, stabbing his fork into a stack of pancakes and placing them on his plate. He drizzled maple syrup on top. "We walked all around the house and checked all the doors and windows."

Annie explained how she watched the house on the hill after everyone had turned in for the night. She told Dan that she saw someone on the deck looking out at the ocean.

"You're just seeing things, Annie," Dan snorted, taking slice of toast from a small plate and slathering it with blackberry jam. "We checked the place out thoroughly. There is no one inside. The house is locked up tight, and no one is there."

"Maybe there is a ghost in that house," Marie shuddered.

"There is no ghost, Marie," Annie insisted. "What I saw was a human being."

"Maybe someone in the neighborhood is using the deck, knowing that the place is vacant," Lizzy suggested. "It is a nice place to view the ocean."

"What Lizzy says makes sense," Dan said. "If you are so sure there is someone inside, figure out how to unlock the doors, and I will go with you to check out the house."

Annie glanced at Donald, who looked back and grinned. Donald knew what Annie was thinking. She would go to the house and pick the lock on the door. Then she would call Dan to meet her. She would not be committing any crimes by picking the lock on a property she owned.

Breakfast continued with chatter about the underground house and wound up with Rand telling Donald he wanted to take Oscar out for a ride this afternoon.

"You and Oscar go out and have a ball, Dad," Donald laughed, as he stood and carried his plate to the kitchen sink. He rinsed the plate and put it in the dishwasher. "I'm off to work. I need to be in a meeting in twenty minutes." Donald wiped his hands on a paper towel and made his way to the office.

♦ ♦ ♦

It was noon when Annie approached the work counter in Ocean Loads of Paper to find Lizzy finishing an order for the shop. Lizzy looked up to see Annie standing near her.

"I had been thinking about an idea that might help bring in more sales with our online customers," Lizzy proclaimed. She closed her laptop and turned to face Annie.

"I'm listening," Annie said, excited that Lizzy was taking an interest in making more sales. Lizzy was in her business mind set, and this was a time when Lizzy always had great ideas.

"Well, I was thinking if we created kits of cards and boxes, people could make without all the struggles of measuring, cutting, and scoring," Lizzy said, presenting a prepared card set. "I asked Daisy to create a sample. We could make four and eight card sets, along with a box for storing or gifting the set. Different message tags could be in the packages and the customer would create the card using the pieces we provide. We'll place the pieces in cellophane bags and display them in the store as well as selling online."

"We can do an assembly line of tags, layering card stock, and embellishments," Annie added writing down notations on a pad of lined paper.

"I can do the tags and help with packaging," Marie stated, as she walked up to the counter where Annie and Lizzy were brainstorming.

"I'm in," Daisy said, following behind Marie. "When do we start?"

The four women spent the next hour working out the details and having fun deciding what types of cards they were going to make. Notes were made on individual notepads and when they had decided they had a solid outline, the notes were given to Annie to make the final plan.

"I'm hungry," Annie said, putting all the notes together in one stack. "How about I go to Ione's and get sandwiches?"

"Today is split pea soup day," Marie said.

"Soup sounds good," Lizzy agreed.

"I wouldn't mind a cup of soup and a half of a sandwich," Daisy said.

"How about a cup of soup and a half sandwich for each of us?" Annie suggested. "Then I will go to Salty's for four chocolate truffles from the candy counter. And while I am out, I want to stop by Spencer's Gallery and see how Jacquie is getting along."

"Annie," Lizzie said. "Your class is at one o'clock and it is now noon. If you stop and visit with Jacquie, you will never get back in time to eat before class begins."

"I won't be that long."

"Marie and I can help out," Daisy countered.

"I can get the soup and sandwiches," Marie offered.

"And I will pick up the truffles," Daisy said.

"Sounds like a plan to me," Annie approved, entering her office to get money from her wallet. She walked out of the office and handed the money to Marie and Daisy. "My treat today ladies."

Having a plan in place, Annie, who was holding the door open on the ocean side of the shop, watched as Daisy and Marie made their way out. Annie followed, walking directly to Spencer's Gallery.

Annie heard familiar voices inside as she opened the door to Spencer's Gallery. Walking inside the gallery, she received a warm greeting from Jacquie.

"Annie!" Jacquie said, as she walked out from behind a counter. "So nice of you to drop by."

"Please don't let me interrupt. I can wait," Annie insisted.

"Nonsense," Jacquie said. "Annie, I want you to meet Laura Wooster. She and her husband, Leo, moved here about a year ago."

"Welcome to Bridgewater Harbor," Annie said. "I believe I've seen you in some of my classes. You look familiar."

"I think Daisy was teaching the two classes I signed up for last month, but I saw you in the store," Laura replied. "This is such a lovely town. Leo and I have been so busy remodeling our house that we have not been very good at introducing ourselves around town. We hope to change that when construction is completed."

"When will that be?" Annie questioned.

"Well," Laura said, then paused a moment to think. "It has been twelve months so far. We expect to finish before Christmas."

"Wow!" Annie exclaimed. "You must have torn the house down to the studs."

"Not really," Laura reacted with a bit of sarcasm in her tone. "Just the kitchen, the master bedroom, floors, siding, a new porch, new roof, and a bathroom."

Annie and Jacquie laughed. Laura said she was running late and needed to leave. Jacquie promised to call when the shipment with Laura's order arrived. Annie bid farewell to Laura and watched as she left through the street-side doorway.

"What brings you here, Annie?" Jacquie inquired.

"I wanted to find out how things were going here, and see if you and John had found a house yet."

As Annie told Jacquie about the house on the hill behind her house, Jacquie's eyes lit up and she smiled widely.

"John and I have been looking at that house, but our Realtor told us it was not on the market," Jacquie said. "She said it had been vacant for some years."

"I just found out that I own that house, and several other properties in town," Annie said. "You're not seriously interested in the house, are you?"

Annie decided it would be best to explain about the unidentified person gaining access to the house without her permission. She told Jacquie how Dan and other police officers had checked out the house and found it locked up.

"Do you think the house is haunted?" Jacquie mused.

"No! It is not haunted, Jacquie," Annie said. "But there is something strange going on there. I think I will go over after work and check it out."

"Oh, please let me come with you," Jacquie begged. "I want an opportunity to see the inside of the house. John is in Portland today and won't be back until early evening. I can meet you at your shop. Just send me a text when you want me to come over."

Annie thought about it for a moment, then said, "Okay. It wouldn't hurt to have the company. If you like the house, then you can have a second look with John."

"Thank you, Annie," Jacquie said.

Annie left the gallery and headed back to Ocean Loads of Paper. She thought about having Jacquie and John as neighbors and smiled to herself. The house had an incredible view of the ocean and a low maintenance yard. Annie could not wait to talk to Donald about the house on the hill, and the possibility of new owners.

♦ ♦ ♦

Annie picked up crafting tools from the classroom tables as the class dispersed with their newly made treat boxes. Once the students completed the boxes, Annie supplied each one with wrapped chocolates to add to their finished craft project. The classroom area was clearing and Annie emptied the scrap bins into the trash can she carried around the tables. As she did so, she noticed her favorite seniors taking their time leaving the class area.

"What did you think of the project we did today in class?" Annie asked the four, approaching the table to clean up the left-overs.

"Top notch as always, Annie," Millie commented.

"Do you ladies have plans for the rest of the afternoon?" Annie asked.

"We are on a mission for Detective Weston," Lorraine announced in a lowered voice.

"A mission?" asked Annie, leaning in and using an equaled lowered voice.

"Well," said LaVerne. "Not exactly a mission he wants to know about. All the same, we are investigating the suspicious circumstances occurring in that house behind your house. The one on the hill."

"We've seen lights on in different windows during the night," Elsie said. "They turn on and then they turn off."

"Someone seems to be moving from room to room with a light of some kind," LaVerne reported to Annie.

"I was going to show the house to Jacquie tonight after work," Annie told the ladies.

"LaVerne and I will meet you there," said Lorraine. "Millie and Elsie are going to a cooking class at the senior center tonight."

"I'll keep your friends out of trouble," Annie said to Millie and Elsie with a sly smile. Annie was not sure who would be keeping her from getting into trouble.

With the classroom cleaned and everyone gone, Annie walked to the counter area where Lizzy was busy on the laptop computer. She straightened a couple of shelves and returned items to their proper display areas.

"So...," Annie said to Lizzy. "I was thinking of going to the house on the hill with Jacquie to show her around." Annie told Lizzy that Jacquie and John may be interested in the house.

"Oh, I want to go too," said Marie.

"You mean you want to go to the haunted house on the hill?" Lizzy asked Marie, using her best impression of a spooky vampire voice.

"The house is haunted?" asked Marie, color draining from her face.

"The house is not haunted, Marie," Annie said, glaring at Lizzy.

"I was just kidding, Marie," Lizzy apologized. Then, as Marie turned and walked over to the windows on the street side of the shop, Lizzy mouthed the words to Annie, "The house is too haunted."

Annie rolled her eyes and said, "Anyway, Jacquie and I are going up thereafter work. Marie, you are welcome to join us. It will be fun to go inside. I have never been in that house."

"What's going on outside with Donald's dad and that police officer?" Marie asked Annie.

Annie and Lizzy walked to the street-side door where Marie was looking out the window. There they saw Rand Harper standing on the sidewalk talking to Officer Kathy Barrel. Next to Rand was Donald's truck with an easily identifiable passenger. Annie walked outside and stood near her shop door where she could hear the conversation between Rand and the officer.

"Mr. Harper," Officer Barrel addressed Rand while looking at his driver's license.

"Doctor," Rand corrected the officer.

"Dr. Harper," said Officer Barrel, not looking too impressed. "And who is the gentleman in the passenger seat of your vehicle?"

"Oh, that's Oscar. He's a patient of mine," Dr. Harper dead panned, attempting to ease the tension.

"From the looks of him, it doesn't say much about you as a doctor, does it?" Officer Barrel said.

"Yeah, I warned him about smoking cigarettes."

Officer Barrel handed Rand his license back and then said, "Dr. Harper, would you throw a blanket over your friend there. He is freaking out the folks in town."

Rand Harper nodded and returned to his truck, not noticing Annie standing by her shop door.

Annie was about to go back inside her shop when Officer Barrel approached her and said, "Hello, Annie. I saw your mother at the courthouse today. I was attending a court appearance on a burglary charge. Your mother said she was working on a big research project for you and Donald. I hope she found what she was looking for."

"Uh, me too," Annie remarked.

"Have a good day," Officer Barrel said, as she put her notebook in her back pocket.

Annie watched as Officer Barrel continued down the sidewalk to her patrol car. She walked back into the shop.

"What was that all about?" Lizzy asked.

Annie explained what she heard of the conversation between Officer Barrel and Rand Harper.

Lizzy giggled and said, "People are going to think he is off his rocker."

Annie was beginning to wonder herself about her father-in-law. She decided to send a text to Donald. As she walked to her office to grab her cell phone, Annie thought about Donald's sense of humor. He was a lot like his father. Was Donald going to be escorting Oscar around town next? The sound of a ringing phone jolted Annie back to reality. When she looked up and noticed Lizzy answering the shop phone, Annie continued to her office to retrieve her cell phone.

A few moments after sending a text about the occurrence with Donald's father, Donald responded and said he would ask his Dad to leave Oscar at home. He thought his Dad might be bored and looking for some excitement. Donald told Annie that he overheard his mother and father discussing traveling north up the coastline to Washington.

Annie felt a pang of sadness thinking that her in-laws were leaving. She had known they would be leaving soon, but not this soon. She was just getting to know them and loved having them nearby. Donald often commented on how he enjoyed the family all being together. She wondered if Donald's parents should live in the house on the hill. They could pay to fix it up the way Rand and Patty liked.

Annie thought about John and Jacquie. She did promise to show Jacquie the house first. She was getting ahead of herself now. Rand and Patty may not be interested in living in Bridgewater Harbor, considering their past quarrels with Robert and Helen Harper. What was that quarrel about anyway?

The chirping of her cell phone surprised Annie. It was Donald asking if she was still there. He had asked her when she was planning on coming home and what she planned for dinner.

Annie walked back to the counter area of the shop and asked Lizzy, "What should we have for dinner tonight? Any ideas?"

"I'll take care of dinner tonight," Lizzy said, closing her laptop lid. "It's about time Dan and I made the dinner plans." She picked up her cell phone and sent a text to Dan.

"And by taking care of dinner, you mean ordering Chinese food?"

"Would you rather I cooked a meal myself?" Lizzy said, looking up from her cell phone. "I have never made a meal in my life. We had a chef when I was growing up. I am not sure I could even tell you what our kitchen looked like."

"It's five o'clock!" announced Jacquie as she burst through the shop door. "Are you ready to go?"

"Let me gather my things, and we'll be on our way," Annie informed Jacquie.

"Should I tell Dan what you are doing?" Lizzy whispered to Annie.

"Marie," Annie called out. "Are you ready to go? I am leaving now." Annie turned back to Lizzy and said, "Tell him we're ghost hunting."

CHAPTER 12

Thursday Evening

Annie, Marie, and Jacquie walked to Annie's house in record time. Annie had been excited to finally find some time to check out the house on the hill. The women looked as an approaching car honked at them. It was LaVerne and Lorraine, two Silver Sleuths who appeared to be on a mission.

"We are off to check out the house behind your house, Annie," LaVerne said, leaning out the driver's side window of her car.

"So are we," Annie said.

"Well, hop on in and go with us," Lorraine offered.

"I would, but I need to stop by my house and pick up a few things first," Annie said.

"I want to grab my sweatshirt," Marie said, as she left the women and made her way up the front path of the house.

Annie could feel a chill in the air and decided she, too, should find a light jacket.

"I'll ride with you, if you don't mind," Jacquie said to the ladies in the car. She walked to the vehicle and opened the door to climb inside. Sitting in the back seat, she rolled down the window. "We'll meet you up there," Jacquie exclaimed. With a wave of her hand, the car took off.

"Wait for me before you go into the house," Annie called out to deaf ears. She shook her head, keeping her eyes on the vehicle. She cringed at the sound of screeching of tires, as the car careened around the corner and out of sight.

Entering her house, Annie met Donald and Laddie coming from the office. "Hi, Donald," Annie said, giving Donald a kiss. "Marie and I are going to explore the house on the hill."

She set her purse on a kitchen table chair and walked to the laundry room in search of a flashlight and gloves.

"I have an evening meeting in a few minutes or else I would go with you," Donald said, placing his coffee cup in the dishwasher. He leaned against the counter and watching Annie pack her small tote bag with a flashlight and various items. "If you wait another thirty-five minutes, I will be out of my meeting and finished for the day."

"Oh, Donald," Annie said, stopping what she was doing and looking up. "LaVerne, Lorraine, and Jacquie are already there waiting for us. Marie is going with me."

Donald reached for a dog treat from the jar on the counter. He broke off a piece and held it out for Laddie. "I'll meet you up there later then. Wait for me. I am curious what the house is like on the inside. By the way, Annie, how are you planning on entering the house? Dan told you it is locked up tight."

Annie thought for a moment, "Any idea where I could find a key for that house?"

"No, but you could practice picking the lock," Donald said with a sly smile. "If all else fails, I am sure Lorraine will be able to help you." Donald bid good luck to Annie and walked to his office. Annie picked up her tote bag, satisfied with herself for earlier having added the lock picks.

"Marie?" Annie shouted up the stairs. "I am ready to go."

♦ ♦ ♦

Annie and Marie stood in front of the house on the hill, staring at the front door. LaVerne, Lorraine, and Jacquie were nowhere to be found. Did they go to the wrong house, Annie wondered? Where is LaVerne's car?

"Where are they?" Marie asked.

"I was just thinking the same thing," Annie responded. Where are her friends? They should be waiting for her and Marie. Annie sensed something was not right.

"I guess they'll catch up with us," Annie said, feeling a bit of chill in the air. "Maybe they forgot something and will return shortly."

"Let's go find out if they are inside the house," Marie suggested.

Annie walked up to the front door and tried the doorknob. It was locked. She glanced at Marie, and then pulled out her lock picking set from her bag. Kneeling down at the front door, Annie began to systematically attempt to pick the lock. She recognized the device as a higher-level deadbolt.

"This might take a while," Annie said to Marie.

Marie stood behind Annie for a few moments, and then began walking around the yard. Annie was aware of Marie checking the garage door, attempting to look through the windows on the front of the house, and looking under rocks.

"What are you doing?" asked Annie.

"Nancy Drew always looks for clues."

"Okay, Nancy Drew," Annie said. "Let me know when you find a clue." Marie giggled.

As Annie worked the lock on the front door, she stopped for a moment to listen. Was that a noise inside the house? She listened for a moment more. Not hearing another sound, she continued with her task. Suddenly, the door opened with a jerk and Annie toppled across the threshold, dropping her lock picks.

"I found a clue," Marie said, standing inside the house, in front of Annie.

Annie lifted herself off the floor and said, "Indeed you did. How did you get inside?"

"The patio door is unlocked," Marie answered.

"Didn't Dan tell us that the house was locked up tight?" Annie asked Marie. She dusted off her clothes, picked up her tools and placed them in her bag.

"Yes, but maybe he missed the patio door."

Annie was sure Dan would not have missed a door or window. He was very thorough about such things. Then it dawned on her. Of course, she thought, Lorraine had picked the patio door lock, because it was in a more secluded area of the yard, not in public view of the neighborhood. She should have done the same thing. It dawned on Annie that she is not cut out for a life of crime.

As Annie and Marie walked into the house, Annie was surprised that the house appeared clean. How was it possible when the house had stood vacant for years? She breathed in the scent lemons. Furniture polish? Yes, furniture polish. That waxy kind in a spray can. Yet, the house was devoid of furniture.

Continuing to walk through the living room, Annie and Marie entered the open concept dining/kitchen area. It looked as if it had been remodeled within the last year. The appliances appeared new and the floor tile also new. There was no dust on the wood floors of the dining room and living room. Who was cleaning the house? Could that person have left the patio door unlocked?

Annie, determined to find the answers to her questions, walked through the house. She ventured upstairs to the bedrooms, inspecting the closets and looking around, but found nothing of interest. The place was clean, and showed no sign of someone living there.

Marie followed Annie back to the kitchen. There was nothing left to do, but go through every cupboard and drawer in the kitchen. She began opening and closing doors and drawers of the counter area. She pulled open the cabinet door under the sink.

"Oh!" Annie said, initially startled by what she found. There, standing all by itself, was the can of lemon scented furniture polish. She pulled out a tissue from her bag and wrapped it around the can, lifting the can to the marble-topped island.

"What's wrong?" Marie asked, as she closed an empty drawer on the island.

"I think I found the reason for the smell of lemons in the house," Annie said, setting the can of spray on the island counter top. "This scent doesn't last long. Someone has been cleaning this house recently."

"Who?" Marie asked, about to pick up the can in front of her.

"Don't touch the can, Marie," Annie said. "We will turn it over to Dan and find out if he can obtain fingerprints off of the sides."

"Good idea," Marie said, tucking her hands in her pockets, so she would not be tempted to pick up the can.

Annie noticed a door in the kitchen she had overlooked. It was stained wood and smelled of lemon spray wax. Turning the lock on the door and pushing it open, she realized it was the entrance to a basement. As she walked onto a landing beyond the dimly lit doorway feeling for a light switch, she was bumped from behind by Marie, which sent Annie forcefully forward. She desperately reached for a stair railing, grabbing hold just as her right foot dropped down onto the first stair.

"Marie?" Annie said in a stern voice.

"Someone pushed me!" Marie shouted back.

Annie turned and looked in horror as she glimpsed a dark hooded figure pulling the door shut. She listened to the clicking sound of the lock be turned. Racing back toward the door, Annie frantically tried to turn the knob. She stopped, realizing that they were locked in the dark basement.

"What do we do now?" Marie asked, her voice quivering.

"Let me think," Annie answered. She began searching her bag, trying to find the flashlight she brought with her.

"Annie? Marie?" came a voice from the dark depths below.

At first Annie was startled, but then she realized who was speaking.

"LaVerne? Is that you?" speaking into the black hole before her.

"Yes," LaVerne shouted back, sounding relieved to upon hearing Annie's voice.

"Oh," stated the voice of Lorraine. "Thank goodness you found us."

"Is Jacquie with you?" Annie asked.

"Yes," Jacquie answered. "And let's not mention this to John. He already worries about me and the trouble I seem to find myself in lately."

"Fair enough," Annie laughed. "Unfortunately, we are locked inside this basement."

Annie pulled out her flashlight and turned it on. She focused the beam of light down the stairs then across the room. There, in a huddle, stood her three friends. Pointing the light at their feet, Annie and Marie slowly descended the stairs to the basement floor. They joined LaVerne, Lorraine, and Jacquie in the center of the room.

The basement, from what Annie could distinguish using the dim lit flashlight, was not large and seemed to be without furniture. The floor was carpeted and three walls were finished with drywall and white paint. One side had a wood texture design covering the entire wall.

Annie looked around the room and trained her light on a small cot with a sleeping bag and pillow, a camp chair, a towel draped over the chair, and several articles of clothing folded neatly at the foot of the bed. A large bin sat next to the chair; the top of the bin was being used as a side table.

"Someone is living in this basement," Annie remarked.

"The same person who locked us in here." LaVerne said.

"Your car was not outside," Annie stated. "Did you park down the street?"

"A horrible hooded man took my purse and car keys," LaVerne said. "He took Jacquie's purse too!"

"He didn't notice my fanny pack. I still have it with me." Lorraine informed Annie. She lifted her sweater to reveal a small bulging black pack belted to her waist. "I have a little flashlight, but the batteries died soon after I turned it on."

"We were hoping you would find us," Jacquie said. "We kept hearing scary noises."

"That was probably Annie and I walking around upstairs," Marie spoke up. "We were opening and closing cabinet doors and drawers in the kitchen."

"Oh, we heard you," Jacquie said, agreeing with Marie. "But the noises are coming from down here. Groaning noises."

"A ghost?" Marie said, her voice quivering.

Even in the dim light Annie imagined Marie's eyes widening as she spoke. "No ghost, Marie," Annie said, attempting to calm Marie's anxiety. Marie was looking all around the room. "Don't let your imagination get the best of you in the darkness. I'm going upstairs and try to figure out how to get out of this mess. Who wants to join me?"

Marie, followed closely behind by LaVerne, Lorraine, and Jacquie, carefully climbed the stairs following behind Annie. The landing was large enough allow all the women to stand as they surveyed the door. Annie handed her flashlight to Jacquie and began searching her tote bag for anything to use as a tool on the door.

"If I could find something to try and loosen the pins on the door hinge, we might be able to pull the door open enough to get out." Annie said, rummaging through her bag.

"Would a screwdriver work?" asked Lorraine.

"You have a screwdriver?" Jacquie asked.

"I carry a bit of everything in my bag," Lorraine replied.

"Except batteries," LaVerne added.

"Now I know to add batteries to my collection of items," Lorraine retorted.

"Ladies, please!" Annie spoke in frustration. "Lorraine, do you have a screwdriver?"

"Of course," Lorraine said. She unzipped her fanny pack as Jacquie shined the flashlight in her direction. Lorraine began pulling items from her pack and placing them into the opened hands of LaVerne.

Annie watched, fascinated as Lorraine pulled out brass knuckles, bear repellent, a small measuring tape, small scissors, tape, glue, a small voice recorder, gum, a small sticky pad, a pen, handcuffs, tie wraps, a small magnifying glass, band-aids, and finally a yellow stubby-handled screwdriver. She handed it to Annie. Annie stood amazed for a moment, then turned to the door.

Jacquie focused the light on the door as Annie attempted to force the door pins from their slots. The pins were seated in tight. Jacquie handed the flashlight to Marie. Pushing her foot on the base of the door and using her strength to pull up on the doorknob, Jacquie signaled for Annie to again try using the screwdriver to loosen the pins. This time the pins came out with less effort.

Annie inserted a pin in the center hinge, only to the first loop, using the pin to pull the door toward her. The door began to creak as it allowed a small opening.

"Great job, Annie!" Lorraine exclaimed. "If that door were any tighter, you would never be able to pull it open."

"Alright, ladies," Annie said. "Who's going first?" Annie stood behind the door to keep it from falling. LaVerne, Lorraine, and Jacquie exited first.

Jacquie held onto the door from the other side, allowing Marie to squeeze through the door where she turned to wait for Annie. Annie was about to maneuver through the door when she stopped.

"Come on, Annie," Marie urged.

"Just a minute," Annie said. "That's the sound of barking downstairs. It is coming from the far wall."

Marie squeezed back through the doorway to Annie's side. Jacquie looked to LaVerne and Lorraine. She was still holding the heavy door. Lorraine reached past Jacquie and attempted to help to keep the door from falling on her friend. LaVerne moved in to help, and the three ladies were able to safely pull the door out and move it against the wall.

"I wish we would have thought of that sooner," LaVerne said, looking to Lorraine. "Too bad we didn't have a flashlight."

"Well, next time you bring the flashlight," Lorraine said.

"I had a flashlight, but it was taken along with my purse and car keys," LaVerne stated.

"Ladies!" Jacquie interrupted. "First of all, next time...be sure to ask me along."

Annie could hear the ladies laughing and wanted to hush them. She was trying to listen for the barking sounds.

"Woof. Woof. Woof," came the animated dialogue of a familiar dog.

"Laddie!" Marie shouted. She ran down the stairs with the only flashlight in hand. When she reached the far wall she searched for a doorway. "Laddie? Do you hear me. It is Marie."

"Marie?" asked a voice from behind the wall.

"Donald!" Annie cried for joy. "Donald, where are you?"

"I'm at the top of some utility stairs in a tunnel. We found keys to the door in the sump pump room," Donald stated. "Annie, are you and Marie alright?"

"Yes, and we're here with LaVerne, Lorraine, and Jacquie. We are all fine." Annie listened as Donald shouted to someone in the distance, letting them know the women were fine.

"Let me try to open the door," Donald said. "Stand back."

A heavy thump sound came from the wall.

"Ouch," Donald yelled, and then there was a moment of silence. "Okay, that didn't work."

Annie strained to listen to shouting from afar, but could not make out what the person was saying. Moments later, she heard a latch being slid aside and the wall opened up, revealing Donald and Laddie. Laddie ran to Annie and then quickly to Marie. He looked upward to the top of the stairs and gave a quiet woof.

"We're fine, Laddie," Annie told the smiling dog, giving him a pat on the head. "You know LaVerne, Lorraine, and Jacquie." Laddie wagged his tail when the ladies at the top of the stairs began to talk all at once.

Annie hugged Donald tightly. "We were pushed inside and locked in by the person who has been hiding out here." Annie told Donald the story of how they got locked in, and how they were escaping when she heard Laddie barking.

By now, the other three women were downstairs and standing in the doorway in the wall. Down the utility stairway they could see Detective Dan Weston kneeling next to a body. Several paramedics were maneuvering around the body.

"Good heavens," LaVerne shouted. "It's Felix, the landlord of the senior apartments."

"Felix?" Lorraine asked. "What's he doing here?"

"Is he dead?" Jacquie called out to Detective Weston.

"He is not dead," Dan said, and then added in a quieter tone, "Not yet."

"Come on, ladies," Donald urged. "Let's leave Dan to handle this." Donald herded the group upstairs. He told Dan that he would wait with the ladies outside.

"Officer Kathy Barrel is on her way to meet you. Wait with her. I'll be there as soon as I can." Detective Weston ordered.

"Well, that was a kick in the pants, ladies," LaVerne remarked, as the group reached the top of the stairs and entered the kitchen area of the house. "We got ourselves out of a sticky situation."

"Annie and Marie got us out of a sticky situation," Jacquie said.

"What about poor Felix?" Lorraine questioned. "What happened to him? Oh, I do hope he will be okay."

"More importantly, why was he in my house and how did he get down those stairs?" Annie said out loud. Then to herself, she wondered if Felix was the one leaving roses for Lizzy. He was on the utility stairs leading to the back of her yard. The cot in the basement did not make sense, though. Felix had no need to sleep on a cot when he had his own apartment at the senior apartment complex. Annie made a mental note to talk to Dan as soon as she could.

Donald led the ladies to assemble on the front porch of the house. There were no chairs, causing everyone to stand while waiting for Dan.

Annie was all too willing to wait outside. Being trapped in a basement was not her idea of fun. She breathed in the salt air and raised her face to the sun peeking out between the clouds spotting the sky. Marie sat down on a step just as Officer Barrel pulled up in a patrol car.

Donald met with the officer and Annie at the squad car while the ladies stood nearby and listened in on the conversation. It was decided that Donald, Annie, and Marie would go back into the house with Officer Barrel and speak to Dan. The other ladies were asked to go home for now.

"But my car is missing!" LaVerne said. "And my purse was stolen by that dastardly character. He took my purse and the keys to my car."

"He took my purse as well," Jacquie added. "I can't even call my husband, because my cell phone was in the purse."

Officer Barrel pulled out her notebook and began taking notes for a report. She took the statements of LaVerne and Jacquie first. Lorraine added bits of information, such as the description of the hooded thug who surprised them inside the house.

Annie pulled her cell phone out of her pocket and handed it to Jacquie, who thanked her and began punching in a set of numbers on the keypad. Annie turned her attention back Donald and Officer Barrel. Just as she did, she was distracted by the conversation between Jacquie and John.

"John," Jacquie started the conversation. "I found the perfect house. You must come to see it. It's the one on the hill behind Annie and Donald's house. What? Yes, I am here with Annie right now. You are? Wonderful. Can you come over right away? You are going to love this house. Great. I will see you soon. Love you!"

Jacquie moved closer to Annie and handed her the phone. "Thank you, Annie. I told John about the house. He is coming to pick me up and wants to see the inside. I hope that is okay with you?"

"I happened to overhear your conversation," Annie said. "You didn't seem to mention the mishap in the basement." Annie smiled at Jacquie, waiting for a reply.

"No need to worry the poor man," Jacquie said, passing off the incident as nothing more than an annoyance. "If you really want to sell the house, John and I would certainly like to be the first to take a look around."

A car pulled up to the house and John Spencer exited the vehicle, noticing the patrol vehicle and numerous people in the yard. He met Jacquie, who was standing near Annie. Jacquie explained that the house was for sale, but a man was found hurt inside. She pulled John aside to quietly discuss what had happened.

Donald turned to Annie. "Jacquie and John want to buy this house?" Donald asked. "Are you ready to sell it?"

"As soon as I talk with Charles Conklin," Annie stated. "Letting the house remain vacant will only cause trouble. Hopefully, Dan can find out who is setting up camp here soon."

Donald turned to Jacquie and said, "I will have all the locks changed and the house professionally cleaned as soon as possible."

"In the meantime, if you and John want a tour, Donald and I can walk you through the house tomorrow," Annie offered. "It's getting late and Lizzy is in charge of dinner tonight."

Donald gave a quick, concerned, look at Annie. "Lizzy is making dinner?"

"No. I said she was in charge of dinner," Annie said. "She's picking up Chinese food tonight." Annie turned to Jacquie and John, "Would you both join us for dinner?"

"Are you sure there is enough?" John asked.

"Lizzy was not expecting us," added Jacquie.

"We will have plenty," Donald said. "There are always leftovers when we have Chinese food."

"So, please feel free to join us," Annie stated. The Spencers agreed and after the paramedics took Felix to the hospital, Donald locked up the house. Dan added a special security lock to the outside doors. The group made their way to Annie and Donald's house.

It was late in the evening when everyone sat down for dinner in the dining room. Dan was quiet while listening to Annie, Marie, and Jacquie tell their stories of what had happened in the house. When he would ask a question, it was in his 'police mode' which sometimes irked Annie.

"I talked to Charles Conklin today, Annie," Stella offered, just to change the subject. She could see that Dan's manner was irritating Annie. "He confirmed what I have been researching at the county courthouse today. Robert did own the house on the hill and you inherited the property. Would you be surprised to find out that there are more properties which had not been filed in the estate records? The properties were purchased within the last six months."

"How many more?" Annie asked.

"What properties?" Donald asked immediately after Annie's question.

"Charles Conklin wants to meet with you next week and review the new findings," Stella said.

Annie decided to call Charles Conklin as soon as she could the next day. How was she going to deal with more properties? What other properties did she and Donald now own? How did her life get so complicated in such a short time?

CHAPTER 13

Friday

I t was six o'clock in the morning and Annie was quiet as she closed and locked the front door. She paused at the top of the porch steps for a moment to take in the quietness of the neighborhood. As dawn was awakening, Annie heard the ocean waves crashing on the shoreline not far from where she was standing. She smelled the familiar salty ocean air and smiled to herself at the good fortune bestowed upon her in recent events. How could she have been so lucky to find and fall in love with a man like Donald?

Deep in thought, Annie made her way to the shop only a few blocks away. In a matter of minutes, she was standing in line at Ione's Bakery & Coffee Shop ready to order her usual chocolate croissant and coffee.

"Good morning, Annie," came a familiar deep voice behind Annie.

Annie turned to see Dan, placing an ear bud into his left ear. He turned the volume knob of a portable police radio and dropped it into his jacket pocket.

"Good morning, Dan," Annie returned. "You're up early this morning."

"You seem to keep me busy."

"I am curious, why you are going to the office a couple hours early today?"

"Paperwork," Dan answered. "The only time I am buried deep in paperwork, you somehow seemed to be involved."

Annie gave Dan a smirk that was all too familiar to him. She moved to the front of the line and greeted Ione, who handed Annie her usual order. Ione appeared to want to say something to Annie, but kept looking beyond her to Dan. Annie decided Ione must have heard something about the happenings in the house on the hill last night. Nothing gets past Ione in this small town, Annie thought.

"Once Lizzy and Daisy arrive at work, I will be back for one of those new chocolate donuts," Annie told Ione. Ione nodded, acknowledging their secret understanding of each other. Annie moved aside to pick up a napkin from the dispenser while Dan moved forward and ordered his coffee.

"Movie and pizza night tonight, Dan," Annie reminded Dan.

"I'll be there," Dan replied. Pulling dollar bills from his wallet and handing them to Ione.

Annie left the coffee shop and walked next door to Ocean Loads of Paper. Once inside the shop, she locked the door and checked it twice to make sure it was really locked. She wanted no surprises this morning.

Just as Annie turned away, there was a sharp rap on the door. Startled, she turned back to find Lizzy peering in, her dark curly hair moving wildly in the wind. Annie quickly turned the lock and pulled open the door for Lizzy.

"I ran into Dan outside the coffee shop," Lizzy said. "He was leaving, and told me that you had just walked out."

"Yes," Annie said. "I didn't think you would be here so early today."

"Since Dan was up, I figured I would get an early start on the day," Lizzy said, setting her purse and a box of donuts on the counter. "Besides, I want to hear your side of what happened in that house. We didn't have time to talk last night."

With coffee and donuts in hand, Lizzy listened intently to the past evening events. Neither Annie nor Lizzy could answer the question of who was camping out in the basement of the house. Their first concern was that it might be related to Lizzy's stalker. It made sense, since the stalker was caught on the back yard camera lurking around the cottage and leaving a rose on Lizzy's desk. The stalker could have had access to the utility stairway.

Annie realized that the person living in the house might not have been watching her house, but Dan and Lizzy's house across the street. The person had a perfect view, and with a telescope, could see into the living room window if Lizzy left the curtains opened. Annie mentioned her thoughts to Lizzy.

"Well, that person would not see much, because I close the curtains when I get home," Lizzy stated. "Dan and I use the family room in the back of the house during the evenings to watch TV. I doubt anyone can monitor what we are doing in the house. At least not from the street."

"Well, someone is aware of your coming and going, Lizzy," Annie said. "And sometimes the person follows you to work. You definitely have a stalker."

"I have no idea who it might be," Lizzy said. "Annie, I've lived here for years. I have no enemies."

"But you do have lots of admirers.,"

"At least one creepy admirer," Lizzy said and shivered at the thought of some unknown person watching her every move.

♦ ♦ ♦

Once Annie unlocked the doors, customers arrived in a continuous flow throughout the day. By mid-afternoon, Annie was prepping her classroom for a box-making event, which had a filled roster and a few extra tourists begging Annie for a spot in the class. Annie and Daisy had squeezed in as many chairs as they could round up within the shop. Fortunately, Annie kept a few folding chairs in the storage room.

It was three o'clock when the bus from the senior center pulled up in front of Annie's shop. The door to the shop opened and Annie noticed Dan enter ahead of the steady stream of regulars from the senior center. Without breaking his stride, he pulled Annie aside, and directed her to the office area.

Once in the office, Annie sat down on her desk chair and watched as Dan paced a moment, deciding what to say to Annie.

"What happened? Annie asked. She could feel it. Something bad happened. She fidgeted a bit in her chair.

"Felix didn't make it through the night," Dan said, once he stopped pacing. He stood tall and dark in his olive-colored trench coat looking down at Annie.

"Oh, no!" Annie exclaimed. "Were you able to find a next of kin?"

"Yes," Dan said. "He came into town late last night and was able to see his dad minutes before Felix passed."

"Well, at least he was there," Annie said, sad that someone in their town had passed. She did not know Felix, but her senior friends did and she felt sad for them.

"That's not the point, Annie."

"I don't get it," Annie said, suddenly realizing that Dan was upset about something else, not just the death of Felix.

"Remember the conditional contract you found in Robert's office?"

It suddenly dawned on Annie. The contract gave the seniors two weeks to find a particular gold ingot to claim the senior apartments as their own.

"I need to talk to the Senior Sleuths right away," Annie said, standing and heading for the door.

"Let me know what you find out," Dan said, he raised his cell phone up to view a message. "I have to go." With that, Dan exited the shop from the ocean-side door.

Annie walked to the classroom area of her shop and watched as the last of the seniors entered and found seats in the crowded classroom. Was it her imagination or was the entire Silver Sleuth's group in attendance? She saw a line of older people seated in walkers and chairs against the windowed wall of her classroom. She was sure they were not registered for the class.

Annie found LaVerne and Lorraine at the table in the front of the class. Seated next to them were Elsie and Millie. She made her way through walkers and chairs to the front of the class, greeting people she knew as she moved forward.

After announcing the various boxes being made, Annie began with the instruction portion of her class. Packets of materials were placed in front of each registered member of the class. Annie had a TV monitor set up on the wall of her classroom so students could view her instructions step-by-step from an application on her laptop. Daisy and Marie were helping out due to the number of students present. At times, one or the other would leave the classroom to help Lizzy with customers.

One of the class projects was a box which held eight greeting cards on a platform inside the main box. An acetate top was decorated with cut-outs and pre-made die-cuts arranged as a frame meant to be added on top of the acetate lid. Annie walked around the room, sometimes squeezing between walkers and people, surveying and helping students.

She stopped and backed up. There it was. Right in front of her. A tourist who frequently stayed in the rental condos at the north end of town and took many of Annie's classes was working on her lid with the framed die-cut. Instead of placing the die-cut on the top of the acetate lid, she placed it on the inside of the lid. She layered the die-cuts to create a framed papercut art piece.

How clever, Annie thought to herself. This made Annie think of ideas for a card with a raised centered die-cut piece showing through the clear box cover edged by decorative paper. Annie went to her notebook at the counter in the front of the class and made some quick notes. Her attention was diverted by LaVerne calling her name. Annie walked over to LaVerne and the main core of the Silver Sleuths.

"Did you have a question about something?" Annie asked as she looked up to see the seniors lined up against the wall lean in closer to LaVerne.

"We have something to tell you," LaVerne said, stopping what she was doing and tilting her body to the middle of the table near Annie. "Our bus will be here to take us back to the senior center right after class, so we need to tell you now."

Annie pulled her stool up to the end of the table and leaned forward to hear what LaVerne had to say. It must have been important news, or the ladies would have waited until Annie got home in the evening.

"I'm listening," Annie said in a whisper.

"My car was found two blocks from the senior apartments," LaVerne stated.

"The purses were inside and untouched," Lorraine added.

"That's not the big news though," Millie noted.

"It's not?" Annie asked. "It is certainly good news."

LaVerne sat up straight and looked around the room. All senior eyes were on her at the moment. Annie looked around the room. Some of the seniors looked concerned and some looked angry.

"Felix Bankford passed away last night," LaVerne announced. "He was the owner and manager of the senior apartments."

"I know," Annie admitted. "Dan told me earlier, before class began."

"Did Detective Weston tell you that Felix had an only son?" Elsie asked.

"Felix's son arrived late last night," Lorraine said. "He is staying in Felix's apartment. Apparently, he has keys to the building."

As the tone around the room was indicating a lack of trust for Felix's son, Annie thought again about the conditional contract. She made a mental note to contact Charles Conklin directly after class today.

LaVerne continued to explain that the residents of the senior apartments were concerned that Felix's son was planning to sell the complex property to a developer in the very near future. Apparently, it was rumored that there was an offer already made on the property.

Annie was shocked. How could there be an offer on the property so soon? Unless...the offer was already in the making and Felix knew he could not sell the property without first offering it to the senior residents. Felix's son had somehow made it in record time to his father's side.

"Does Felix's son have a car?" Annie asked.

"Not that he parked in our lot at the apartments," Morty offered.

Annie realized that the entire class was listening to this conversation. She whispered to LaVerne that she would discuss it with Dan and talk to the Silver Sleuths later, when there were not so many others listening. Annie told LaVerne that she had some very important information to tell her about the senior apartment property. LaVerne agreed and passed the word on to the others.

It was nearly four-thirty in the afternoon before Annie could make it back to her office. She dialed the number for Charles Conklin and identified herself to the woman answering the phone. The woman explained to Annie that Mr. Conklin was not currently available, but did have documents for Annie to sign. She made an appointment for Monday morning to have Annie come to the office and sign the papers. She shared that Mr. Conklin also had information and documents to give to Annie. Annie asked what they were, and the woman said she was not able to provide that information to Annie over the phone. Annie understood, but it was worth a shot to ask.

Tonight was 'dinner and a movie' night at Annie's house. Annie received a call earlier from her mother that a roast was in the crock pot with potatoes, carrots, and onions instead of pizza. It was one of Annie's favorite meals. Dan will be disappointed, Annie thought. He loved pizza.

Annie was wondering if it was too late to pick up a couple of loaves of crusty bread when William appeared in her office doorway. Marie stood next to him...rather close, Annie noticed.

"Ione asked me to bring this to you," William handed Annie the bag of bread.

"Thank you, William."

William smiled shyly and left, followed closely by Marie. Annie could hear them chatting at the door of the shop. Then it dawned on Annie that the shop must be empty. She stood and walked to the counter area and looked around. Not a single customer was seen. Annie took in a deep breath and exhaled. Silence at last, well except for the giggling she heard a short distance away. Annie watched Marie hold the door open for William. He backed out saying good bye at least a dozen times. It was obvious that William was smitten with Marie. They were a sweet duo.

Looking down at the bag of bread, Annie discovered a note attached on the outside of the package: "Your mother called and asked if bread could be delivered to you for tonight's dinner. Dinner sounds good! I put it on your tab. Ione."

Annie was amused to find out she had a tab at Ione's. She decided to run over and pay the 'tab' before she forgot about it. Letting Lizzy know where she was going, Annie headed out the door with her purse in hand.

Annie entered Ione's Bakery & Coffee Shop to find it devoid of customers. Ione cleaned tables, while William and two other employees were cleaning floors and restocking paper supplies at the counter. It seemed like the town had closed up shop for the day.

Ione looked up at Annie and motioned for her to sit at a table. Annie pulled out a chair and sat down.

"Would you like anything to drink? A donut?" asked Ione.

"I'd better not," Annie replied. "You know what I am having for dinner. I don't want to spoil my appetite. I just came to pay for the bread."

Ione sat down at a chair across the table from Annie. She set her cleaning rag in front of her and placed her chin in her hands while resting her elbows on the table. Annie scooted her chair closer to the table.

"I heard Felix passed away last night," Ione started. "I find it interesting that he was found in the old house once owned by Marie's grandparents."

"The house on the hill was Marie's grandparents' house?"

"Oh yes," Ione said, sitting up, absentmindedly straightening her cleaning cloth. She paused and looked straight at Annie. "Haven't you heard that story? I guess not. You were away at college, when Marie and her mother moved from her grandparents."

"I thought Marie and her mother lived next door to Helen and Robert, before Marie's mother died," Annie responded.

Ione went on to tell Annie that Marie and her mother lived with Marie's grandparents in the house on the hill from when Marie was born until she was around six or seven years old. After the grandparents passed, Robert and Helen Harper bought the house, and they helped Marie's mother purchase the house next door to the Harper's. It was a smaller and more affordable house to maintain. Unfortunately, Marie's mother developed cancer and, at some point, was not able to take care of Marie or the house. When she passed away, Robert and Helen were representatives of Marie's mother's estate and became guardians of Marie.

As Ione continued, Annie discovered that Robert and Helen sold Marie's mother's home and built an apartment above their garage to allow Marie to live with them, but have her own independence. Ione told Annie that this same house is the one that Sharon and Gregg Pinehouse now lived in, with their grandson, Oliver.

"How old is Oliver?" Annie asked. Annie wondered if she had seen him.

"He's about 15 years old," Ione stated. "He rides his bike everywhere. In fact, he has a little business to earn some spending money. You may have seen him around here. He helps me out once in a while."

"I might have," Annie said. "What does he do?"

"He will deliver anything for five bucks!"

A chill went up the back of Annie's neck.

CHAPTER 14

Friday Night

Annie asked Ione to describe him.

"Is he in any trouble?" Ione asked. "I could call Sharon and report him if he is. She's the one who called me and asked if I had deliveries he could make to earn extra money. She told me he was a good boy."

"No," stated Annie. "I just wondered if I had seen him around. I may have a time when I need to have crafting supplies delivered to the north part of town where the condo renters stay."

"I doubt he would go that far, but you could always ask," Ione said. She paused and eyed Annie suspiciously for a moment. Then she went on to describe Oliver, "He is tall and skinny, usually wears dark jeans and a dark hoodie type jacket. I bet he stays in shape from all the bike riding. Apparently, he keeps busy throughout the week making deliveries at any hour of the day."

Ione continued to talk while Annie thought about Lizzy's stalker. A fifteen-year-old boy delivering diamond jewelry? Was it possible that Oliver knew Lizzy's stalker? Annie realized she was getting side-tracked in her thoughts when she heard Ione talking about Felix.

"And to think his son arrived just moments before Felix died," Ione said. She took a breath and then looked at Annie. "Did you hear me?"

"Ah, yes," Annie fibbed. "I was just thinking. The Silver Sleuths told me this afternoon that Felix had passed away. In fact, Dan had told me just before they arrived. I feel so bad for Felix's son."

"Oh, I wouldn't feel too bad for him," Ione muttered. "He and Felix have never gotten along well. In fact, I could have sworn I saw his son in town last week. Felix had been upset about something that happened between he and his son."

"Do you know what?" Annie questioned.

"It had something to do with the sale of the senior apartments," Ione explained. "Felix told me not that long ago that he had a very generous offer for the land. Apparently, a developer wanted to buy the land and build condos, or something like that, on the property. It sounded as if the seniors would be out of a home if Felix sold the property. There isn't any other place around here for the seniors to live."

"That's true," Annie acknowledged. She thought about how horrible it would be for so many of the seniors who lived at the apartment complex.

"Well," Ione continued. "I asked Felix if he was really going to sell the property. He said he couldn't, because he had an agreement with Robert Harper. He wouldn't say what that agreement was, but I wonder if Robert purchased part or all of the property to help Felix in some way. Everyone knew Felix was a gambler at the casino up north. Sometimes he would get himself in deep, and then the next thing you know he was out of trouble again."

Ione really does know everything going on around town, Annie marveled to herself. Felix was using the rent money to pay for his gambling debts. But that just got him in deeper, because he failed to pay his mortgage or property taxes. Why was Robert Harper helping him out, other than to save the seniors from losing their homes? Did Robert really have a soft spot in his heart for the seniors?

Annie looked at her watch and stood up. It was five o'clock now and she needed to help close up shop for the day. She paid Ione for the bread and headed back to Ocean Loads of Paper.

When Annie walked through the door of her shop, Lizzy greeted her with exciting news.

"This is the best day in sales we have had in a long time," Lizzy announced, closing the cash register and taking an envelope to the safe in the office. She continued to talk about how busy the shop had been, and that they had not seen such activity all summer. She appeared in the doorway and stopped to look at Annie. "What's up?"

"I just had a very interesting discussion with Ione," Annie said. She walked past Lizzy and into the office to set her purse on the desk.

"And...?" Lizzy questioned.

Annie walked back out and stood at the counter next to Lizzy. She looked around the room for anyone listening. Daisy and Marie were in the classroom setting up for the next class on Saturday. Annie knew it was a small class, so she had to talk fast.

"Well, first of all," Annie began. "I found out that the house on the hill once belonged to Marie's grandparents. Marie and her mother lived there after Marie was born."

Annie continued to tell Lizzy what Ione had relayed to her. Lizzy listened intently as she slowly sat down on a stool near the cash register.

"You don't really think the 15-year-old kid is my stalker, do you?"

"Well, first of all," Annie stated. "He doesn't earn enough money to buy you diamonds from Tiffany's."

"True."

"I believe he is just delivering the packages for a fee," Annie continued, as she straightened papers on the counter. "That's his business. He delivers anything for five dollars a delivery."

While talking, Annie moved to the sample table and began cleaning the rubber stamps with baby wipes. She put the stamps away in a tray on her table, then walked back to the counter where Lizzy was still sitting on the stool.

"We need to find Oliver and ask who pays him to deliver gifts and flowers to you." Annie said in a lowered voice.

"I should tell Dan," Lizzy offered.

"Let's wait until we talk to Oliver first," Annie suggested. "I would bet a chocolate donut that Oliver was the person in dark clothing who left you that rose in the cottage. He lives right next door and could have easily hopped the fence in the corner of the property. The cameras would not have picked him up, because he was behind the RV."

◆ ◆ ◆

Annie and Marie walked through the door of their home to find Stella in the kitchen tossing a salad for dinner.

"I was hoping you would get home soon," Stella stated. "I have some news for Donald and you."

"I have some interesting news for you as well," Annie said, as she picked up a cherry tomato and popped it into her mouth.

Marie walked to the refrigerator and opened the door. She stood looking inside for a long moment until Stella turned and told Marie to go wash up, as dinner was just about ready.

"Do you need any help?" Marie asked.

"No, thank you," Stella said. "I had a few hours this afternoon to get the dinner table set up."

"I thought we were going to watch a movie tonight?" Marie said. "Don't we eat pizza and watch a movie on Friday nights now?"

"Tonight, it is pot roast and potatoes," Stella announced. "Now go wash up."

Marie pouted and turned to go upstairs. "I wanted pizza."

Annie chuckled as she watched Marie leave the kitchen and head upstairs.

"You can pick out the movie," Stella shouted up the stairs. She turned to Annie, "Now, what is your news?"

"You go first," Annie said. "Mine might take a few minutes to tell."

"I was searching records at the courthouse in Newport today," Stella offered. "I have copies of the records of when Robert Harper purchased the house on the hill. Did you know that he was the one who sold the property to Felix where the senior apartments are located? Robert built the complex and then sold it to Felix."

"I didn't know that," Annie said, and then presented her news to her mother. "I talked to Ione this afternoon and she told me that Marie's grandparents owned the house on the hill." Annie lowered her voice in case Marie should walk in the room and overhear their conversation. She told her mother what she learned from Ione.

"I remember Marie and her mother moving into the house next door to Helen and Robert," Stella remarked. "I am not sure, but I think Marie was about five years old then. I think they lived in that house close to fifteen years."

"The house was sold to Gregg and Sharon Pinehouse," Annie shared. "They currently have a grandson living with them. His name is Oliver."

"I think I have seen him riding a bike around town," Stella said. "He's kind of a skinny kid. Always wearing black."

"Yes," Annie stated, standing straight up. "He makes deliveries for five dollars a trip. AND...he dresses in dark clothing."

"You can't be suggesting that Oliver is Lizzy's stalker?"

"Better than that," Annie said, smiling slyly. "He knows who Lizzy's stalker is and probably how we can contact the stalker."

"You have to tell Dan right away," Stella demanded.

"Not until Lizzy and I have a talk with Oliver first," Annie said. "Ione said that Oliver is a good kid. He is just making deliveries. I don't want Dan to scare him."

"True," Stella agreed. "If Dan scares him, he could tell the stalker and then we would not get anywhere with the stalker's identification."

"Thanks for understanding, Mom."

Annie told her mom about how she believed Oliver came over the fence from his house, into her yard, and behind the garage without the cameras picking him up. Stella agreed.

"Maybe I should plant some thorny bushes back there so he doesn't try that again," Stella laughed.

Donald emerged from his office with Laddie. He took Laddie through the laundry room and let him out in the doggie run. After a few minutes, both Donald and Laddie appeared in the kitchen. Donald went to Laddie's treat jar and pulled out a crunchy-style dog bone. Laddie bounced around with joy waiting for Donald to give up the treat.

"I had a late meeting tonight," Donald said, reaching into the salad bowl and pulling out a cherry tomato and popping it into his mouth.

"Dinner is ready," Stella said, slapping Donald's hand away from the bowl of greens while he was searching for another tomato. "We are waiting for Dan and Lizzy."

As if on cue, Dan and Lizzy rapped on the front door twice and entered the house. Dan took his coat off and hung it on the hook on the wall. He then helped Lizzy off with her light jacket and placed it over his. Lizzy added her purse to the hook and walked into the kitchen, with Dan following.

"Where's the pizza?" Dan said, rubbing his hands together. "I'm starved. Donald, you want a beer?" Dan said, walking to the refrigerator and opening the door.

"It's pot roast tonight," Marie said. She had entered the kitchen behind Dan.

"No pizza?" Dan said, turning to talk to Marie.

"Close the refrigerator door and get seated for dinner," Stella reprimanded.

"But I was looking forward to pizza and beer tonight," Dan frowned.

"Me too!" Marie stated. "Just pizza. No beer."

Stella reminded Marie that she could pick out the movie for tonight. Excited about the compromise, Marie said she wanted to watch a movie in the theater downstairs. Stella agreed and the group sat down to dinner.

♦ ♦ ♦

As the meal progressed, Dan asked the group at the table, "Anything exciting happen today?" He looked up from his plate as the room was suddenly quiet. Dan looked to Lizzy, who was engrossed in her salad. He then looked to Annie, who was trying desperately not to look at Dan. He next looked to Stella.

"Did you get potatoes, Dan?" Stella asked, then picked up a dish of potatoes and shoved them toward Dan.

"Is there something going on that I should know about?" Dan asked.

Everyone looked at Annie. Annie had just stuffed a forkful of pot roast in her mouth. She was not ready to tell Dan about Oliver just yet. She had to think of something quick. She stopped chewing, swallowed, took a drink of water, then said, "Lizzy and I want to take another look at the conditional contract that Robert Harper had with Felix Bankford. There is something in it that we are overlooking."

"Like what?" Donald asked, grabbing another slice of bread from a platter in front of him.

"I can't put my finger on it at the moment," Annie said. "But knowing what I know today, I think reviewing the document might give me an idea."

"I can help until my meeting tonight," Donald said.

"Count me in," Dan said, slicing through his pot roast and stabbing a piece with his fork. "You've got my full attention. Let's go now. I'm finished." Dan put his fork down and pushed his chair out.

"Dan," Stella admonished. "Can't you at least wait until the rest of us finish dinner?"

"I've eaten about as much as I can, Mom," Annie said. She stood and took her plate to the kitchen.

"I'm right behind you," Donald stated. He reached for another slice of bread, sticking it into his mouth, and then carried his plate to the kitchen sink.

Lizzy followed with her plate and after rinsing the plates in the sink, she placed them into the dishwasher. Stella and Marie stayed behind to finish dinner and clear the table.

"I guess it's just you and me tonight," Stella said to Marie.

"Good," Marie replied. "We can watch a romantic comedy instead of an adventure movie tonight."

♦ ♦ ♦

Upon entering Robert Harper's office, Annie walked directly to the desk where she found the file of the senior apartment complex. She picked up the file and opened it to find the conditional contract signed by Robert Harper and Felix Bankford. She sat down in the green leather upholstered chair and read the document aloud to Donald, Lizzy, and Dan.

"Let me get this straight," Dan started. "If the property comes up for sale due to Felix wanting to sell, or passing away and his only son inherits the property, the seniors have fourteen days to find a particular gold ingot to pay for the property."

"Otherwise," Lizzy added. "The property goes to the son to do with as he pleases."

"And the seniors are given thirty days' notice to vacate the premises," Donald said, finishing the recap of what Annie had read in the document.

"Exactly," Annie replied.

"The question is then," Dan said, "where is this particular gold ingot? Is it in the vault room?"

"Not that we have seen," Donald remarked. "Annie and I can take some time tomorrow and go through the vault drawers."

"Why would Robert Harper keep the particular gold ingot?" Lizzy pondered.

"I am not sure he did," Annie answered. "I need to talk to the Silver Sleuths tomorrow and see if they know anything about this document."

Closing up Robert's office, Annie and Lizzy, followed by Donald and Dan, headed downstairs to the theater room. The door was open and Annie could tell from the way the characters spoke that it was an old movie.

Annie sat in a chair behind Stella and Marie.

"What is the name of this movie, Mom?" Annie whispered.

"Shop Around the Corner," Stella answered. "You may know the remake of this movie as You've Got Mail."

"Oh, I love that movie," Lizzy announced, as she stepped inside and sat next to Annie.

"That's a chick-flick," Dan said, as he quickly turned and walked into the bar. "Donald, you want a drink?"

"I wouldn't turn one down." Donald said, following Dan into the bar.

"I could have told you Dan would not want to watch a romantic comedy," Lizzy commented in a soft whisper to Annie.

"Just as well," Annie whispered back. "Where's the popcorn, Mom?"

CHAPTER 15

Saturday

Annie looked up from her notebook of box design sketches and ideas when she heard a chime from her phone. It was six-thirty in the morning on a drizzly Saturday. The fog had set in over the ocean to the point where she could not see the jagged rocky point in the bay below her house.

A message from Lizzy appeared on the screen of Annie's cell phone. She picked up her phone and viewed the text message.

"Let's walk to work together today," Lizzy wrote.

"I was going to wait for Marie to get up and dressed, but since Mom wanted to come to the shop today, I'll leave a note for Marie to walk with Mom. I am ready any time you are."

"Great," Lizzy replied. "I will meet you in front of your house."

♦ ♦ ♦

Annie shook her rain jacket just outside the shop door and walked inside to her office to hang the wet garment on a hook to dry. She had worn waterproof boots and brought a pair of shoes with her to change into after she reached the shop. It was a miserable day weather-wise so Annie was not expecting many customers. Good thing yesterday was busy, she thought to herself. This was typical weather for the Oregon coast. Bright and sunny one day, rainy the next.

Lizzy followed Annie into the office and hung up her soaking wet jacket. She went back out to the shop area and began opening routines.

"I don't have much hope of seeing lots of customers today," Annie said, as she walked around the shop turning on lights. She stopped by the thermostat and raised the temperature setting. She shivered at the dampness in the air. "I think I will call Mom and tell her and Marie to stay home."

"I'll text Daisy," Lizzy said. "She might enjoy a day off."

"What do you think of closing on Sundays and Mondays?" Annie paused at what she was doing after blurting out the question to Lizzy. She was not sure she actually wanted to close the shop on the weekend, but noticed the majority of boutique shop owners closed on Sunday and Monday. Now that she was married, and her family had grown considerably, she realized that she enjoyed the family gatherings. She wanted to spend more time with Donald.

"...And I wouldn't mind spending more time with Dan, since he only has Saturdays and Sundays off," Lizzy said. "Annie, stop daydreaming and listen to me."

"I'm listening," Annie said, knowing that she was fibbing a bit. "You want to spend more time with Dan."

"I also said if we could let Daisy and Marie handle Sunday and Monday, we could be open, but take those days off."

"Do you think Daisy is ready to open and close the shop?" Annie asked Lizzy.

"She's been doing a great job so far," Lizzy answered. Lizzy took a sip from her coffee cup and then said, "I can work with her on opening and closing and you could work with Marie on handling the cash register for returns and credit cards. I think it is a possibility."

Annie and Lizzy decided to set a plan in motion to allow them to have the days off. If the shop got too busy, Daisy could always call Annie or Lizzy and help would be a few minutes away.

Annie heard knocking on the street-side shop door and turned to see a very wet Daisy, hands cupped against the glass door peering inside. Annie ran to the door and turned the deadbolt to unlock the door. She swung the door open and stood aside as Daisy rushed in.

"This is the worst day ever," Daisy said, taking her light jacket off. "I drove and parked in the lot across the street. I got this wet just walking the short distance here."

"Didn't you get my text?" Lizzy asked Daisy, as she looked at Daisy in surprise.

"Oh," Daisy said, pulling her cell phone from her bag. "I heard the chime of my phone, but I was driving and forgot to look at it when I parked." She studied the message, put the phone back in her bag, and looked at Lizzy and Annie.

"If you don't need me, I'll run some errands and go home," Daisy said, putting her jacket back on and hoisting her purse strap onto her shoulder. "I have the class set up and packets are on the counter in the basket. There are only six people in the class today. All from the senior center."

"I think I can handle that on my own," Annie told Daisy. "Take the day off and enjoy yourself."

Daisy looked at the constant rain falling outside, turned to Annie with a shrug, and then waved good bye, exiting out the street-side door and turning toward Ione's Bakery & Coffee Shop.

"You're right, Lizzy," Annie said. "We can let Daisy and Marie handle Sundays and Mondays."

"Great!" Lizzy said, making a note on a pad of paper near the cash register. "We'll begin tomorrow."

"You take the day off," Annie insisted, "and I will open the shop and give Daisy and Marie the news."

◆ ◆ ◆

It was just after lunch and Annie was daydreaming out the ocean-side windows of the shop. She was correct in thinking the rain would keep many tourists from shopping downtown. Not even half a dozen people entered the shop that morning.

Annie's attention perked up when she spotted a tall, skinny, young man move hurriedly to Ione's Bakery & Coffee Shop. He was wearing a dark knit jacket with a hood and walking his bicycle on the boardwalk. She watched as the young man placed his bicycle up against the windowed wall of Ione's shop.

"Lizzy!" shouted Annie. "I think I see Oliver heading into Ione's shop. I'll be right back."

Before Lizzy could reply, Annie was out the door. Lizzy moved to the windows to watch Annie enter Ione's shop.

A bell chimed as Annie pushed through the glass door of the bakery. She stepped in line behind the tall thin person dressed in dark clothing.

"Excuse me," Annie said, tapping the left shoulder of the person in front of her. "Are you Oliver?"

"Yeah," the young man said. He slid back the hood on his head, revealing a blond-headed kid of around fifteen years old. His slightly curly hair was flying in all directions after being released from cover.

"I heard you make deliveries for five dollars," Annie said, thinking quickly to find a way to get Oliver to her shop and question him without others around. "I was wondering if you could make some deliveries for my shop."

"Sure," the young man replied. "Where is your shop?"

"Next door," Annie said, pointing in the direction of her shop. "Ocean Loads of Paper." Was Annie's imagination running away with her, or did Oliver appear to be surprised?

"Uh, okay," Oliver said. "I can come over as soon as I get my donut and hot chocolate."

"That would be wonderful," Annie responded. Annie realized she did not have money with her to purchase anything. "It seems I forgot my wallet. I will see you next door soon." Annie waved to Ione, and turned to leave.

Attempting to stay as dry as possible from the rain, Annie practically ran to Ocean Loads of Paper and pushed through the shop door. Annie's entrance startled Lizzy, who was using the laptop on the counter.

"Are you okay?" Lizzy asked with alarm in her voice.

"I found Oliver!"

"What? Are you sure it's him?" Lizzy asked.

"I talked with him at Ione's," Annie said with excitement in her voice. "He's coming over here under the pretense that I need him to make a delivery. We can question him when he gets here."

Lizzy looked frantically around the shop, wondering what item they were going to have delivered and to whom. She ran to a shelf area and picked up a pre-packaged pack of white paper cardstock.

"Here!" Lizzy said, setting the pack of paper on the counter. "We'll ask him to deliver this to...who?"

"I'll send a text to Jacquie and tell her that someone is delivering paper to her," Annie said. She pulled her cell phone from her desk and began typing quickly. "I told her I would explain later. I asked her to accept the package and not say anything."

"Here he comes!" Lizzy shouted with obvious nervousness in her voice.

"Lizzy, calm down," Annie said. "He's not the one stalking you. We need to question him as to who is sending you flowers and gifts."

Lizzy stood tall and stiff as Oliver entered the shop. Annie tried her best to look natural, but ended up with the same posture as Lizzy. The two stood like statues.

Once Oliver entered and stepped forward to the cashier counter, he looked up at Lizzy and froze.

"Hello, Oliver," Lizzy said in a monotone as she greeted the young man standing in front of her.

"Uh, hi," Oliver stated. He appeared unsure whether he should stay or run out the door. "Did you have something for me to deliver?"

"Yes, we do," answered Annie. "But first I wanted to ask you a few questions."

"If it's about the flowers and things..."

"As a matter of fact, Oliver, it is," Lizzy jumped in before Oliver could finish his sentence.

"I just get a call to meet this guy and he gives me stuff to deliver," Oliver says.

"Do you have a name for this guy?" Annie asked in a soft voice.

"He never told me his name," Oliver replied. Looking at Lizzy, he says, "I just thought it was a guy who had the hots for you or something. I told my grandma and she told me you were married to a cop. She said I should stop delivering stuff from this guy, but he pays me twenty dollars each delivery. That kind of money is hard to give up."

"I understand, Oliver," Annie spoke. "We need to find this guy and talk to him. Do you have any idea where he stays or anything about him?"

"No," Oliver said. "He meets me in different places and watches me deliver the flowers and sometimes gifts."

"Do you see a caller ID when he calls you on your cell phone?" Lizzy said, her voice relaxing in tone.

"No," he said. "The number is always listed as a private caller. I usually know it's him, because everyone else has their number show up when they call. I think he might be a cop, because I noticed he carried a gun under his jacket."

"Police officer?" Lizzy asked.

"Yeah."

Annie and Lizzy looked at each other in puzzlement.

"Did you have a delivery for me to make?" Oliver questioned.

"Oh," Annie said. "Please deliver this to Spencer's Gallery right away." Annie handed Oliver the paper pack in a brown paper bag. "Here is your five-dollar delivery fee, and fifteen dollars if you would please contact me right away the next time this guy wants you to make a delivery." Annie wrote her cell phone number on a piece of paper and handed it to Oliver, along with a twenty-dollar bill.

"Please, don't tell the person we are asking about him," Lizzy pleaded. "Annie and I just want to find out who is sending the flowers and gifts."

"Doesn't he sign his name to the notes?" Oliver asked.

"Unfortunately, no," Lizzy said.

"Well, if you need anything else delivered, get a hold of me within the hour," Oliver advised. "I'm going camping with my cousins until Tuesday or Wednesday and I leave later this afternoon."

"We'll be sure to do that," Annie stated. "Have a great time camping and thank you for speaking with us."

"Hey, no problem," Oliver said, walking to the door. He turned and said, "My granny really likes your shop. She says you're a very nice person."

"I appreciate that, Oliver," Annie said, smiling widely. She was trying to remember the last time she saw Sharon Pinehouse in her shop. Maybe she should find out Sharon's email and get her on the class notification list. Then again, Annie thought to herself, she did know Sharon's address. She could send a postcard and ask Sharon to sign up to be on the class notifications, or she could visit her neighbor and talk to her personally.

"Well," Lizzy said. "We certainly did not learn anything from that interrogation."

"On the contrary," Annie said, snapping out of her thoughts about Sharon Pinehouse. "We know that the mystery guy might be a cop."

"Are you thinking it's Dan?" Lizzy asked.

"Do you know any other police officers?" Annie inquired.

"Wait a minute," Lizzy exclaimed. "If it were Dan, why would he have kicked the Tiffany's bag down the sidewalk if he knew what was in it? And where would Dan get the money for jewelry at Tiffany's?"

"I forgot about that," Annie said. Annie thought for a moment and then said, "Oh, Lizzy...who else carries a gun who is not a police officer?"

"Besides the people who have permits?" Lizzy said, smirking at Annie. "Oh, Annie, you wouldn't be thinking about a bad guy, would you?"

Annie could see Lizzy shuddered at the thought.

"On the other hand," Lizzy said, looking at Annie, appearing to have the answer. "I bet he's an armed messenger. It makes sense. He's delivering jewelry. Oliver said the guy watches him make the deliveries. Maybe he's not a bad guy at all."

"Okay," Annie agreed. "But who is sending the flowers and gifts?"

"I don't know."

"At least we know you won't have any deliveries until Tuesday or Wednesday when Oliver gets back from camping," Annie said.

Annie suggested Lizzy tell Dan over dinner. Lizzy told Annie that they would not be around for dinner, as Dan was taking Lizzy out to eat in Newport tonight for a date night. Lizzy said that if the opportunity came up, she would tell Dan. Annie knew Lizzy would never find the chance to tell Dan, because she did not want to spoil the evening. Dan was not happy about the anonymous flowers and gifts being sent to his wife.

The shop had few customers all afternoon. At three o'clock, Annie saw the bus from the senior center pull up to the curb. She watched as LaVerne, Lorraine, Millie, and Elsie exited the bus. No one else appeared to be following them. She was sure she had a couple more seniors registered for her class.

Annie opened the shop door and greeted the Silver Sleuths as they entered. She watched as they made their way to the classroom and sat down. They seemed sullen for some reason. Did someone die? Annie hoped not.

"We have some terrible news to tell you, Annie," Elsie stated, setting her purse on the table as she sat down.

Annie sat down across from the women. "What's happened?" She noticed Lizzy approaching and taking a seat at the end of the table so she could watch for customers entering the store.

"Are we the only ones in the store?" Lorraine asked.

"At the moment," Lizzy answered. "It has been so slow today due to the rain."

"It has been downpouring all day," Millie said. "We took my car to the senior center. I'm afraid it is not a happy place right now."

"Did someone pass away," Lizzy asked.

"If only it were that simple," Elsie stated.

LaVerne, who had been quiet up until now, spoke up, "Felix Bankford's son just handed out thirty-day notices to all of the seniors in the apartment complex."

"Oh no!" Annie spoke up in surprise.

"That's right," Lorraine said. "He has a buyer for the property and plans to turn it into expensive condos. The plans are to tear down the apartment complex and build horrible, high-density, housing."

"He has drawings and everything," Millie said.

"Oh, Annie," Elsie said. "All of our dear friends will be homeless. We don't know what to do."

Annie looked to Lizzy as if to ask if she should tell the ladies about the conditional contract which she had found. Lizzy motioned by nodding her head up and down. She told as much as she could about the document between Robert Harper and Felix Bankford. It all made sense, except for the location of the particular gold ingot bar.

"Wait a minute, ladies," LaVerne said. She paused to think. "Do you remember...oh, it was maybe four to six months ago...Robert Harper had coffee with us at Ione's?"

"Yes," Millie stated. "It was a bit odd that he would come over to our table and sit down with us."

"Oh!" Elsie exclaimed. "He told us that if we were the top-notch detectives we said we were, then he would challenge us at some point in the near future to a great mystery."

"Of course, he died and we never gave it another thought," Elsie added. "He never told us what the challenge was. He only said that things were looking up."

"Robert Harper was planning for you ladies to find the gold ingot that would pay for the apartment complex," Annie explained. "He wanted you to turn the apartment complex into a co-op ownership of all who lived there."

"But why tell us?" Millie asked. "We weren't living at the senior apartment complex."

"YOU weren't, Millie," LaVerne said. "But at the time, Lorraine, Elsie, and I were living there."

The next half an hour was spent discussing where the gold ingot was hidden, and how were they going to find the clues that would lead them to save the senior apartment complex.

"Apparently," Annie said. "You only have fourteen days to find this ingot from the day that Felix's son gave you notice."

"That's not much time at all," Millie cried. "Oh, dear, where do we begin?"

"Start with Ione," Annie instructed. "She knew Robert well and spoke with him often. I have an appointment on Monday with Robert's attorney, Charles Conklin. He may have more information."

"Didn't Robert build the senior center?" Lizzy asked. "Could the ingot be hidden there?"

"We'll search every nook and cranny for the ingot at the senior center," LaVerne stated.

"As well as the senior apartment complex," Lorraine added. "Robert Harper built that, too!"

"Good gracious," LaVerne said. "Lorraine is absolutely on to something. It has to be somewhere the Silver Sleuths would have access to, and something he had a hand in building."

"We are usually good at figuring out puzzles," Elsie said. "Though where are the clues to this puzzle?"

CHAPTER 16

Sunday

As the sun rose from the east and splashed on the water far below, Annie rested, with her legs tucked under her, on the sofa in the sitting room of the master suite. She watched the sky gradually brighten the ocean beyond her.

A puzzle, Annie thought to herself. There must be something for the Silver Sleuths to solve. Did Robert Harper die before he was able to complete a set of clues for the ladies?

Annie reached for her cell phone when she heard the familiar 'ding' of someone leaving her a text message.

"Are you up?" Lizzy asked.

"Of course," Annie replied.

"Since Dan and Donald are going crabbing, would you mind if I spent some time in Robert's office?"

"Of course not," Annie messaged back. "I will join you for a while, until I need to open the shop for Daisy and Marie."

"Sounds good," Lizzy said. "We'll be over in a few minutes."

"We?" Annie asked.

"Dan is going crabbing with Donald this morning. Is he ready?"

Annie stood and walked to the bed to find not only Donald sound asleep, but Laddie on the bed next to him with his paws in the air. She called out to Donald, who awoke with a jerk and sat up suddenly.

"What time is it?"

"Time for you to get up, if you are still going crabbing with Dan," Annie replied.

Donald sprang from the bed, throwing the covers over Laddie. Laddie attempted to right himself, but he was getting tangled up in the covers. Annie reached out to help the struggling dog.

"Would you tell Dan I'll be ready in a jiffy," Donald called out from the dressing room.

"He's on his way over with Lizzy."

"I forgot to set my alarm last night," Donald said, as he came hopping out of the bathroom on one foot while attempting to put a sock on the other foot. He sat down on the bed and completed his task. "I can't be late. We have to be there and set up before the good spots are taken."

"Today is looking great," Annie stated. "It is slightly overcast, but the sun promises to shine today. It should be good for crabbing."

"Would you mind taking Laddie out?" Donald said. He gave Annie a quick kiss and hurried out the door.

Annie heard the doorbell ring and the familiar sound of the alarm being disengaged.

"That's your cue to get up out of bed and downstairs, Laddie," Annie told the large black dog taking up space on her bed. Annie quickly made the bed and escorted Laddie to the doggie run outside. She fed Callie and gave her a fresh bowl of water. By the time she had cleaned up Callie's potty box, Laddie was scratching at the door to come inside.

When Annie walked to the kitchen, she noticed Lizzy helping herself to a cup of coffee. Lizzy took another mug from the cupboard and brewed a fresh cup for Annie. Annie sat down and yawned.

"Are you sure you want to open the shop on Sundays?" Lizzy asked. "I could talk to Daisy. You talk to Marie. Let's close on Sundays, at least."

"I would like a day off to spend in Robert's office," Annie announced. "I feel like there is something we are missing about this ingot. It is right in front of us."

"Well," Lizzy started. "If it was, the senior apartment complex would be saved. Why would Robert do this to the seniors?"

"He told Elsie and the other ladies that he had a challenge for the Silver Sleuths," Annie said, as she pondered. "He left the gold ingot somewhere for them to find. He was challenging them to solve the mystery of finding the ingot."

Annie and Lizzy each made a fresh cup of coffee and headed to Robert Harper's office downstairs. They took the stairs behind the bookcase in the small sitting area off the dining room. Annie pushed open the metal door and stood for a moment while lights automatically illuminated the hallway. She walked along the faux wooden fence and pressed on the section of fencing that revealed the closed office door. She turned the doorknob and entered the room. Reaching for the switch, Annie flipped it and watched the lights flood the office and sitting area of the room.

Lizzy walked to the desk and set her coffee cup down. She opened the credenza file drawer and began searching. Annie chose to search the workspace island with the large drawers containing architectural drawings and files of notes. Both Lizzy and Annie worked quietly, unless they came across something of interest. Lizzy kept a notepad and jotted down notes on what they found and where to find it again. After two hours of searching, both Annie and Lizzy stood up and sighed at the same time.

"I'm hungry," Lizzy said, putting back a file from the credenza and closing the drawer. "Let's stop for breakfast. I feel like I haven't accomplished a thing this morning."

"Can't argue with that," Annie said from behind the island counter. She closed the bottom drawer and stood up with a groan. "I need more coffee." She followed Lizzy out to the hall, turning off the lights and closing the door behind her. Annie then swung the fake wooden fence back in place, concealing the office door.

Annie and Lizzy made their way upstairs to the kitchen where they found Stella and Marie.

"Would you two like an omelet?" Stella asked. "I just started making breakfast for Marie and myself. There's plenty to go around."

Annie walked to the kitchen sink and after rinsing out her mug, she made another cup of coffee and found a seat at the kitchen table. "I would love a ham and cheese omelet."

"Lizzy, how about you?" Stella asked.

"Same for me," Lizzy said. "Can I help chop up some mushrooms and peppers?"

"Check the refrigerator," Stella replied. "I was waiting for the boys to get back from crabbing, so I prepped different vegetables to put in the omelets. Annie and Marie only like ham and cheese, but I know Dan likes just about everything in his omelet. I am not sure what Donald likes."

"He likes just about everything as well," Annie remarked.

Lizzy opened the refrigerator door and pulled out a couple of small bowls covered in plastic wrap. She set a bowl of chopped mushrooms and a bowl of chopped red peppers next to Stella at the stove.

"Lizzy and I have been searching for the last couple of hours for anything that would indicate a set of clues for the Silver Sleuths to solve to find the gold ingot," Annie said. She watched Stella preparing the perfect omelet on the stove, as she took a sip from her mug of coffee. "Could he have passed away before the clues were written?"

Stella slid the ham and cheese omelet onto a plate and sprinkled grated cheddar cheese on top. Handing the plate to Annie, she leaned against the counter in thought for a moment.

"Knowing Robert," Stella began. "He would have written the clues before talking to the Silver Sleuths."

"But how are the Silver Sleuths supposed to find the clues and solve them?" Lizzy asked Stella.

Stella turned to the stove and began pouring an egg mixture into a small fry pan. "Charles Conklin handled all of Robert's affairs. I would check with him first. He may have the answers."

"I meet with him tomorrow morning," Annie said. "Until then, Lizzy, let's take the day off and do something fun."

Just as the words left Annie's mouth, she heard a vehicle pull up in the back yard. She went to the kitchen door window to see Dan's SUV park by the garage. Lizzy stood behind Annie at the kitchen window and said, "Like clean crab for the next two hours?"

"If we're lucky, they only got a couple of crabs," Annie said. She looked up at the house on the hill, "That reminds me. I promised Jacquie and John that I would show them around the house on the hill tomorrow, after I get back from meeting with the attorney in Newport."

"Oh, can I go with you? I would love to see the inside of the house," Lizzy asked.

"Does that mean we are closing the shop on Monday?"

"No," Lizzy answered. "I'll open the shop with Daisy and get her up to speed on opening and closing. You should be back from your appointment by then. We can have lunch and you can tell me everything you find out."

"Am I working tomorrow?" Marie asked.

"Yes," said Lizzy. "You and Daisy are in charge of the shop on Mondays from now on."

Before Marie could respond, Dan and Donald bounded through the kitchen door, nearly knocking into Annie and Lizzy. They were carrying two large buckets of crabs.

"Oh, my word!" Stella exclaimed. "Take those smelly things out to the patio right now. You are not going to clean them in this house."

"But it might rain outside," Dan said. "And the chairs are wet."

"You can put up that portable canopy that's in the garage," Stella instructed. "I will get you a towel to wipe the chairs down." She walked to the laundry room to get a couple of old towels. Walking out, she handed them to Dan.

Donald and Dan exited the kitchen, trying not to slosh water on the floor.

"I hope you came up with a good excuse to not clean crabs," Lizzy whispered to Annie.

"I suggest we do further exploration of the underground house," Annie stated. "I know! Let's go through the vault room again. We have to find that ingot."

"Lizzy," Stella said, placing a plate on the table. "Here's your omelet. Sit down and eat."

"Thank you, Stella," Lizzy said, moving the table and pulling out her chair to sit down. "It looks delicious!"

Annie was finishing up her breakfast when Donald entered the kitchen and announced that he and Dan had set up the canopy outside and wiped down the chairs. He opened cupboard doors and took out metal bowls of various sizes to place the crab meat as they cracked open the already cooked crustaceans.

"We were able to get the crabs cooked at the dock," Donald said proudly. "We were first in line at the crab cooking station. That's why it is important to get there early. So, who's all going to help with shelling the crab?"

"I will!" shouted out Marie.

Annie and Lizzy looked at each other. They both knew that if Marie was willing to crack crab, they should help as well.

"How many are there?" Annie asked.

"We limited out," Donald said. "Twelve crabs each."

Annie told Donald that they would be outside as soon as they finished their breakfast.

"I'll tell you what," Stella stated. "When you are finished, bring the crab meat inside and I will use part of it for a nice seafood chowder." Stella opened the freezer door and rummaged around inside to check for scallops, clams, and shrimp to accompany the crab.

"That sounds wonderful!" Lizzy said. "I can walk to Ione's and get a couple of baguettes."

"I'll go with you, Lizzy," Annie said, as she sat up in her chair. This meant getting out of cleaning all those crabs.

"You'll have plenty of time after the crabs are cleaned," Stella said. "I will call Ione and ask her to set a couple of loaves aside for you."

"Thanks, Mom," Annie said, trying not to sound too disappointed. She looked at Donald, who was smiling at her, knowing she wanted to get out of cleaning crabs.

"I'll make it up to you," Donald said, mouthing the words to Annie.

As it was, Annie only had to clean four crabs. Donald finished extracting the meat from his six crabs in record time and took one of hers to help out. Marie cleaned one from Annie's pile of crabs and one from Lizzy's. The weather seemed to stay sunny for the time the five were outside working. As soon as they cleaned up and put the canopy away in the garage, a downpour of rain began. Everyone raced inside to stay dry.

Stella divided the crab into storage bags, giving one to Lizzy, setting one aside in the refrigerator for the seafood chowder that evening, and putting the others in the freezer. She announced that she and Marie were going shopping and she would see everyone later in the afternoon.

Once everyone had left the house, Annie told Donald she was off to take a shower and then to find an old movie in the theater room to watch. Donald did the same and within the hour they were sitting in the theater room watching Bachelor Mother starring Ginger Rogers and David Niven. Annie was trying to remember the last time she and Donald had this much time alone together in the afternoon.

♦ ♦ ♦

During dinner that evening, Annie brought up the subject of the Silver Sleuths and the idea that Robert Harper may have left clues to locate the hidden ingot of gold. She explained to Donald and Dan what information she had gathered so far and what the elderly ladies had related.

"If Robert had left any clues," Dan pondered out loud, "He would have put them in a place where the seniors could easily find them."

"Uncle Robert knew about the offer Felix had on the senior apartment complex," Donald further offered. "He seemed to want to keep the sale from happening, so he bailed Felix out of a gambling debt, then devised a plan to allow the seniors to purchase the property and develop a co-op to run the place."

"I believe Charles Conklin will answer all your questions, Annie," Stella said. She stood and leaned over the table to dish out a second helping of seafood chowder.

"I understand that he wrote the conditional contract, but that may be where it all ends." Annie told her mother. She held her bowl out to Stella for a refill of soup.

"Robert may have a vested interest in the property since he originally built the apartments and then sold it to Felix," Lizzy pointed out. "Felix must be paying the mortgage to Robert Harper. That is why Robert left the clues for the seniors. He wants them to have the apartment complex."

"He gave them fourteen days to locate the gold ingot," Annie stated. "Why didn't he just purchase the property back from Felix when he paid off Felix's gambling debts?"

"Maybe he did," Donald said. He put his spoon down and reached for a slice of bread. Dan noticed, and passed the butter dish to Donald. "This conditional contract was just a way of having fun with the ladies. Uncle Robert owned the mortgage on the property. Uncle Robert paid Felix's gambling debts for a price. The property was to go to the seniors all along."

"Wait a minute," Annie said. "The ladies came to the shop and told me that Felix's son just gave the residents thirty days' notice to vacate the premises due to the sale of the property. They didn't know about the conditional contract until Lizzy and I told them."

"It seems I need to have a talk with young Mr. Bankford," Dan announced. "Something doesn't make sense. He suddenly shows up in town just hours before his dad passes away. He doesn't seem to waste time in selling the property. How did he get a buyer so soon?"

"And how does he have the authority to sell the property so soon?" Annie asked. "Is there a Will? Why weren't the seniors told of the conditional contract and their fourteen days to provide the gold ingot to gain control of the property?"

"Oh, my gosh!" Lizzy shouted. Everyone stopped and stared at her. "Dan, did you ever find out why Felix Bankford was found on the stairs leading to the sump pump room? And Annie, didn't you say there was a cot in the basement and clothes?"

"You think Felix's son was the person in the house on the hill?" Donald asked, setting his spoon down and contemplating Lizzy's questions. "If so, could he have struggled with Felix, because he had a buyer for the property and wanted to sell it?"

"And pushed Felix down the stairs?" asked Lizzy.

There was a long period of silence at the table. The only sounds were that of the occasional clicking of spoons in the bowls of chowder.

"Would you pass the bread, please," Marie asked.

Donald picked up the platter of bread and passed it down to Marie. She took a slice and passed the plate to Stella. Stella took the plate and set it down in front of Lizzy.

"Do you think Felix's son may have murdered his father to gain control over the property?" Stella asked Dan.

"Maybe he was trying to convince Felix that since Robert was dead, he could sell the property for a large amount of money to a developer and at the same time pay off the loan. Both Felix and his son would benefit from the sale of the property," Lizzy speculated.

"Except," Annie added. "Felix knew of the conditional contract giving the Silver Sleuths fourteen days to claim the property with the gold ingot."

"Why didn't Uncle Robert just give the property to the seniors?" Marie asked. "Like he did with the Senior Center."

"Because," Donald said. "Uncle Robert probably thought he was going to be alive and he would never have let the property be sold to a developer."

"Here's another question," Annie started. "Robert Harper has been dead for four months now. Where are those mortgage payments going?"

"Was Felix making those payments once Robert died?" Lizzy asked.

"I believe I have a whole new investigation to begin first thing in the morning," Dan replied.

CHAPTER 17

Monday Morning

*L*ate in the evening, Annie was turning lights off in the kitchen and getting ready to go to bed. She looked out the kitchen window and noticed that there were no lights on in her mother's apartment. Her mother must have been tired and went directly to bed. Out of curiosity, Annie looked up to the house on the hill. A light was shining through a window. A dark figure stood in the window, staring out over the ocean.

Annie found herself at the front door of the house on the hill. She stood still by the door. Keys jingled in her hand...a hand that was now trembling. She was finally going to discover who it was occupying her house. She saw her shaking hand raise up and place a key in the lock. She turned the doorknob and pushed open the door to a sparse, but expensively furnished living room. Someone was living in her house!

There, by the window, still looking out toward the ocean, stood a tall man in a fedora hat. He wore a sleeveless vest, a long-sleeved shirt and khaki pants. Annie questioned if what she was seeing was real. This man could have stepped right out of a jungle movie. An explorer. An adventurer. Who was he? As if to answer her question, the man slowly turned to face her.

"Robert Harper!" Annie shouted out. Even though her mouth felt like it was moving, no sound came out. It can't be! Robert Harper is dead.

Robert stared at Annie for a long time. He moved closer to her, tilting his hat upward with the index finger of his right hand. A smile grew across his face as he recognized Annie. He motioned for her to follow him with a quick jerk of his head. He opened a door and waved her through. She found herself in a long corridor. It was void of any color and she could not see an end. She wondered where Robert was guiding her and why.

It seemed like she only took a few steps and she was standing directly in front of another door. She opened the door and stood staring into Robert's office. She turned to Robert, who walked past her into the room and pointed in the direction of the island counter.

"Robert!" Annie could hear herself saying. "Why...?"

"Annie!" Donald shouted. "Wake up. You are having a bad dream." Donald sat up next to Annie in bed. "Are you okay?"

Realizing she was sitting up in bed, Annie turned to Donald, "I had a dream that Robert Harper was alive and living in the house on the hill," Annie said. "He wanted me to see something in his office." She sat there desperately trying to focus on her dream and what Robert wanted to show her. Each moment she spent on thinking about the dream, the dream seemed to further escape her. Parts of the vision were fading quickly.

"It has something to do with the island counter in his office," Annie said. She was still trying to grasp the details of her encounter with Robert. Only the main parts were coming to her. Even Robert's face was evaporating quickly from her mind. His smile remained. A smile that was trying to tell her something.

"It seems like your sub-conscious knows the answer," Donald suggested. "Could it be the plans of the new development for the senior apartment complex property? Those plans were in the top drawer of the island counter."

"I need to look at those plans, Donald," Annie said.

"You have an early appointment with Charles Conklin today," Donald stated. "I can go to the office and pull out the plans for you. I will leave them in a secure place in my office."

"I'll come straight home after my appointment in Newport," Annie said. "If you have time, will you go through the plans with me?"

"Do you want me to take a look before you get back?" Donald asked.

"Only if you have the time," Annie said. "I don't want to keep you from work."

Annie looked at the clock. It was nearly six in the morning. Later than she usually got up on a work day. She had a very busy day ahead and wanted to have an hour to herself to prepare. She watched Donald walk to the bathroom, and decided to get out of bed.

♦ ♦ ♦

Driving south on Highway 101 heading to Newport, Annie spotted the Yaquina Head Lighthouse high above a rocky point jutting out into the Pacific Ocean. She had visited the lighthouse on numerous occasions, even before the museum, a short walk away from the lighthouse, was built. Her Federal Park day pass lay on the dash of her vehicle, giving her unlimited access to the park.

The drive to Newport was beautiful to Annie, even in the rain. But today, the sun was out and clouds were few in the sky. It was perfect for a drive down the coast. Annie loved driving on her own. It gave her time to think, plan crafting projects, work out problems. Today was no exception. She was racking her brain to figure out what additional properties she might own besides the house on the hill. What did Helen get her into with the house and its secrets?

As if on auto pilot, Annie pulled into a parking space at the office of Charles Conklin. She was a few minutes early, but decided to go inside anyway. She was sure she was the first appointment of the day. The sun was warm, and Annie chose to take her jacket off and leave it in the backseat of her SUV. Making sure she had her keys in her hand, she pushed the lock on the door, closed it, and tested the handle to make sure the doors were locked. Double-checking for her keys was a habit Annie developed after she had once locked herself out of her car.

Annie entered the attorney's office. The main reception room was pleasant, but not overly done. The furniture was fresh, modern, and new. A young, 20-ish looking woman occupied a seat behind a long counter. Annie introduced herself to the young woman, who had a microphone extending beyond the side of her face. The receptionist pressed a button on a communications panel and announced the arrival of Annie. She then asked Annie to take a seat.

Moments later, a middle-aged woman with short blond hair opened a door and walked up to Annie. Annie recognized her as Lori, Charles Conklin's assistant.

"Hello Ms. Harper," Lori said. "It's good to see you again. May I offer you some coffee or tea?"

"I am a bit nervous being here," Annie began. "Maybe coffee. Dark roast if you have it." Annie knew that this office brewed coffee from individual pods and did not make a full pot of coffee and leave it sit for hours. She felt safe getting a decent cup of coffee here. Not that she was a coffee snob...okay, she was a coffee snob. She's had coffee in the past that she thought was brewed from shredded cardboard.

"I remembered," Lori told Annie. "Follow me and I will get you seated in Mr. Conklin's office."

Annie followed Lori through a doorway and into a corridor lined with glass-walled offices. At the end of the hallway was the office of Charles Conklin. Lori opened the door to the office and ushered Annie inside. She pointed to a chair at a small conference table and Annie made herself comfortable. Before Lori disappeared, she advised Annie that Mr. Conklin would arrive shortly.

"Good morning, Annie," a slightly gray-haired man said as he hurriedly entered the office and set a stack of files on the table. Annie rose to shake his hand.

"Good morning, Mr. Conklin," Annie said.

"Please call me Charles, Annie," Charles instructed.

After a brief conversation with Charles on the well-being of Stella, Marie, and Donald, Lori entered the room with the coffee for Annie. She set it down in front of Annie and then sat down next to Mr. Conklin. Lori began pulling files from the stack placed on the table by the attorney.

"First, let's start with your appointment with Sheryl Doxie," Charles stated.

"Who?" Annie asked.

"Your accountant," Charles said, looking up over the top of his glasses at Annie. "Annie, did you read the packet of information I gave you over a month ago?"

"I'm still trying to go through it all," Annie fibbed. She had in fact completely forgotten all about it over the last month. So much had happened to her since she
inherited the house, fell in love, and got married. Then there was the mystery of the painting she helped solve. Not to mention the mystery of her new home and all its hidden secrets.

"Then, I really do have an accountant for R&H Enterprises?" Annie asked innocently.

"Yes," Charles said. "Her name is Sheryl Doxie. She has an office in town about a block away from your place. It is on the south side of the floral shop."

"Yes, I actually know where that office is located," Annie said. She remembered the vendors suggesting the name Sheryl Doxie during their meeting.

"When I contacted her this morning," Charles said. "She said she had not heard from you. She wanted an appointment to meet you and discuss R&H Enterprises and the senior center accounts."

"The senior center accounts?" Annie questioned.

"Annie," Charles said, sounding a bit exasperated. "Read the papers left to you by Helen Harper."

"I promise that I will read them tonight," Annie said, running through her mind what she had on her calendar for the day. She thought about meeting Jacquie and John after work to show them the house. If not tonight, tomorrow, she thought to herself. She wished she had asked Donald to come to this appointment with her. Whatever properties she was finding out about would certainly concern Donald.

Charles looked at Annie suspiciously and then said, "I might as well tell you the story behind the senior center and the senior apartment complex. I have my suspicions that you might not get to the papers tonight."

Annie sunk in her chair momentarily, but as she listened to Charles, she found her body straightening upright.

Charles began with the land where the senior center now stood. As it was explained, the land was owned by Robert and Helen Harper, now Annie's property due to her inheritance. The building was custom made for the seniors by Robert Harper. He gave the building to the seniors and entered into a contract with the city whereby they would pay R&H Enterprises one dollar a year, due in January of each year, for ninety-nine years.

Annie listened intently, not wanting to miss any detail of what Charles was relaying. "Should I be taking notes?" Annie asked.

"Lori will take notes and email them to you," Charles said.

Annie looked to Lori and thanked her.

"Now," Charles continued. "The wide strip of property between the senior center and the senior apartment complex is, or was, owned by Robert and Helen Harper. That property is now yours. There is a service that maintains the grounds and fountain that sits on the property near the entrance of the senior apartment driveway."

"Who is the service and how do I pay for the service?" Annie asked.

"Sheryl Doxie actually takes care of all that for you," Lori offered. "I will be giving you a list of things you need to attend to immediately."

"Oh," Annie responded. "A list. Thank you. I can handle working off a list." Annie was thinking it was Lizzy who should have come with her, not Donald. Lizzy would have had all of this taken care of the second she knew about it.

"Next," Charles continued. "The senior apartment complex. I am going on record to say that I never agreed with the sale of the apartments to Felix Bankford. After doing a background check on him, I advised Robert not to sell. Sometimes, Robert Harper had a soft spot for people, and he could not be reasoned with to see the whole picture. After Robert agreed to sell the property, Bankford made good on the payments for about a year, and then got into trouble due to gambling debts. He got far behind in the mortgage payments. Robert should have foreclosed on the property, but he didn't. He bailed Bankford out against my advice. And though Bankford assured Robert he would quit gambling, that didn't happen. When Robert believed Bankford would fall behind on payments again, he came up with a plan to turn the property over to the seniors and have them form a board of trustees to maintain the property."

"The conditional contract I found in Robert's office," Annie stated. "Unfortunately, that document requires the seniors to solve clues and find a gold ingot in fourteen days. They have no idea what the clues are or how to solve them."

"Lori, do you have a copy of the document for Annie?" Charles asked.

Lori dug through her stack of papers. She pulled out two sheets stapled together and handed them to Annie.

Annie recognized the familiar top page of the conditional contract. She flipped to the second sheet and was surprised to see a set of instructions for the seniors to follow to find their gold ingot. Robert did leave them the information they needed to find the money and save the apartment complex.

Annie smiled at Charles Conklin and said, "This is exactly what we were looking for in Robert's office. This document will help the seniors find what they need to save their apartment complex from developers."

"I have to tell you, Annie. Robert never told me where he hid the gold ingot. The ingot is concealed and only Robert knew its location. He believed he would be around to help the seniors find the gold if they were unable to solve the clues. I can't help you with that," Charles told Annie.

"But the conditional contract only allows the seniors fourteen days to find the ingot," Annie exclaimed. "How are they going to do that in fourteen days? If they don't find the gold, the property is turned over to Felix's heir...his son, who has already found a developer to purchase the land and tear down the apartments. The son has already given the seniors thirty-day notices to vacate the premises."

"Sadly, Robert expected to be alive when he drew up this agreement," Charles announced. "It was really a game between himself and the Silver Sleuths, whom he often talked about as being the craftiest ladies around town. I was against the whole thing from the beginning."

Annie smiled at the thought of Robert's fondness of the Silver Sleuths. Yes, the ladies were indeed crafty, but could they solve this mystery without Robert's help? She realized that Robert Harper did have a soft spot in his heart for people. She wanted to call Donald that moment and tell him what she had found out. Focus, she scolded herself.

"I hope these clues will help the seniors find their gold," Charles said. "Otherwise, Annie, the son can take the property and do with it as he wishes. From what I am hearing, there was a buyer in place before Felix passed away. There is no time to waste in finding the gold."

"The thirty-day notice has started," Annie said. "The clock is ticking."

"Not exactly," Charles said. "The thirty-day notice takes effect after the fourteen days. If the Silver Sleuths do not find the gold ingot, then the clock will start counting down thirty days. I will send a letter to Felix's son by messenger today to remind him that the Silver Sleuths have fourteen days before the thirty-day notice begins."

"I appreciate that," Annie said. She paused for a moment in thought and an idea came to mind. "Can Donald and I just pay for the property for the seniors?"

"The details explain a particular gold ingot," Charles said. "It was meant to be a test of the Silver Sleuths skills as detectives. Robert often talked of testing their skills. Of course, he made no mention that they could not receive help."

"Were you and Robert Harper close?" Annie just had to ask.

"I handled his business and personal affairs for several decades," Charles said. It was obvious to Annie that he missed Robert. "He was a good man." Charles removed a handkerchief from the inside pocket of his suit jacket. Removing his glasses, he wiped the lenses and placed the glasses back on his face.

"I plan on helping them as much as possible," Annie said, determination building inside her. "But I can't let everyone know about the gold ingot, as there could be people racing to find it and tearing the town apart. Even then, I worry that someone would steal it and the seniors would lose their homes."

"Keep me posted," Charles requested, closing the file folder in front of him. "Let's move on to the next issue."

Charles Conklin began discussing the house on the hill behind Annie and Donald's house. Lori handed a packet of papers to Annie as Charles explained what the packet contained. The house was owned by Robert and Helen Harper, and Annie inherited the property.

Annie relayed to Charles Conklin that she had found out the house was once owned by the grandparents of Marie. She shared that Marie and her mother lived with Marie's grandparents until the grandparents passed away. It was then that Robert Harper purchased the house from Marie's mother and helped her purchase the smaller house next to Annie and Donald's house; the house where Sharon and Gregg Pinehouse currently live with their grandson, Oliver.

"Mom was researching files at the county records office and told me about the property owners being Robert and Helen Harper, I assumed it would be something I had inherited," Annie said, continuing that she may have a buyer for the house.

"Annie," Charles said, setting his glasses on the table and folding his hands in front of him. Turning to Lori, he asked her to wait outside for a moment. She nodded and left the room. He watched to make sure the door to his office was closed. Facing Annie and in quiet tones, Charles said, "The house on the hill and your house are connected."

CHAPTER 18

Monday Afternoon

Annie stared at Charles Conklin for a moment before speaking. "Connected? How is that?" she asked.

How much did Charles Conklin know about the underground house? How far under ground did the house extend? How was the house on the hill connected to her underground house? How many more secret areas were there? Annie was wishing she had asked Donald to come with her after all. She was feeling anxiety she had never felt before. Does Charles Conklin know why the underground house was built?

Leaning forward, Charles Conklin lowered his voice even more and said, "How much of the house have you explored?"

Annie realized he was testing her knowledge about the secrets of the house. "I know about the vault room," Annie said hesitantly.

"That's a start for now," Charles responded. He leaned back in his chair.

"I also know about Robert's underground office, the underground house, under the cottage, the garage, and the beautiful craft room." Annie said, leaning forward and speaking in a loud enough whisper.

"Then you have read the papers left by Helen!" Charles said, sitting back up in his chair.

"All of that is in the papers?"

"Annie, I beg of you," Charles said with exasperation. "Read the papers from Helen."

"I promise!" Annie exclaimed. She made a mental note to place that on her priority list today.

"Only Robert, Helen, a few trusted local workers, and myself know about the underground rooms, Annie," Charles said. "It would be in your best interest to keep it that way."

"To be honest," Annie began. "My family knows about it, but they have all sworn to keep it a secret. We have been enjoying ourselves. It is like being on a holiday whenever we want. Come to think of it...I believe the Silver Sleuths may have some knowledge of what is underground."

"Lorraine's husband was one of the contractors working on the house and other rooms," Charles said. "Her husband signed a non-disclosure, so I am not sure how much they really know as a group. Her husband was an honorable man."

"Have you any idea who might have been remodeling the house on the hill?" Annie asked, remembering that someone had modernized the kitchen and cleaned the house.

"I am sure I can find out," Charles said. "There must be permits on file at the county office. I can ask Lori to check on that for you."

"Actually," Annie spoke up, thinking out loud. "This may be a perfect task for my mom. She loves research and knows the county office staff well."

"Very well then," Charles said, signaling for Lori to return to the office. "Let's get all the paperwork signed and you can be on your way. There will be a matter of a few months for the county to register the deed to the property, so hold off on selling until I contact you."

Annie was glad to wait, as it would give her and Donald time to search the house and find out how it was directly connected, not just through the detached sump room...then again, she could read the documents Helen gave her.

◆ ◆ ◆

Traveling north on 101, or Highway 101 as outsiders called it, Annie's mind was reeling from thoughts about the house on the hill and the senior apartments. It was mid-morning and she could not wait to tell Donald what she had discovered during her appointment.

By the time she turned into her driveway and parked the SUV in the garage, she realized she had driven from Newport to Bridgeport Harbor, but did not remember the drive at all. Her mind was so wrapped up in everything she had learned, that the drive was a blur. She gathered her packet of papers, pulled the key from the ignition, and raced to the kitchen door. The kitchen was quiet as she maneuvered her way around the table and into the living room.

Reaching the office, she pushed open the door, closing and locking it behind her. She rushed to Donald's desk and picked up a remote control to close the long curtains of the window facing the patio.

"Can you take a break right now?" Annie asked in anticipation.

"Sure," Donald said. "I was thinking about getting an early lunch. Do we have any lunchmeat in the refrigerator? I was thinking that a sandwich sounded good."

"No time for that right now," Annie said, moving to the bookcase and sliding it down the wall, exposing the safe and then the stairway going down. "I have some exciting news." Annie began walking down the stairs.

"You found the gold ingot?" Donald said, closing the bookcase and trying to keep up with Annie on the way downstairs."

Annie stopped and turned to look at Donald, "Well, not that exciting. Not yet, anyway."

After entering Robert's office, Annie quickly moved to the large counter island and dropped her armload of packets on top. She sorted through the packets and pulled out the one containing the conditional contract Mr. Conklin had given her. She pulled the papers out and handed them to Donald.

"The conditional contract," Donald said, looking at the first page. He flipped to the next page and read. "The clues! Annie, you found the clues. We can solve the mystery and the seniors will have a place to live."

"Not so fast, Donald," Annie said. "The clues have to be solved first. That's no easy task."

"You're right. It's time to call on the Silver Sleuths," Donald said, sounding like a stricken citizen calling for the help of a group of superheroes.

Annie tried her best to present a look of distain at Donald's mocking of her statement, but all that came out was a giggle. She pulled the document from Donald's hands and made her way to the copy machine. Fortunately, she had left it on so the machine was ready to go. Once the copies of the clues were made, she handed one to Donald, and put the rest in her purse to distribute to the Silver Sleuths. She kept a copy of the original for herself.

Annie and Donald decided to put the packets of documents in the vault for safe keeping. They closed up the office and walked to the vault. Once inside, Donald moved to the counter with all the locked drawers and began looking for the locking mechanism of the bank of drawers further down and next to the bank that contained jewels. Annie, in turn, opened the safe marked with an "H" and placed the papers inside. Donald had written all of Annie's pass codes into a secured password application on her phone. She was finding that quite handy now.

A low whistle came from Donald across the room. Annie turned and noticed that Donald had opened a drawer in the counter. She closed and locked the safe. She met up with Donald and stared in amazement.

"The gold ingot is here?" Annie asked Donald. She was staring at three drawers containing ingots, each embedded into their own velvet lined space. She counted out loud to eleven, noticing the empty space where Donald was pointing.

Inside the empty bed, where the ingot once may have been, was a handwritten note. Donald picked up the note and read aloud to Annie. "This particular ingot has been stamped with my initials and hidden in a place for the Silver Sleuths to locate."

"And it is signed by Robert Harper," Annie added. "Can't we just use one of these other ingots? Who would know?"

"What do you think Charles Conklin would say?" Donald asked.

"No," Annie replied. Donald was honest at least, Annie said to herself. She was not so sure she could be that honest, especially when it came to saving the seniors from losing their homes. "Let's go upstairs. I will make you some lunch and tell you what else I learned today."

Annie and Donald worked in perfect harmony preparing a lunch consisting of sandwiches, salad, and flavored carbonated water. They took the plates of food to the kitchen table and sat down.

As Annie explained details of her meeting with Charles Conklin, the most intriguing part of the conversation for Donald was the fact that the house they lived in and the house on the hill were directly connected somehow. Both Annie and Donald decided that they might have some time over the next few weeks to find the connection.

When Annie told Donald about needing to read all the papers that Helen had left to her, Donald offered to help her out and read them for her. Donald told Annie he knew she was busy trying to run the shop, and that the seniors' homes were at risk, and how it all weighed heavily on Annie's mind. Annie agreed, and on that note, they finished lunch.

After clearing the lunch dishes, Annie kissed Donald good bye and headed out the kitchen door to the garage to drive her SUV to her shop. She could not wait to tell Lizzy what she discovered during the meeting with Charles Conklin.

Pulling into the parking lot and locking up her car, she looked both ways before crossing the street. It was quiet in town and she was thankful for that. Down the block, she could see Fred outside of Fred's Hardware, sweeping the sidewalk and picking up trash that had blown in front of his store.

As Annie reached her shop, she saw a black Mercedes convertible with California license plates parked in front. She did not give it much notice since tourists arrived in Bridgewater Harbor from all over the United States. Just as she placed her hand on the door to enter her shop, she heard someone calling her name.

"Annie!" shouted a male voice from across the street. It was Russ from the realty office waving his arm high in the air. He was trying to get her attention. Standing with Russ was a smartly dressed gentleman who appeared to Annie to be in his forties. He was very tan, probably from a tanning bed, she thought. His hair was light brown and had a dusting of gray at the temples. The man followed Russ across the street to where Annie was standing.

"I'm glad I caught you," Russ said, hopping onto the sidewalk and making his way toward Annie. "Lizzy told me you were in Newport today."

Annie noticed that something suspicious was up in town. Many of the shop doors were ajar and some shop owners were stepping outside now. Ione had opened her shop door to the point where it locked into the open position. Annie could feel Ione's presence just inside the doorway.

"What can I do for you, Russ?" Annie said straightforwardly, though her radar was suddenly on full alert.

"I want to introduce Bruce Trendle," Russ stated. "He's a developer from California and wants to talk to you about some properties here in Bridgewater Harbor."

"How do you do, Ms. Weston," Bruce Trendle said, extending his hand in the form of a greeting.

Annie nodded, and made a show that her arms were full of items she was carrying to the shop. She really did not want to shake this man's hand right now. She did not know why, but she had an instant dislike for the guy.

"Annie, is there any way we can sit down and talk for a moment?" Russ asked.

"What is this about, Russ?" Annie asked. She certainly was not going to waste her time today. She had so much to tell Lizzy, and no interest in the man from California.

"Ms. Weston," Bruce Trendle began. "I am purchasing the apartment complex a couple blocks east up the street, and I want to make an offer on the additional properties from the apartment complex down to the street here."

"I've been doing some research for Mr. Trendle, Annie," Russ stated. "I understand that Robert Harper owned the piece of land between the apartments and the senior center. I was hoping that land was part of what you inherited from Helen Harper. I haven't been able to verify that with county records."

"First of all, Mr. Trendle," Annie stated. "The senior apartment complex is not for sale and neither are any of my properties."

Annie could have sworn she heard cheering from inside Ione's Bakery & Coffee shop. She noticed Mr. Trendle's face tighten.

"I am currently in negotiations with the son of the owner of those apartments," Mr. Trendle said. He straightened his body to appear towering over Annie. The residents have already been given notice to vacate within thirty-days."

"You may want to ask Felix Bankford's son about the conditional contract," Annie said. "You can also check with my attorney, Charles Conklin in Newport. I'm sure he would be happy to share what he can about the terms of the contract."

Bruce Trendle's body seemed to shrink a bit from what Annie told him. "Well, I will be checking with the city on selling the property where the senior center sits."

"As I just found out today, Mr. Trendle," Annie said with an insincere smile on her face. "The property the senior center sits on is owned by me. I lease the property to the city."

Mr. Trendle's neck veins bulged as his face grew to deep red. Annie decided that Bruce Trendle was used to getting his way. He turned to Russ and stated, "Apparently, there are circumstances that I have not been made privy to at this time. I will keep in touch." At that, Bruce Trendle turned and walked to his car. Annie and Russ stood still, watching the California Mercedes roar down the street.

"There goes a huge commission," Russ said preoccupied. He turned to Annie and stated, "I knew you were never going to sell. Please believe me when I say I never expected to make a cent off this guy. He wouldn't take no for an answer. He wanted to ask you in person."

"I doubt that will be the last I hear from Mr. Trendle," Annie remarked.

Annie heard cheering coming from the various shops with opened doors. It seemed that they thought Annie had made the right choice in not selling to Mr. Trendle. Annie smiled as she bid Russ good bye and entered her shop.

♦ ♦ ♦

It took nearly two hours for Annie and Lizzy to catch up on all the exciting news Annie had to share. Lizzy was full of questions, and Annie chided herself for not asking Lizzy to accompany her to the lawyer's office.

Annie's dream was what really had Lizzy listening intently. Annie told Lizzy about Robert Harper dressed as a jungle adventurer and how Robert guided Annie down a long hall that ended up in his office under her house.

"What if Robert Harper really is alive and living in the house on the hill?" Lizzy asked, her eyes wide with fascination. "Did they ever find his body?"

"His ashes are in the entwined whale urn in Donald's office," Annie said rationally.

"Are they?" Lizzy questioned. "How do you know?"

"At least most of them," Annie answered. "Some escaped when I bumped into the unstable bookcase and the urn slid off hitting Eddie in the head."

"That's right. I remember the mess. Your mother really tried to get it all swept up and back into the urn." Lizzy shuddered at the thought.

Lizzy told Annie about all the speculation in town of the senior apartment complex being sold, torn down, and a larger apartment complex being built for a younger clientele. Ione had been to the paper shop twice with samples of treats to find out if Lizzy had heard from Annie. No wonder shop owners were trying to be inconspicuous about being outside and listening to her discussion with Mr. Trendle. Everyone was worried for the seniors.

As if on cue, Jacquie entered Ocean Loads of Paper from the street-side door. She seemed to be on a mission and walked quickly to the front counter where Annie and Lizzy were standing.

"I couldn't wait until after work," Jacquie said excitedly. "What did you find out about the house? Is it still for sale? Can John and I take a tour tonight?"

"Yes, and yes," Annie laughed. "The only catch is we may have to wait a few months for paperwork to get finalized. In the meantime, Donald and I would love to show it to you."

"Would you mind if I tagged along?" asked Lizzy.

"Not at all," Jacquie said. "After the last time we were there, the more the merrier. I don't suppose your husband would like to meet us there?"

"I can ask," Lizzy said. She pulled out her cell phone and began tapping a message on the screen.

"He can meet us there at five o'clock," Lizzy said, receiving an immediate return text from Dan.

"John is meeting me at the gallery at four-thirty," Jacquie informed Annie. "We close at five. We'll drive right to the house."

"It's four now," Annie said. "I'll help Lizzy and we'll be closed by four-thirty today. It has been so slow today, we sent Daisy and Marie home."

"Tell me about it," Jacquie said. "The only excitement was you having the conversation with that horrid developer from California. We are all so happy you told him no."

"There was no other answer," Annie said. "But I have a feeling that was not the last of Mr. Trendle."

"Probably not," Jacquie stated. "I need to get back to my shop and wait for John." Jacquie bid Annie and Lizzy good bye and was out the door.

♦ ♦ ♦

Annie opened the door of her house at a little after four-thirty to find her mother in the kitchen preparing for dinner. She had potatoes in a colander in the sink and was just about to turn the water on to rinse the spuds.

"You're home early," Stella remarked, as she wiped her hands and turned her attention to Annie.

Annie told her mother about the visit with Charles Conklin and how Charles knew of the underground. She told Stella about signing the papers for the house on the hill, and mentioned showing the house at five o'clock to John and Jacquie Spencer.

"By the way, Mom," Annie said. "I have a research mission for you if you have the time."

"What is it?" Stella inquired.

"Would you be able to research county permit records and find out who remodeled the house on the hill?" Annie asked. "It has to have been done recently, but before Robert Harper's death."

"Get me the address and write down any questions you have," Stella said, handing a pad of paper and a pen to Annie.

Annie took the pad and wrote down the information, after checking her phone for the address of the property. Earlier she had entered the information into her phone contacts for future reference. Now she was glad she did.

Donald entered the kitchen and gave Annie a kiss on the cheek. "Are you ready to go to the house and show it off?" Donald asked. "I was thinking of taking Laddie, if you don't think he'll be a nuisance."

"I would feel safer with Laddie around," Annie said.

"I taught Laddie everything he knows," Donald said.

Annie looked around Donald to Laddie, who was on the floor licking himself. Laddie stopped, looked to Annie and then Donald, then continued with his licking task.

"Bad timing, Laddie," Donald said to his faithful companion.

After getting keys and flashlights, Annie, Donald, and Laddie made their way to the house on the hill by walking around the block to the next street. Lizzy joined them, stating that Dan would meet the group at the house. They arrived before everyone else and Annie put the key in the lock of the front door. She pushed open the door and moved aside to let Donald and Laddie inside first.

A car pulled into the driveway and Annie recognized the unmarked police vehicle that Dan normally drove home. Dan joined her at the front door and walked inside the house. Annie and Lizzy followed.

Donald and Laddie walked through the main level of the house and then made their way upstairs to the bedrooms. Donald called out that the house was clear. Dan and Donald also checked out the basement area and discovered that it, too, was all clear. There were no longer signs of anyone camping in the basement after Dan had cleared it of the camping cot and other items earlier.

Annie and Lizzy made their way around the house opening blinds throughout the building. Even without furnishings and decorations, the house looked spectacular. Annie found it difficult to remind herself the house was not brand new.

Lizzy opened the sliding glass door leading out to a large deck overlooking the Pacific Ocean. "Wow!" Lizzy stated. "I can see why the Spencers want this house. The view is amazing."

Annie joined Lizzy on the deck. She looked down to her back yard to see her mother walking to her apartment over the garage from the kitchen door. She called out and waved to her mother, her mother waved back. Marie came out from the kitchen doorway and began jumping up and down and waving wildly. Annie and Lizzy waved back and laughed.

The doorbell rang and Annie left to greet John and Jacquie Spencer. Opening the door and inviting them inside, Annie could tell Jacquie and John were smitten with the house. They walked all around the main level, pointing out placement for furniture, before they wandered upstairs. Annie let them have time alone to discover the house.

After watching the couple head upstairs, Annie called to Lizzy and the two opened the door to the basement. The guys had been down there a long time and Annie was hoping everything was alright. She had a feeling they were up to something, as Laddie would have signaled a stranger in the room by barking or growling.

Once they reached the bottom of the stairs, Annie and Lizzy watched Donald and Dan searching for something along the far wall. Laddie, noticing Annie had arrived, hurried over to her. She reached down and instinctively began scratching his head. He sat comfortably next to Annie, as she continued to scratch and pet him.

"What are you guys searching for on the wall?" Lizzy asked.

"Donald told me about the houses being connected," Dan told Lizzy. "It would make sense that the entrance to a stairway be in this basement and on this wall."

"Annie's the door-whisperer," Donald said. Waving Annie over to the wall, he said, "Help us out here."

"I would be happy to, but..." Annie began, as she was about to ask them to wait until the Spencers had finished going through the house. Just then the door to the basement opened and John called out to Annie.

"We're down here, John," Annie called out.

"They're down in the basement," John told Jacquie.

"Oh," Jacquie cried out and appeared at the door. "I was worried something had happened to the four of you."

"We're fine," Annie announced. "Just making sure the basement carpet is dry and checking for any leaks." Annie looked around and decided there were no leaks, covering the big fib she was making. She did not want to let the Spencers in on the secret connection to this house and hers. At this point, she was not sure there was a connection, except for the utility tunnel for the water drainage pipe and sump pump room.

After checking out the house, Jacquie who looked to John, nodded, then told Annie and Donald that they would like to talk about, and possibly make an offer on the house. Annie told the Spencers Russ in the realty office could handle the transaction, but told them that it had to wait until the paperwork was properly filed in the county records. The Spencers were happy to wait, and told Annie to contact them when the sale could happen.

"If you are looking for a decorator," Annie started. "Debbie, Russ's wife, is an interior decorator and has an office inside the realty office. You can talk to her anytime. She does amazing work."

CHAPTER 19

Monday Evening

Walking the Spencers to the front door, Annie said good night and locked the door before returning to the basement to meet up with Dan and Donald. Lizzy followed behind her, after closing and locking the patio deck door.

Annie stood halfway down the stairs, and took in the view of the entire finished basement area. Slowly descending one step at a time, she thought she noticed something strange about the wall across the room. She backed upwards on the stairs, and then walked forward again. She was sure of it!

"Well, wall-sniffer?" Dan asked.

"Door-whisperer," Donald corrected Dan.

Dan looked at Donald and rolled his eyes. Donald smiled a wise-guy grin.

"You're going to eat your words when she finds a door," Donald warned Dan. Donald looked at Annie as if questioning whether she felt she found something that might indicate a door. Annie gave Donald a knowing smile. Donald asked Dan, "Should we make a wager, Dan? Loser mows the lawn?"

Annie felt her cell phone vibrate in her pocket, indicating someone had sent her a text message. She pulled the phone out and looked at the message. It was her mother stating that dinner was ready and asked if they were on their way home. Annie typed in a quick reply and slipped the phone back into her pocket.

"Let's get going," Annie announced. "Mom has dinner waiting for us."

"Which I take to mean you don't have any idea where a door might be in this room?" Dan asked. "When did you want to come over and mow my lawn, Donald?"

"Actually, I do know where the door is located, Surely," Annie said smugly, making her way down the stairs.

"I'll have the lawn mower ready for you when you arrive to mow my lawn, Dan," Donald said, signaling Annie to approach the wall and reveal the door's location.

Annie walked to the wall where Dan and Donald were standing. She moved her hands along the wood slat wall covering, similar to what was in Robert Harper's office. Testing the decorative moldings, she found one that she was able to pull up, discovering it was hinged on the side. Once she pressed on the panel, a door popped open revealing a landing with stairs leading downward.

Dan looked dumfounded and Donald said, "See, she is the door-whisperer."

Stepping in front of Annie, Dan entered through the doorway and turned on his flashlight. He located a light switch and signaled the others to follow him. Annie and Lizzy went next, leaving Donald to close the doorway. Laddie let out a "woof" when they heard the spring-loaded molding pop back into place.

"I hope that doesn't mean we're locked in here," Lizzy said.

"Let's find out where this leads us," Dan stated.

As they descended the stairs, they came to a landing, and then another set of stairs going downward. Finally reaching the bottom of stairs, they then found themselves in a small ten-by-ten-foot room with decorative wall paper. A door stood in front of them.

"It can't be that easy," Donald said, moving to the door and reaching for the handle.

"I wonder if it leads to the underground house?" Annie asked. She looked upward to the stairs and tried to determine how far they had traveled downward.

Donald opened the door and found another door. He looked puzzled, and then pushed on the second door. The room beyond was dark. Both Donald and Dan raised their flashlights to get a better view of the room before them. Donald located a light switch on the wall and flipped on. Light illuminated the small room filled with empty wooden shipping boxes.

"Annie," Donald said. "We know this place."

Annie moved forward, next to Donald. "It's the secret room under the cottage!" Annie exclaimed.

"There's a secret room under the cottage?" Lizzy asked. "Why didn't you tell us before?"

"We forgot," Donald said.

"Actually, we found it before we decided to tell you all about the underground vault, which led to the underground house." Annie explained.

"What was in all these boxes?" Lizzy asked. She moved around the room looking inside the wooden boxes.

"As far as I can tell," Donald said, "these are shipping crates. We don't know more than that at this time."

"Wow!" Lizzy stated. "A secret room under the cottage and a secret staircase to the house on the hill."

"But why did Robert need a secret stairway to the house on the hill?" Dan asked.

"That, my friend," Donald said, looking at Dan, "is the mystery." Donald closed the door on the inside of the stairwell and then closed the door on the inside of the room under the cottage. The door seemed to disappear into the wall.

Annie led the way up the stairs to the cottage. She shoved open the bookcase and walked into the cottage office she and Lizzy had set up. The others followed and Donald closed the bookcase.

"Somehow," Donald said. "I believe there is a connection between this cottage and the underground house."

"If we keep looking," Lizzy said. "I bet we can find it."

"Let's look another time," Annie stated. "Dinner is on the table and I'm hungry."

With that said, the group left the cottage and joined Stella and Marie for dinner. Stella had just placed the last dish of food on the table when she heard the kitchen door open.

"Just in time," Stella announced. "Marie, dinner is ready."

Marie turned off the television and entered the dining room. She sat down and began looking over the plates of food set before her. "What do we have for dessert?"

"You haven't eaten yet," Dan said from across the table.

"I could eat dessert first and then eat dinner," Marie said with a giggle.

"I could too," Dan said. "But I don't think Mom will let us." Dan passed the platter of sliced meatloaf to Marie.

"Stella, you are the best," Donald said, passing the bowl of vegetables to Annie. "Meatloaf with mashed potatoes and gravy...my absolute favorite."

"I made two meat loaves, because I know you boys like meatloaf sandwiches," Stella remarked.

"I like meatloaf sandwiches, too!" Annie blurted out. Lizzy and Marie nodded in agreement.

"There's plenty for everyone," Stella said.

"By the way, Dan," Annie said, forking a couple of green beans into her mouth and chewing before continuing. "Lizzy and I happened to talk to Oliver before he left to go camping with family."

Dan stopped eating and looked up at Annie, "Just how did you happen to see him?"

"He came by the shop to make a delivery for us," Lizzy said, not looking at Dan.

"He just happened to be making a delivery for you?" Dan questioned.

"Okay, Dan," Annie said, yielding. "We saw him and lured him to the shop on the pretense of making a delivery for us. The fact is, we got him to talk!"

Dan asked tersely. "When did you talk to Oliver?"

Annie thought for a moment...when did she talk to Oliver? "Saturday. That's it! It was Saturday," Annie stated. "I saw him go into Ione's Bakery & Coffee Shop and I followed him in there."

"And this is the first I am hearing about it?" Dan asked.

In an effort to avoid Dan's last question, Annie told Dan that she asked Oliver to come to the shop to pick up a delivery. When he came, Annie and Lizzy questioned him about the items being left for Lizzy. Oliver told them that he did not know the man's name. He would receive a call to meet him, and the man would always watch Oliver make the deliveries.

"He also said that the guy had a gun under his jacket," Lizzy added. She noticed Annie give her a sharp look. She quickly dug into her mashed potatoes.

"What?" Dan asked. "Why didn't you tell me this sooner?"

"Don't get excited, Dan," Annie cautioned. "Lizzy and I think the person is an armed courier from a jewelry store."

"The jewelry is from Tiffany's, after all," Lizzy added.

"Who is sending you expensive jewelry from Tiffany's?" Dan asked.

"Certainly not you," Annie replied.

Dan gave a sharp look to Annie. Everyone else turned to Lizzy, who looked up and stopped eating long enough to shrug her shoulders about knowing who was sending her expensive jewelry.

Dan inhaled deeply, as if thinking about his next statement. "I need to talk to Oliver right away," Dan stated. "Where can I find him?"

"He went camping with his cousins and won't be back until Tuesday night or Wednesday," Annie replied. "I asked him to call me when this guy hires him to make another delivery."

"And when Oliver calls you, you will call me immediately. Right?" Dan asked.

"Of course," Annie said. "That was the plan."

Dan eyed Annie suspiciously, "I mean it, Annie. Call me immediately. This guy could be dangerous."

"I will. I will," Annie assured Dan.

"Annie," Stella said, attempting to change the subject. "Tell us about the clues for finding the gold ingot."

Annie told the group about her visit with Charles Conklin and finding the list of clues on a sheet attached to the conditional contract. She made copies to give to the Silver Sleuths in hopes that they could solve the clues, and find the gold ingot in time to save the senior apartment complex.

Then there was the property between the senior center and the senior apartment complex. After some discussion of what Robert Harper had in mind for the property, Annie asked Donald, "Could we build an apartment complex on that site for the seniors?"

"We could possibly build, at the most, ten cottages," Donald said, stopping to take a sip from his water glass. "But that won't help the one hundred or more seniors needing housing."

"Our only hope is to figure out the clues, and find the particular gold ingot before the deadline expires," Annie said reluctantly. She set her fork down and pushed her plate forward.

A moment of strained silence crept over the dinner table. Lizzy took several sips from her water glass. Setting the glass down, she said, "I guess this might not be a great time to ask, but Annie did you tell anyone about the developer who spoke with you today?"

"What developer?" Donald asked.

"His name is Bruce Trendle," Annie stated. "He wants to purchase all of the property from the apartment complex down the hill to the main street."

"He wants to buy the building that houses the Chinese Restaurant and Bridgewater Inn?" asked Dan.

"Worse than that, Dan. He wants to purchase the senior center, the property that is between the senior apartments and senior center, as well as the building housing the Bridgewater Inn," Annie explained. "I told him no. Donald and I own everything from the plot of land next to the senior apartments to the street."

"And beyond, if you count the building your shop is located," Lizzy stated.

"I thought the senior center was owned by the city." Dan commented.

"Donald and I own the senior center. We apparently lease the building to the city for one dollar a year," Annie stated. "Which reminds me, Lizzy. I must make an appointment with Sheryl Doxie tomorrow. I hope you'll want to go with me."

"I will make arrangements with Daisy to cover the shop while we are at the appointment," Lizzy said.

"I can help at the shop while you are gone," Marie spoke up. "I am learning all about how to cash out customers. Daisy is teaching me."

"I heard you were very good with customers," Stella complimented Marie. "Before you know it, you and Daisy will be running the place."

"That's my goal for you, Marie," Annie said, proud for Marie taking steps to move out of her comfort zone.

"Daisy and I have been learning the art of quilling for the class coming up on Tuesday," Marie added, blushing from the compliments. "We know the basic stuff. Now we are learning how to make harder projects."

"That reminds me," Annie said, suddenly remembering a task from her mental 'To Do' list. "I have frames for your customers to use to frame their projects once they finish the quilling class. I will get them together tonight and bring them to the shop tomorrow."

"Are you talking about the framed art pieces I gathered from the other shops?" Lizzy asked.

"Yes," Annie replied. "They're still piled up in Robert's office."

"If you want, I can help you now and we can have them ready in no time," Lizzy suggested.

"Perfect!" Annie said, gathering her dinner plate and other items to place them in the kitchen sink.

"Donald?" Dan asked, as he stood and took his plate to the kitchen. "Would you mind if I take a look at the back of the underground house? We really haven't explored there. I am curious if there is a connection from the underground of the cottage to the underground of this house."

"We can try," Donald said with a wide smile. "But I warn you, we may need to engage the help of the secret door-whisperer." Both Donald and Dan looked to Annie.

"No way!" shouted Lizzy from the dining room, where she was helping to clear the table. "Annie and I are busy tonight prepping for the class at the shop tomorrow."

"Don't you have a lawn to mow, Dan?" Annie called to Dan.

◆ ◆ ◆

Lizzy walked into the former office of Robert Harper ahead of Annie. She flipped the switch for the lights, and proceeded to the island counter on the north side of the room. The pile of framed art lay against the wall on the floor near the island. Lizzy picked up a couple of frames and set them on the counter.

In a set of shallow drawers next to the filing cabinets, Lizzy found needle-nosed pliers and a screw driver. The two women began the task of carefully removing the sheets of intricately cut papers and stacking them in a pile on the counter of the island.

Annie found glass cleaner and paper towels in the adjacent crafting room and took care cleaning the glass of each frame. As she finished each panel of glass, she carefully handed it to Lizzy, who placed it back into the frame. There were two panels of glass for each frame. One for the front and one for the back. Lizzy cleaned the frame itself and by the time they were finished, a stack of fourteen sparkling-clean frames stood before them.

"What do you want to do with these papers?" Lizzy asked Annie.

"Not much we can do but throw them away," Annie said, gathering up the papers, folding them in half, and tossing them in the trash can by the desk.

Picking up half of the stack of frames each, Annie and Lizzy made their way to the office door, closing it behind them. Annie signaled to Lizzy to set the frames down, and motioned her to follow as she made her way down the stairs to the underground house.

The downstairs was a buzz of activity with Stella in the kitchen cleaning, Marie in the movie theater watching a romance-comedy movie, and the men playing pool in the pub room.

"Would you like an iced tea by the swimming pool?" Annie asked Lizzy.

"Now that is an offer I can't refuse," Lizzy said, following Annie to the kitchen.

Time seemed to pass quickly as Annie and Lizzy talked about anything and everything under the sun. Annie found Lizzy bright and adventurous as Lizzy spoke about her childhood and the places she and her family traveled around the world. Where Annie had a small doll house and miniature furniture, Lizzy had a full-sized, small cottage with life-sized custom furniture in her back yard. Annie and her family would travel to Disneyland, Lizzy and her family traveled around the world.

"Are you two going to stay down here all night?" Donald asked. "I'm going to bed. Everyone else went upstairs."

◆ ◆ ◆

MYSTERIOUS PAPERCUTS

Annie crawled into bed with the packet of papers left to her by Helen Harper. It was late and she was not certain she was going to keep her eyes open for long. Donald turned off the light on his nightstand and rolled away from Annie. Sounds of deep breathing were soon coming from Donald's side of the bed.

Annie pulled out an envelope from the packet. She took the papers out of the envelope and unfolded them. A key slipped from the papers and dropped onto her lap. She picked it up and noticed it was not shaped like a typical key. Looking at the letter in her hand, she read:

My dearest Annie,

As you will find out, I have left you and my nephew, Donald Harper, vast wealth. It is my wish that the two of you will form a relationship to help the citizens of Bridgewater Harbor.

Robert was particularly fond of the seniors in the community and especially a small group who call themselves the Silver Sleuths. Mystery was a hobby of my dear Robert. He sometimes challenged the ladies to solve mysteries. Robert usually created a mystery just to keep the ladies busy in their golden years. He often said it was to keep their minds sharp. He would secretly reward them upon their solving of the clues he left.

Which brings me to the point of this letter. At the time that the owner, Felix Bankford, decides to sell the senior apartment complex, he must first give the Silver Sleuths a chance at solving the clues left by Robert. Charles Conklin will have the information you need to pass on to the ladies.

Enclosed is the key to a special box. It is very important you keep the key in a safe place. You will know when to use it. This key will provide the seniors their reward for solving the mystery given to them.

I leave the task to Donald and you to help the seniors should they be stumped. They will only have two weeks to complete this task. You will know what to do.

With all my love, Helen.

Annie ran her fingers over the odd-shaped key. She yawned deeply and looked at the clock on her nightstand. It was nearing eleven o'clock. She put the papers back into the packet and placed them in her nightstand drawer. She thought about Robert and his tendency toward mystery. It all began to make sense. The hidden rooms, the secret underground house, the concealed passageways...they were all part of creating a mystery to Robert.

Judith Dickenson Ackaret

Taking the key, Annie decided to hide it within the cover of her cell phone. She popped a corner of the cover open and slid the key inside. She checked to make sure the cover was securely back in place and put the phone back into the charger on the nightstand. Turning the light off, it wasn't long before Annie fell into a deep sleep.

CHAPTER 20

Tuesday

Annie closed the drawer of the cash register and picked up her donut to take a bite, when Lizzy came up to the door, unlocked it, and entered the shop. She appeared tired, yet dressed like she walked out of a fashion magazine.

"I need coffee!" Lizzy announced. She set her purse and jacket in the office and returned, plopping herself on a stool.

Annie slid a covered cup of coffee toward Lizzy, who removed the top and took a long drink of the now warm, not hot, liquid.

"I may need an espresso," Lizzy stated. "Dan and I were up until midnight talking about Felix Bankford and the clues." Lizzy pulled her laptop computer from her carry bag and placed it on the counter. She opened the laptop and booted it up.

"He doesn't have much faith that the Silver Sleuths will solve the clues and retain the senior apartment complex," Lizzy remarked. "I disagree with him. We have this bet going now. Annie, we have to help the Silver Sleuths solve this mystery. I am not one to lose a bet."

"First, we need to meet with Sheryl Doxie, our accountant," Annie said. "I just called her office and made an appointment for ten o'clock this morning. Daisy and Marie can handle the shop until we get back."

"Great! Then we'll work out the clues," Lizzy stated excitedly.

"Actually, we'll meet the Silver Sleuths for coffee and donuts at the senior center in one of their private meeting rooms," Annie countered. "We can give them the list of clues and let them know that we will try our best to help them. I want to ask the ladies about the mysteries Robert had them solving in the past and what kind of rewards they received."

"I don't understand," Lizzy said, looking questioningly at Annie.

"I read one of the letters left to me by Helen," Annie said. She continued to tell Lizzy what Helen had written about Robert challenging the Silver Sleuths to mysteries and rewarding them when they solved the clues.

"From the sounds of it, we may be less help and more of a burden to this group," Lizzy commented.

"It does sound like they have a lot more practice than we originally thought," Annie added. "I sent a text to LaVerne to meet us at the senior center at one-thirty this afternoon. We can go over the clues and see if they have any idea where Robert is leading them to obtain the gold ingot."

Annie and Lizzy turned upon hearing the door chime and greeted Daisy. Daisy turned the sign from 'closed' to 'open' and held the door for the approaching Marie and Stella. She greeted them, and they walked together to where Annie and Lizzy were standing by the other door. Annie had already turned the sign on that door to 'open'.

"I have some errands to run," Stella told Annie. "I thought I would drive Marie to the shop and see if I can get anything for you."

"Thanks, but I think we are good for now," Annie said.

"Text me if you think of anything last minute. I will be in Newport," Stella stated. "I will try and get that information you asked for the other day." With that, Stella exited the shop, and Annie watched her get into her little sports car and drive away.

At ten minutes before ten o'clock, Annie and Lizzy exited Ocean Loads of Paper and walked a block and a half to the accounting office of Sheryl Doxie. They first met with Pam, the office manager, who introduced them to Sheryl.

Sheryl was a tall woman in her forties with short blond wavy hair and a broad smile. She had the ability to make anyone in her presence feel instantly at ease. Annie found Sheryl outgoing and funny. Sheryl and her fireman husband, Rex, were known by reputation as a generous and caring couple. After asking around, specifically asking Ione, Annie discovered that Sheryl and Rex were also known for their compassion in fostering and finding homes for stray dogs and cats.

Sheryl led Annie and Lizzy to a small conference room and the three sat at a round wooden table. Annie listened while Lizzy asked questions, made notes, and reviewed the files with Sheryl. Although

Annie followed and understood everything being discussed, her heart was not into the actual financial management of the shop or R&H Enterprises. Which is why she was grateful for Lizzy being so excited to handle the entire business.

As Sheryl continued her explanation of taxes and the various accounts set up to maintain payment of the taxes and maintenance of the buildings, Annie's attention was diverted when two small kittens pushed through the door, which had been left ajar, and chased each other through the small room. Annie reached down to pick up one of the kittens.

"That's Katy," Sheryl announced. "She and Daisy are sisters. Rex and I are fostering them until we find them a good home. They came to work with me, because I did not want to leave them home alone with the dogs."

"We have a young woman working at our shop named Daisy," Annie said, petting the purring mound of fur in her arms.

Lizzy picked up the smaller kitten, who looked very similar to Katy. She held the little tortoise colored kitten up and began cooing. "I think I am in love," Lizzy stated to Annie, as she held the little girl close to her chest.

"I named this kitten Daisy, because I love the name," Sheryl said, pointing to the kitten being held by Lizzy. She explained that the kittens were only a few months old. The accountant told her clients she was hoping to keep them together since they were sisters and enjoyed each other's company. Noticing that Lizzy was smitten with the kittens, Sheryl hinted that no one else had shown an interest in the cute little kitties yet.

Lizzy looked again to Annie. Annie, herself, was wondering if Callie would get along with two kittens in her home. What would Laddie do with kittens running around the house?

"Do I ask Dan what he thinks about having kittens?" Lizzy asked Annie. "Or, should I just bring them home, and hope he falls in love with them?"

"Why don't you take them home and let Dan fall in love with them?" Sheryl said.

Annie realized that Sheryl was not only a good accountant, but a great salesperson. Lizzy now had both kittens in her arms, and they were purring loudly.

"Annie," Lizzy said. "Meet my girls...Katy and Daisy." Lizzy held up each kitten as she spoke their names. She continued to hold the now sleepy little girls in her arms as Annie took over note-taking while the meeting progressed.

As promised by Charles Conklin, Sheryl Doxie provided Annie and Lizzy with a list of accounts, projects, services, maintenance needs, and various other items requiring attention. Sheryl explained that she was handling the properties until the heir was available to take over the company. Annie thanked her for taking on the task, and assured Sheryl that R&H Enterprises would continue their accounting business with her in the future.

After the meeting ended, Sheryl produced two cat carriers, one with the name Daisy and one with the name Katy. Lizzy helped place the kittens in the carriers and made a list of items she would need to purchase before she went home today.

"I can text mom with a list of kitten supplies," Annie said to Lizzy, as she slung the strap of her tote bag over her shoulder. "She said to text if we needed anything from Newport. There is a great pet store there."

"You don't think she would mind?" Lizzy asked. She picked up Katy's carrier in one hand and Daisy's in the other, thanking Sheryl while heading to the door.

Walking back to the shop, Lizzy fretted, "I hope Dan doesn't mind. He knows I was wanting a cat. Two kitties would keep each other company, right?"

"Frankly, Lizzy," Annie said. "I don't think Dan would mind the kittens. Anyway, we know he can't say no to you."

Lizzy laughed, and told Annie that it went both ways.

Annie was already thinking that if Dan had a fit, she would be happy to have the little kitties. It was her backup plan just in case. She was also sure her mother would take them. Either way, the kitties would have a good home.

Daisy, the human, ran around the counter as Lizzy entered the shop carrying a carrier in each hand. "Oh, kittens!" she cried out as Lizzy set them on the counter. "Can I hold one of them?"

"Sure, this is Daisy," Lizzy stated, opening the door of Daisy's carrier and pulling the little fluffball out. "I think the more they get used to being held the better."

"What a perfect name for you, Daisy," Daisy cooed at the kitten.

"Where is Marie?" Annie asked Daisy.

"William asked her to have lunch with him," Daisy said, holding the kitten in the air, and then kissing her on the head. "They are at that table out on the boardwalk." She pointed to a round table between Ione's Bakery & Coffee Shop and Ocean Loads of Paper.

"Are they holding hands?" Annie practically shouted, as she walked to the window to spy on the couple outside.

"It's okay," Daisy said, she traded the Daisy kitten for Katy. "I've been watching them. It is sweet."

"Annie!" Lizzy scolded, as she walked from the office and noticed Annie. "Move away from the window. They might see you."

Annie reluctantly moved from the window and walked over to the counter where Lizzy and Daisy were cuddling the kittens.

"Let's put them in the office to run around. I don't think they'll cause too much trouble," Annie said, peeking into the office and surveying the surroundings. "They'll need a potty box."

"I have their food and water dishes here," Lizzy announced. "Sheryl gave me the supplies she brought in with them today."

"I can make a shallow potty box for the kittens," Daisy offered, as she handed Katy to Lizzy and walked to the storage room. Annie heard the whirl of the paper shredder. Daisy appeared in moments with a small shallow box filled with shredded paper for the kittens. She placed the box on the floor of the office. Annie was wondering how long it would take the kittens to spread the tiny bits of paper all over the floor.

Annie and Lizzy made a list of things needed for the new kittens. Annie sent a text to her mother, who quickly replied that she was overjoyed to have the babies in the family. Stella sent another message that she would be happy to pick the kittens up and take them home until Lizzy got off work. Both Annie and Lizzy thought that would be a great idea, as the kittens were a distraction to them both, and Marie was not aware of them...yet.

It was not long before the kittens were in the office and settling in nicely. Marie walked through the ocean-side door of the shop and stopped when she noticed Annie, Lizzy, and Daisy, the human, all standing next to each other in front of the office door.

"What's wrong?" Marie asked.

"Mew!" came a loud sound followed by scratching from the other side of the office door.

"Is that a cat?" Marie shouted. "We have a cat in the store? I want to see the cat."

Annie gave a grimaced look to Lizzy and they moved to the side to let Marie see the kitties in the office.

"Kittens!" Marie exclaimed loudly. "We have kittens!"

"We don't have kittens, Marie," Annie said, as she grabbed Katy trying to make an escape from the office. "Lizzy and Dan have kittens."

"I can babysit," Marie offered, looking up at Lizzy. "You can leave them with me when you go on vacation."

"Why don't you keep them company until they take a nap," Lizzy suggested. "Make sure to keep them in the office."

"I will," Marie said, closing the door to the office behind her.

♦ ♦ ♦

Annie and Lizzy arrived at the senior center promptly at one-thirty and were escorted to a quiet conference room. There, sitting at a long conference table, were LaVerne, Lorraine, Elsie, and Millie with cups of tea in front of them.

After some brief greetings and casual conversation, LaVerne said, "You didn't bring us here for chit-chat, Annie. Let's get to it."

"LaVerne!" scolded Elsie. "Give her a minute to catch her breath. It's not easy walking up that hill."

"We're fine, really," Annie assured the ladies. She pulled out a few papers and handed them to each of the Silver Sleuths.

After briefly reviewing the words written on the page, Lorraine said, "This looks like Robert Harper's work."

"Indeed, it does," stated Millie. She set the sheet of clues down on the table and began rummaging through her purse.

"Charles Conklin, my attorney, gave this paper to me yesterday," Annie began to explain. "I made copies for each of you. You have a mystery to solve and only have a short time to complete the task."

Millie pulled out a magnifying glass and began to closely inspect the document. She pointed out areas of the document to Elsie and Lorraine. LaVerne was deeply absorbed in reading the contents of the paper. The room was quiet for several minutes while the seniors reviewed the document.

Annie began to relate the information about the clues leading the seniors to the gold ingot that would allow the seniors to stay in their apartments. At one point, tears welled in her eyes once she realized that the senior apartment complex may be closing for good. She sat up straight with determination that such a thing would not happen if she could help it.

"Oh, that Robert," LaVerne exclaimed. "He thought he was so smart challenging us with mysteries to solve."

"We solved every challenge he put forth," Lorraine added. "He'll not win this one either."

"I read a note written to me from Helen last night," Annie said. "She mentioned that Robert presented a reward for each mystery solved. What were the rewards, if I may ask?"

"The senior center for one," Elsie stated. "He built a large kitchen extension in the building after one case we solved."

"The last investigation we did resulted in the beautiful fountain on the property between the senior center and the senior apartment complex," Millie said. "I believe he was thinking of turning that property into a park with benches and other water features."

"Sadly," Elsie said, "that never happened. Robert passed before the additional work was even started."

LaVerne looked up from her paper, "Ladies, we have work to do. Let's get busy."

"Annie," Lorraine stated, "we'll check in with you tomorrow to give you an update on the clues. Never fear! The Silver Sleuths will solve the mystery." With that, the senior ladies stood and exited the conference room.

"What's your backup plan, Annie?" Lizzy asked, as the two women made no move to get up from the table.

Annie sighed.

◆ ◆ ◆

Later in the afternoon, after Stelle had picked up the kittens, Daisy and Annie began setting up the classroom for the quilling class. Annie pointed out the frames, to be used for the finished art pieces, to Daisy. Daisy inspected the frames and commented on how nice they were. Annie told Daisy the frames were being reused from an old project. They both agreed that the students would be excited to take home framed work.

Marie walked into the classroom with a box of donuts, followed by William who was wheeling in the coffee server on a cart. Annie had set up the cart specifically for serving coffee and other beverages for the class students. Marie placed a stack of napkins near the box of donuts.

"I miss the kittens already," Marie stated, looking glum.

"Maybe you can go home right after the class ends, and help Stella take care of the kittens," Lizzy suggested. "But for now, you need to help Daisy with the class."

"I will help until the class is over," Marie said. "Then I will go home and babysit the kittens."

Marie became more excited as the students of the quilling class began to arrive. Annie watched for a few minutes until class began. This was Daisy and Marie's class, so Annie decided to quietly leave the classroom and make her way to the other side of the shop. She could hear Daisy and Marie introducing themselves as she left the area.

"I don't have a backup plan, Lizzy," Annie remarked, as she walked up to the counter. She had been thinking about Lizzy's question from the meeting at the senior center. What were Donald and she going to do if the Silver Sleuths were not able to solve the clues and find the gold ingot? Would they try and buy the property or was it already a done deal with Bruce Trendle?

"Let's take a look at those clues while the shop is quiet," Lizzy said.

It seemed like only a few minutes had passed, and yet Annie noticed the students in the class exiting out both doors of the shop with frames in their hands. Annie chided herself for not trying to see the work the students completed before the class was over.

"The frames were a big hit, Annie," Daisy announced excitedly, as she pointed out a framed piece of Marie's quilling project.

"Marie," Annie said, "your work is beautiful."

"Thanks!" Marie said smiling widely. "I am going to take it home and give it to Mom." She headed to the office to retrieve her tote bag and jacket. She waved good bye and was out the door, heading home.

Over the next hour the shop remained quiet. By five o'clock, Annie was ready to lock up for the evening. Turning off the last light, Annie made her way to the shop door, followed by Daisy. Lizzy stood in the doorway, holding the door open.

A man in dark clothing stood on the sidewalk next to an expensive model vehicle with his back turned to them. He kept his head down and appeared to be looking into the window of the car. Suddenly, he turned and made a dash for the shop door.

"Oh!" Lizzy shouted. "I dropped a cat toy." Lizzy moved quickly past Annie, back into the store, leaving Annie holding the door open.

Annie was suddenly in darkness as a bag was pulled over her head and she was being whisked away by strong arms!

CHAPTER 21

Tuesday Night

Annie struggled, trying to swing her legs out and kick her assailant, but she was only making contact with air. She hit her head as she was being shoved into a vehicle. The force of being pushed into the car caused her to fall on the seat. She found herself lying on her side, her head aching.

Annie's heart raced as she felt the motion of someone hurriedly getting in the front seat of the car. Hearing the engine start, Annie thought the only thing to do was to fight. She sat upright, bag over head, and tried to fumble her way to stopping the driver from leaving the area. With one hand she was trying to get the bag off her head, and with the other she was reaching for the hair on the driver's head.

Feeling a soft mound of hair, she grabbed with all her might and pulled the man's head back as far as she could. The car lurched forward and made a sharp turn to the right. The man was trying to grab her hand to remove it from his hair. As he tried, he swerved left and then right again, causing the vehicle to weave down the block at an accelerate speed.

"Stop this car and let me out now!" Annie's muffled voice screamed into the man's ear.

The car swerved again, this time side-swiping a parked car on the street. Annie was knocked back into the seat. She was attempting to regain her balance while trying to remove the dark canvas bag. Using both hands, Annie pulled the bag with all her strength. She glanced at the bag and realized it was a laundry bag from Bridgewater Inn, the bed & breakfast across from her shop. She threw the bag onto the seat and once again sat up.

The vehicle took a sharp left turn to head up the hill. This action caused Annie to once again fall back into the seat. She forced herself up and with both hands, reached around the headrest and placed her hands over the man's face.

"Hey!" the abductor cried out. "Don't do that. I can't see where I'm going."

"Stop this car now!" Annie screamed again. Looking over the headrest and out the front window, Annie saw a someone crossing the street. Annie removed her hands and screamed, "Stop!"

The man, seeing the pedestrian immediately in front of him, swerved right while screaming, "Get out of the way!"

Once again, Annie was knocked back, but this time she hit the left side door with the full impact of her body. "Ouch," Annie cried, as she sat up rubbing her shoulder. She pushed herself forward again attempting to get the attention of the driver.

The kidnapper, regaining control of his vehicle, turned and looked at Annie. "Hey!" said the man, whose face suddenly blanched. She could see the fear in his eyes. "You're not Lizzy!"

The car veered to the left, still speeding up the hill, as the captor had his head turned toward Annie. Annie looked out the front window in time to see Morty with his walker slowly making his way down the sidewalk to the senior center. He was in the direct path of the out-of-control car. Annie lurched forward and attempted to grab the wheel of the vehicle. Her hand made contact with the steering wheel, sending out a long blast on the horn.

Morty, hearing the long loud horn, froze for an instant, at the mass of metal approaching him. The elderly gentleman looked both ways and jumped to the side as the car hit his walker and sent it flying into the air.

"Hit the brakes!" commanded Annie.

The assailant did as he was instructed by Annie, and the vehicle made a sudden stop within inches of the fountain in the park-like lot between the senior center and the senior apartment complex.

Annie flew back into the rear seat with such force that it nearly knocked the breath out of her. She sat stunned for a quick moment, then regained her senses and grabbed the door handle. She realized the child-locks were not allowing her to open the door.

"Let me out of here," Annie shouted at the man in the front seat. There was a moment of silence, and then Annie heard a clicking sound. She reached for the door handle again and opened the door. Bailing out of the back seat, Annie stood for a moment, breathing hard, and watched as her kidnapper opened the front door and slowly exited the vehicle. Annie noticed that he seemed a bit dazed.

"You're not Lizzy," the man stated. "You're supposed to be Lizzy."

Annie, who was furious at this point, lost all control and with one swift kick, sent her assailant to the ground, clutching his lower anatomy. He cried out in pain as Annie stepped back in shock at what she had just done. He deserved it though, she consoled herself.

"Annie!" came the voice of an out of breath woman running to Annie's side. "Are you alright?"

"I'm fine." Annie replied to Lizzy, who was now doubled over trying to catch her breath after running a block uphill trying to catch up with Annie.

Lizzy stopped and looked at the man on the ground in a fetal position breathing hard. He was groaning and near crying from the pain.

"Reggie?" Lizzy asked.

"Reggie?" Annie questioned, looking at Lizzy. "You know this guy? He wanted to kidnap you and got me instead. Who is he?"

"My ex-fiancé," Lizzy said quietly to Annie, as now there were people crowding around the scene.

Before Annie could answer, she heard sirens coming up the hill toward them. The vehicle screeched to a halt and Detective Dan Weston hopped out and raced to Lizzy.

"Are you alright?" he asked Lizzy.

"Yes, I'm fine," Lizzy answered as she hugged Dan tightly.

"I'm fine too," Annie said sarcastically. "Can't say the same for the kidnapper there," pointing to the man on the ground who was now beginning to sit up with his legs outstretched before him.

"I'm not a kidnapper!" yelled the man on the ground. "I came here to talk to Lizzy."

"Well, placing a bag over my head and forcing me into the backseat of your car makes you a kidnapper!" Annie yelled back. She was angry he had put her through this harrowing experience. Annie quickly moved closer to the man. With her foot behind her ready to swing forward and make contact with the man on the ground, Annie felt strong arms around her, lifting her up and pulling her to the side.

"This is like childhood all over again," Dan said, as he set her down, turned her around and grabbed her shoulders. "Knock it off. I will deal with this."

Annie had a flashback of the many times Dan had rescued her from retaliating against a bully. At times it was good to have a big brother. Still frustrated, Annie pouted a bit as she walked to the back of the vehicle.

Frozen in mid-step, Annie saw the prone body of Morty laying perfectly still across a low box hedge bush. Annie gasped and called out his name. People turned their attention to Annie, who was racing over to Morty's still body. Just as she drew nearer to the old man, Morty sat up quickly and slid to the ground.

"Morty," Annie called out. "Are you okay?"

"Well, that was a kick in the pants!" Morty said, shaking dried leaves from his head. He looked up at Annie, "Am I in heaven, because I see an angel before me?" Morty smiled a toothless smile at Annie. He reached up and felt his mouth. "My teeth! I lost my teeth. Help me find my teeth!"

More sirens signaled the arrival of the fire department paramedics. Annie waved them to her location, where they began helping Morty stand and locate his missing teeth.

Moving to the fountain, Annie noticed Morty's walker in the pool of water. She pulled the bent-up walker out of the water. As she was setting it on the ground to inspect for damage, her eye caught a brass plate attached to the fountain bearing the names of Robert and Helen Harper. She smiled, thinking of the generosity of the Harpers.

Annie's attention was drawn away by Lizzy, who was calling her name. Annie returned the walker to Morty and walked quickly to Lizzy's side. She noticed Lizzy's ex-fiancé was now standing and brushing the dried grass from his slacks.

"Can I just talk to Lizzy, please?" pleaded Reggie.

"How about you talk to me down at the police station?" Dan answered, turning Reggie around to place handcuffs on him.

"Lizzy, please!" Reggie once again pleaded. "Your dad sent me to talk to you."

"Dan, wait!" Lizzy shouted.

Dan stopped and turned the cuffed man to face Lizzy.

"Lizzy," Reggie said, in a voice that pleaded for her to listen to what he had to say. "Your dad asked me to come here to talk to you since you won't respond to his messages."

"Messages?" Lizzy responded. "I haven't received any messages from my father."

"According to the private detective that your father hired," Reggie said, standing up straight, looking a bit confused, "he left you several messages...along with flowers and gifts."

"Oh my!" Lizzy said, slapping her forehead. "It all makes perfect sense now. How could I not see it?"

"Maybe you could help the rest of us see it more clearly, Lizzy," Dan asked, sounding irritated. He was still holding on to Reggie's elbow.

Lizzy began to explain that her mother was currently in Italy, spending time with her family. With her mother gone, Lizzy assumed her dad had time to think about how his actions nearly ruined his daughter's life.

"And what does that have to do with this gentleman?" Dan asked.

"Let me finish," Lizzy demanded.

Lizzy continued to relate that her mother spoke of how Lizzy's dad was feeling happy that Lizzy had found a wonderful, smart, intelligent, handsome...

"Yeah, we get it. Move on," Annie said.

"Well, Mom told me earlier that Daddy was also feeling upset with himself for trying to push me to marry Reggie," Lizzy explained. "He knew Reggie was all wrong for me. It was more of a business arrangement with Reggie's father. The two have been friends for decades. They came up with this stupid idea that their kids should be married to each other." Lizzy continued to explain how she thought that the flowers, jewelry, and candy were signs of her father expressing regret.

"You are telling me that your father apologizes with expensive jewelry?" Dan asked.

"Yes," Lizzy said excitedly. "My mother's collection alone could put the Queen of England to shame."

Annie was almost certain Lizzy was exaggerating, but then again having seen Lizzy's mother at the wedding, she was not sure it was an exaggeration. From the looks of Lizzy's mother, there was a lot of asking for forgiveness going on from Lizzy's father.

"That doesn't excuse him from kidnapping my sister," Dan said in his authoritative tone of voice. "I am still charging him with kidnapping."

"Wait!" cried out Reggie. "I only wanted to talk to Lizzy without a bunch of townspeople realizing who she was and who I was. Please, Lizzy! I don't want to be arrested. My father will disown me forever."

Annie heard the implorations of a spoiled rich boy. She thought of Lizzy and how Lizzy went to great lengths to protect her identity all these years. Lizzy was the best friend she ever had. Annie did get in a good, solid, kick to her assailant. Why cause him more distress? Annie looked to Lizzy, who gave her a pleading look back.

"Dan," Annie said, walking up to and standing in front of Reggie. The man took a step back, fearing Annie was going to strike at him again. She stared at Reggie for a moment, turned to Dan and said, "This man mistook me for Lizzy. It was simple mistaken identity. He was not kidnapping me. I am not pressing charges."

"Annie," Dan said, getting close to her face. "You don't have a choice in this matter."

"Let him go, Dan," Annie said, moving closer to his face. "There is no crime here. The worst you have here is reckless driving."

"Did you need to mention that?" whined Reggie.

"It's better than kidnapping," Dan said. He removed the handcuffs and called out to Officer Kathy Barrel to issue Reggie a citation for reckless driving, hit and run, and anything else she could throw at him. Dan followed Officer Barrel, who escorted Lizzy's former fiancé to her patrol car.

"My walker!" came a voice from the other side of the crashed car. "Somebody broke my walker!"

Annie, followed by Lizzy, made her way through the crowd of people to Morty's side. The paramedics were finished and picking up their equipment. Morty stood with the aid of another senior gentleman.

Annie took the opportunity to quickly make peace with Morty. Not wanting Dan to file any further charges on Reggie, Annie spoke up, "I'll buy you a brand-new walker, Morty. That walker was fairly old," she said, pointing to the crumpled-up heap of metal that had recently been his walking assistant.

"A new walker, you say?" asked Morty. Annie noticed from his grin that he had found his teeth.

"Yes. A brand-new walker."

"One of those fancy types with storage under the seat and all the gadgets?" Morty said, obviously taking advantage of Annie's generosity. She didn't mind.

"Yes, Morty," Annie said. "Anything you want."

"I was thinking of one of those power scooters might be good," Morty said. My leg hurts now, you know."

Annie realized she was dealing with an astute gentleman here. She was sure the power scooter was not the end of it.

"How about we buy you both a power scooter and a walker with a storage seat and all the gadgets?" came a voice behind Annie. It was Donald.

Annie quickly hugged Donald. He, in turn, wrapped his arms around Annie and kissed her.

"Daisy called me. I just talked to Dan. He told me what happened." Donald explained, telling her that he had raced up here as soon as Daisy called.

"Oh!" Lizzy cried. "I left Daisy holding my purse and bag, with the shop door unlocked. I'd better get back to the shop."

"I met Daisy at the shop," Donald stated. "I put your stuff in the office and locked up. We'll meet you there when you have finished up here."

Annie was happy she had the forethought to give Donald a key to the shop. It had proved handy in this situation. Annie heard Morty asking his friend to help him back to his room so he could figure out which scooter he wanted to get. The man reminded him to pick out the top of the line and to not forget the walker. Annie chuckled to herself as she watched the two older men saunter back to the senior apartment complex.

CHAPTER 22

Wednesday

"Ding!" came a sound from Annie's nightstand. She lifted her head and studied the clock until it came into focus. It was two o'clock in the morning. Who was texting her at two o'clock in the morning? She pulled her phone from the charger and read the text message.

"I AM A TERRIBLE MOTHER!" It was a text from Lizzy.

"What are you talking about?" Annie sent a message back. Was Lizzy dreaming?

"I FORGOT ABOUT MY KITTENS!" Lizzy explained. "In all the excitement, I forgot to pick up my kittens. I haven't even told Dan yet."

"The kittens are fine with my mother. Don't worry. We'll deal with it in the morning. I'll meet you at eight to walk to the shop. Good night." Annie had forgotten all about the kittens herself. She and Donald had picked up Chinese food and went to bed early last night. Though a note on the kitchen counter informed them that Marie was spending the night at Stella's place, it had never occurred to Annie that it was because the kittens were there.

Annie placed the cell phone on her charger and fell back to sleep. Callie was curled up next to Annie's pillow, softly snoring. Donald was sleeping soundly and Laddie was lying on his own bed with his feet in the air. All was peaceful in the Weston Harper household.

"Hey," Annie heard Donald call out to her. "You going to get up, lazy bones?"

"What time is it?" Annie said from under the covers.

"Six-thirty," Donald replied.

"Oh, good grief!" Annie remarked as she flung the covers off and sprang out of bed. "I told Lizzy I would meet her at eight to walk to the shop." Annie raced into the bathroom and a half hour later she was walking out of the bathroom with wet hair, but dressed for work.

After straightening the bed, Annie began to make her way downstairs, but stopped when she heard the faint sound of meowing. She opened her bedroom door and noticed Callie now asleep in her cat tree.

Hearing the sound again, she walked to Marie's bedroom door. Opening the door, she noticed a small kitten attempting to get out of the bedroom. She picked the little bundle of fur up and held it in her arms. Marie lay in bed, asleep. Annie closed the door and took the kitten downstairs with her.

Just as she entered the kitchen, she could see Stella running across the back yard from her apartment over the garage. She was carrying a kitten. She punched in the code on the back door lock and entered the kitchen.

"I'm missing a kitten!" Stella announced. She then noticed Annie holding the other kitten in her arms. "Marie must have snuck the little furball out last night."

"You can't blame her," Annie said, holding the mewing kitten up and then giving it a kiss on the head.

"Here," Stella said, "you hold this one and I'll go get their belongings before I get too attached to them." She exited, leaving Annie with two kittens in her arms.

Donald and Laddie came into the kitchen, and Laddie immediately noticed the little creatures. His nose was in full action, sniffing the unfamiliar animals in Annie's arms.

"Leave it!" Donald told Laddie. Laddie backed up and sat down, never taking his eyes from the kittens.

"Are those ours now?" Donald asked.

"No, Lizzy is going to get them after work," Annie answered. "I think I might have to have Marie stay home with them here today. Mom is getting too attached to them."

"I'll keep Laddie in my office with me," Donald said, taking one of the kittens from Annie's arms. Laddie stood and walked to Donald, sniffing the kitten, which purred against Donald's chest. Laddie licked the kitten and then yawned.

"Laddie's afraid he is going to end up living with a house full of cats," Donald said. "He says it is only fair to get another dog."

"He says that, does he?" Annie said. She turned to Laddie and said, "You're safe, buddy. The kittens belong to Lizzy."

"What kittens belong to Lizzy?" asked Dan, who had just walked into the kitchen.

"Don't you ever knock?" asked Annie.

"I did, and when you didn't answer, I heard voices and used my key to open the door," Dan replied. He was looking at the kittens. "Did you say these were Lizzy's kittens"

"Yours and Lizzy's," Donald said, handing a kitten to Dan.

Dan held it out to inspect the fuzzy miniature cat.

"Her name is Katy," Annie said. "I have Daisy."

Annie heard her cell phone ding, indicating she had a text message. She handed Daisy to Dan and pulled her phone from her pocket. The message was from Lizzy, "Is Dan over there? His car is still here, but I can't find him in the house. He doesn't know about the kittens yet."

"He does now," answered Annie. Lizzy did not respond back.

A few minutes later, Annie heard a knock and opened the front door. Lizzy walked in and froze in her tracks when she saw Dan holding two kittens.

"I am a terrible mother, Dan," Lizzy said, walking into the kitchen and taking Katy from Dan's arms. She held the kitten up and then kissed it on the head. She cuddled Katy to her chest. "I completely forgot about these little girls after all that happened yesterday."

"I was not aware that we were parents of cats," Dan responded. He continued to hold Daisy against his chest.

"I really meant to tell you. They are rescued kitties. They need a loving home. How could I resist?"

"Well, how much trouble could two little kittens be?" Dan said.

Stella came bounding through the kitchen door carrying two carriers, a tote bag of food and toys, a cleaned litter box, and a small bag of litter. Donald raced over to help her with the load of supplies for the two little kittens, which Dan was so sure would not be much trouble.

◆ ◆ ◆

Ocean Loads of Paper, on this sunny Wednesday morning, was teeming with customers. Summers were great for shoppers and the regular tourists planned their vacations with some crafting in mind. Annie always had samples of projects, some easy and quick, and some which took more time and materials. Her shop was a favorite, alongside Ione's Bakery & Coffee Shop and Salty's, the much-loved hamburger café.

Annie and Lizzy were busy with shoppers, while Daisy was ringing up customers who were standing in line waiting to check out with their crafting finds. Annie was talking with a woman, who was trying to decide on a choice of paper products, when she glanced out the window and noticed the four Silver Sleuths exiting Jerry's Leatherworks. She thought it odd that these ladies would be interested in leather, but dismissed it when her customer began asking more questions.

It was lunchtime when Lizzy pushed through the ocean-side shop door carrying an armload of food and drinks. She set the food on the counter and began distributing the hamburgers to Annie and Daisy.

"You'll never guess who was at Salty's just now!" Lizzy said. "I'm glad I called our order in ahead, because it is packed with tourists over there."

"Who did you see?" asked Daisy, taking a sip from her drink.

"The Silver Sleuths," Lizzy answered. "They were at the chocolate counter talking to Salty. It was busy and I couldn't get over to them. Besides, my arms were full."

"Let's take our food to the office and eat," Annie suggested.

"I'll stay out here and eat at the counter," Daisy said. "I can watch for customers from here."

Annie and Lizzy went to the office. Annie set her hamburger, fries, and iced tea on her desk. Lizzy sat down in a chair in the corner of the office. With the door open, Annie and Lizzy could comfortably talk with Daisy, who was seated at the cashier counter.

"Donald called me while you were out," Annie said. "He thinks Dan is warming to the idea of the kittens. Dan has already been back to our house to check on Katy and Daisy."

"Oh, that's wonderful!" Lizzy said, taking a sip from her iced tea.

"Apparently, Donald said Dan made the excuse that he thought he left his jacket at the house." Annie told Lizzy.

"He was wearing his jacket when he left," Lizzy added dryly.

Annie continued to tell Lizzy that not only was Dan checking up on the kitties, but her mom was in the kitchen cooking up a storm.

"Any idea what she is making for dinner tonight?" Lizzy asked.

"Donald says it is lasagna. Lots of pans of lasagna. Apparently, she is planning to freeze some of it. Marie is helping when the kittens are napping."

"I hope Stella doesn't mind if Dan and I eat at our house tonight," Lizzy stated. "We haven't had the kittens home yet. They're going to get used to living at your house and not want to be at our house."

"I doubt they are attached to any place at this time of their lives. They only care about eating, playing, and sleeping," Annie said, attempting to console Lizzy.

Annie and Lizzy were finishing their lunch when Daisy announced that the Silver Sleuths had just entered the shop through the street-side door. Annie quickly cleaned up her desk, making good use of the office trash can. She left the office to greet the ladies. Lizzy followed, quickly discarding her trash, as well.

Annie greeted the ladies and offered them a seat in the classroom area.

"We don't have much time, Annie," LaVerne said.

"We're on a mission to find the answers to the clues," Lorraine stated.

"Are you making any discoveries?" Lizzy asked.

LaVerne leaned in close to Annie and Lizzy and said, "We believe the shops hold the answer. Each clue leads us to a shop."

"A shop that is housed in a building owned by R&H Enterprises!" Millie added.

"Well, that makes sense," Lizzy said. "Robert did own the buildings and he was the one making these clues."

"I have a suggestion," Annie said. "Let's all work together and try and solve the clues. Tomorrow is going to be another sunny day. Let's meet at five for dinner and then everyone can work on a clue."

Annie suggested a barbecue outside in the back yard. The ladies were in agreement and went on their way to do more sleuthing. Annie called Donald and told him about her idea. He said he would handle the barbecuing and would call Dan to take care of the drinks. Donald also said he would tell Stella, who was now napping on the sofa with kittens curled up next to her. He was keeping an eye on Marie in the back yard with William, who had come over an hour ago to visit the kittens.

"By the way, Annie, my parents are on their way back to Bridgewater Harbor and should arrive before dinner," Donald announced.

"I hope they had a good time traveling up north," Annie said.

"It sounds like they did. They're excited to tell us all about it later."

After a few more minutes of talking, Annie realized the shop was now getting busy with customers again and bid Donald good bye.

At four-thirty, Annie was nudged in the shoulder when Lizzy spotted Reggie entering the shop with another man. Reggie introduced the man to the women as the private detective hired by Lizzy's father to deliver the jewelry and notes to Lizzy.

"I was to deliver the last gift and note to you today, but I haven't been able to get a call through to the young lad I was using to make the deliveries," said the private detective.

"His name is Oliver," Annie spoke up. "He has been camping with his family and should be back sometime today."

"You know about him then?" the detective asked.

"It's a small town," Annie said. "Everyone knows what's going on."

"You said you have one more delivery to make?" Lizzy asked.

"As a matter of fact, yes," said the private detective. He opened the flap on a black leather messenger bag, which was draped over his shoulder, and after reaching inside, pulled out a small square package. He handed it to Lizzy.

Lizzy opened the familiar jewelry store box and looked inside. "And that completes the set," she said, pulling out a chain with a diamond encrusted heart shaped pendant. "I now have the bracelet, earrings, and pendant. Time to call my father and let him know I forgive him." She turned to Annie and said, "Not that I ever held it against him in the first place. I am just a stubborn girl who has to do things her way...a trait I got from my father."

"I believe he already knows that," Annie laughed.

Annie spoke with Reggie and the private detective, the latter informing Annie that he was not aware the notes were to be obviously from Lizzy's father. The communications were coming from the secretary of Lizzy's father and there was apparently some miscommunication along the way.

Lizzy finished her call with her father, and announced that all was good again. Lizzy had told her father of the damage caused by Reggie. Her father promised to pay for all damages and hire an attorney to handle Reggie's charges. When she told Reggie that he was to return home immediately, he stated he would be more than happy to do so.

After the detective and Reggie left, Lizzy informed Annie that her allowance had been reinstated and her dad was going to buy her a new convertible. She asked Annie what she thought Dan would think, being married to an heiress. He had married her thinking she was a poor working girl, after all.

"Frankly, Lizzy," Annie said laughing, "I believe Dan will be thrilled. He may want to retire from the police business and take up fishing."

"No way!" Lizzy commented. "Dan loves his job. He just wants a slower pace of life."

"Are you planning on quitting and being a bon-bon eating, soap opera watching, lay around the house, rich girl?" Annie asked.

"I think you know me better than that, Annie," Lizzy laughed. "I will quit when you quit."

"I guess we're here for the long haul, Lizzy," Annie admitted. "But let's close up and go home for now. Donald's parents are coming back, and I want to spend some time with them this evening."

"And I want to pick up a pan of lasagna for Dan and me tonight," Lizzy said.

"As well as the two kittens?" Annie asked. "By the way, with your new found wealth in the form of an allowance from your father, you can now hire a cook and housekeeper."

"Oh, good grief, Annie," Lizzy said. "I really am a terrible mother. I keep forgetting my kittens! And why should I need a cook and housekeeper? We eat at your house, and Dan and I are doing a great job keeping the place clean ourselves."

Annie laughed, walking out of the shop and locking the door behind Lizzy. Daisy joined them on the walk home, as she wanted to see the kittens again and then walk home with her brother, William. When they arrived at Annie's house, they spotted Dan carrying kitty supplies across the street to his house.

"I don't think Dan is going to have a problem with the kittens, Lizzy," Annie stated as she walked up the stairs to her front door.

Stella opened the door before Annie had a chance to reach for the knob. "The kittens are already at your house, Lizzy. Marie and William are over there watching them until Dan can get their kitty box, food, and water all set up."

"Well, I guess I will see you tomorrow, Annie," Lizzy stated, as she began walking down the stairs.

"Wait!" Stella called out. "I have a lasagna for you and Dan to eat tonight for dinner." Stella stepped out from the doorway and handed a pan of food to Lizzy.

"Thank you, Stella," Lizzy said. "Come visit the kittens any time." She turned to walk down the sidewalk.

"I'll go with you," Daisy said, running after Lizzy. "I want to see the kitten named after me, and you'll also need help prying William away from the kittens."

"Send Marie home for dinner," Stella called out to the two women leaving the yard.

CHAPTER 23

Thursday Late Afternoon

The next day, Annie walked through the door at four-thirty, greeted by Laddie who was anxious to go outside. She hung her purse over the stair banister and walked to the kitchen. Laddie ran to the kitchen door and whined. Looking out the window, she noticed Donald cleaning the grill. She opened the door and Laddie made a dash to Donald's side. Annie greeted Donald with a kiss and looked around the yard.

"You escaped early from the shop today," Donald remarked.

"Lizzy kicked me out," Annie said. "She'll close at five and stop by to check the kittens before she comes over. Dan is planning to be here at five-thirty."

"Your mom and Marie went to the grocery store," Donald said. "They should be back any minute now."

Annie heard her mother's sports car coming up the drive. Marie had only worked a half day, so she was able to help with grocery shopping for the dinner with the Silver Sleuths tonight.

The afternoon was sunny with a light breeze in the air. Perfect for a barbecue. The flowers in the yard were still in full bloom, which gave Annie the idea to create a flower arrangement for the table. She found a pair of clippers in a large old mailbox on a post next to the garage, which Stella had been using as a tool storage bin. Annie clipped roses from various bushes and returned the clippers to the mailbox bin.

"Oh dear!" exclaimed Stella, looking at her watch. "It is later than I thought. Marie, please help me get the table set outside."

"I'll help as soon as I get these roses in a vase," Annie shouted from the laundry room. She pulled a vase from the cupboard and filled it with water. Placing the roses in the vase, she gave them a careful fluff so as not to stick her finger on the thorns.

Judith Dickenson Ackaret

Annie walked into the kitchen to find a frantic Stella pulling groceries from the bags and putting them away. Marie was looking for a tablecloth in the pantry for the outside table.

"I am ready to help," Annie said to Stella. "What do you want me to do?"

"How about we set up the table first," Stella suggested, "and when everyone is here, Donald can begin to grill the steaks. I have potato salad in the refrigerator, as well as a raw vegetable tray. Once you and Marie finish setting the table, you can butter the bread. Then sprinkle one loaf with Parmesan cheese and the other loaf with garlic."

Annie and Marie quickly prepared the table on the patio. Just as they finished placing the last plate down, Annie heard the familiar chatting of the Silver Sleuths approaching up the driveway. She walked out to greet the ladies.

"Annie!" said Lorraine. "We are so excited to discuss the clues with you tonight."

"I see Rand and Patty arrived back home safely," Millie stated, handing a blueberry pie to Annie. "It must be nice for Donald to have his parents so close."

"What's for dinner?" LaVerne interrupted before Annie could respond to Millie's comment, simultaneously placing an apple pie in Annie's other hand.

"Steak, potato salad, and bread," Annie answered, looking at the Harper's motorhome and wondering if they were going to join the party for dinner. Donald and she had stayed up until midnight talking with Rand and Patty the night before.

Annie ushered the ladies to the patio area, and asked them to take a seat. After getting drink orders, she excused herself and went to the kitchen with the wonderful smelling, still warm, pies. Returning quickly with lemonade, iced tea, and sparkling water on a tray, she handed out drinks to the guests.

"Have you figured it all out?" Annie asked, feeling a bit excited to solve the mystery.

"Let's have dinner first, then go inside and discuss the clues," LaVerne said.

"The trees have ears, Annie," Millie said, leaning in to speak to Annie.

The four Senior Sleuths looked to the house on the hill.

"Donald changed all of the locks on that house," Annie said, following the ladies gaze to the house behind her back yard. "I doubt anyone has entered since."

"One can never be too sure about that, Annie." Lorraine stated.

Donald walked up and greeted the ladies, announcing that he was going to put the steaks on the grill. He took orders for how each lady wanted their steak cooked, and left to begin his task.

Dan and Lizzy appeared, walking up the driveway to the patio area. Dan greeted the ladies cordially and then met Donald at the grill. Lizzy excused herself and went to the kitchen to get a drink. She returned, followed by Stella and Marie, to join the ladies on the patio.

"Lizzy," Elsie asked, "how are your adorable kittens doing in their new home?"

Lizzy paused for a moment before asking, "How did you know we had kittens?"

"Well," stated Lorraine, "Pam from the accounting office told Myra from the flower shop, who told Charles at the chiropractic office, who told..."

"Do you really want an answer to that question, Lizzy?" LaVerne cut in.

"No, I guess not," Lizzy answered. "It was a silly question, wasn't it?"

LaVerne smiled and then said, "That's alright, dear. It's a small town."

Patty and Rand emerged from the motorhome looking as if they had just awakened from a long nap. They greeted everyone and after some brief conversation, were invited to join the ladies. Rand moved more chairs to the seating area for Stella, Marie, and Patty, and then joined Donald and Dan at the grill.

The wind was starting to pick up just as the group was finishing dinner, so Stella suggested they go inside for dessert. Marie escorted the group to the dining room and everyone took a seat at the large table. Donald brought over a couple of the kitchen chairs to provide enough seating for twelve people.

Marie helped Patty and Stella dish out plates of pie, ice cream, and coffee. Stella brought out a chocolate cream pie for Annie, since she knew Annie did not care for fruit pies. Anything with chocolate was about the only dessert Annie liked.

As the group dug into their desserts, Annie decided to get the ball rolling on the clues. "I think it is important to try and solve the clues Robert Harper left for the Silver Sleuths," Annie began, looking at Dan who did a slight roll of his eyes. "But I think it is also important to figure out a backup plan. What if we can't find the gold ingot?"

"If we don't find the gold ingot, then the seniors will lose their home," stated Millie.

"Some of the people have already moved out since they received a thirty-day notice from Felix's son," Elsie said. "Morty has nowhere to go. Where is he going to live?"

"What if Annie and I try to outbid the developer and buy the place?" Donald suggested.

"Patty and I would help with that," Rand said.

"I bet I could get my father to buy the place for me," Lizzy spoke up. "He's feeling guilty right now, so it's a good time to hit him up for the money."

"What?" Dan asked, looking curiously at Lizzy.

"Didn't I tell you about my father?" Lizzy asked, acting a bit too innocent in Annie's view. Dan was seeing through it all anyway.

"We'll talk later," Dan said. "It seems like we have a lot of catching up to do."

"We can go away for a few nights," Lizzy said quietly to Dan.

"I'll kitten-sit," shouted Marie, who was sitting next to Dan.

"I am REALLY a terrible cat mother," Lizzy said looking dejectedly at Dan. "I completely forgot about the kittens."

"I can take good care of them," Marie stated. "They can sleep with me in my bedroom."

"Looks like we have a sitter for the kids," Dan said, giving his absent-minded bride a kiss on the cheek. "I'll make the arrangements for Friday and Saturday night this weekend."

"What have you figured out so far about the clues?" Annie asked LaVerne.

"They all seem to lead to various shops downtown," LaVerne stated.

"Only shops owned by R&H Enterprises," Lorraine added. "There are fourteen clues in total."

"The clues indicate these shops having something in common," Elsie said.

"Excuse me a moment," Annie said. "I want to get the original of the conditional contract. There might be something we overlooked." She made her way to Donald's office and pulled the document from the office safe where she had placed it for quick access and safe-keeping earlier.

Annie emerged from the office and went to the laundry room to get a magnifying glass from a utility drawer. She placed the document on the table in front of LaVerne and the other ladies. Even with the magnification, she could not see anything she may have missed earlier. Holding the paper to the dining room light she spotted something.

"There appears to be a watermark of some kind," Annie said. "Follow the papercuts."

There was silence in the room as everyone pondered the message. Suddenly, Annie and Lizzy looked wide-eyed at each other.

"The papercuts!" Annie and Lizzy said in unison.

"Where are they?" Lizzy questioned, jumping up from her chair.

"I put them in the trash," Annie answered.

"Uh, oh," Donald said, standing up from the table and moving to get his jacket off the coat hook near the door. "Would you get me a flashlight from the utility drawer in the laundry room, Annie? I gathered all the trash in the house and took it out to the curb earlier this evening." Annie made haste to the laundry room to get a flashlight. She followed Donald outside to sift through the garbage can, while Lizzy stayed and explained what they were looking for.

"Annie and I took apart framed art that was hanging in each shop," Lizzy began. "They were strange bits of cut out papers that didn't make any sense. We reused the frames for the quilling class. Annie just threw the papers away."

"Were there fourteen of them?" LaVerne asked.

"Yes," Lizzy said.

"That is a good sign," Elsie said. "Those frames are what we were looking for in the clues."

"But Annie and I removed them a week ago, so you were unable to find the commonality of the shops," Lizzy said.

Annie and Donald opened the front door, elated to have found the tossed papercuts. She tore open the plastic bag the papers were in and spread them out on the table. Stella and Patty began picking up the dessert dishes to give more room to spread the papers out.

"There is a letter here on the corner of this paper," Dan said, holding it up and pointing to the bottom right-hand corner. "Does anyone else have a letter?" Everyone signaled that they had found the letter.

Annie went to a utility drawer in the kitchen and pulled out a pad of sticky notes and a marking pen. She asked each person holding a paper to call out the letter. She wrote one letter per sticky note and set her pen down. Everyone stared for a moment, not quite sure what to do.

"I think these letters spell out words," LaVerne stated.

Marie moved next to Annie and began manipulating the sticky notes around to form words. Annie began doing the same. Marie reached over and took one of Annie's letters, forming the word "senior".

"Look!" Annie shouted. "Marie found the word senior."

Everyone gathered around the table near Annie and Marie. Stella patted Marie on the back, congratulating her on finding the first word. Marie smiled and turned her attention back to the next word hunt.

As Annie shuffled the scraps of paper containing the letters, everyone made guesses, some funny and some nonsensical. As Annie moved the papers around again, a gasp sounded from the group. The bits of paper formed the word "fountain".

"It's the senior fountain on Robert Harper's property between the senior apartment complex and the senior center!" Annie exclaimed.

"I'll get a tool kit, you lock up the house and meet me outside," Donald said, grabbing his jacket once more. "Let's take your car and Dad you take my truck." He handed the keys to his father.

"The Silver Sleuths will meet you there," LaVerne said. "Come on ladies. We have a treasure to find!" With that the older ladies were rushing out the door, followed by Annie asking them to be careful.

"Lizzy and I will meet you there," stated Dan. He was already halfway out the front door with Lizzy in tow. Grabbing jackets, Annie quickly locked the door and hurried Stella and Marie out the kitchen door ahead of her. They met Donald at the car and they were off to the park next to the senior apartment complex.

CHAPTER 24

Thursday Night

Annie was surprised to find the Silver Sleuths already parked and getting out of their vehicle when Donald pulled up behind them. As she was getting out of the car, she saw Rand and Patty pull up behind them in Donald's truck. Dan screeched to a halt across the street from Annie's car. Annie waited for Lizzy to meet up with her. Stella and Marie followed Donald to the fountain, carrying flashlights, tool kits, a shop blanket, and a battery powered lantern.

A group of seniors were exiting the apartment complex and making their way to the fountain area. Annie was amazed how the word got out in the short time it took to drive to the fountain from home. Morty was in the lead with his newly acquired motorized chair. Annie was hoping he would slow down before he ran into the group already at the fountain.

"Everyone, stand back and give these people some room to work," ordered Dan in his best police tone of voice. "Come on people, move back. Let them work."

"Word gets around fast in this town," Lizzy whispered to Annie.

Annie looked at the growing crowd. There must have been fifty people already, and the crowd appeared to be growing. The Silver Sleuths were up front and waiting anxiously as Annie and Donald began circling the fountain looking for any obvious clues as to where the gold ingot could be hiding.

"Do you think it's concealed in the cherub at the top of the fountain?" Donald asked Annie.

Annie walked around the fountain slowly. She viewed the top of the fountain from all angles, deciding it was too high for the seniors to access. Then she walked around the fountain another time, this time viewing the base of the fountain.

"Donald," Annie leaned over and lowered her voice. "I think the best hiding place would be behind the brass plaque at the base of the fountain."

"Well, that would make it way too easy for me to get to it," Donald said happily.

"It's got to be there," Annie said, moving closer to the plaque. "The rim of the fountain is about..." Annie pulled a small tape measure from her purse, "fourteen inches deep. That's enough room to build in a small nook and conceal it with a brass plaque."

Donald and Annie approached the brass plaque and examined the screws holding the plate in place.

"These are not ordinary screws," Donald revealed. "I can't use a regular screw bit."

Annie hopes were suddenly dashed. How could they come this far and not be able to find out what was behind the brass plate? Was there anything behind the brass plate? Were there clues to find to remove the screws? Annie's mind was suddenly filled with doubt about finding the gold ingot. Then she thought of prying the plate from the concrete fountain wall. She was brought back to reality when she heard Donald ask her a question.

"Would you focus the flashlight on that screw at the top?" he asked Annie. Donald reached for a black case and opened it to reveal a battery-operated impact driver. Examining the screw head, Donald reached into his case and produced a small plastic box with various sizes and shapes of bits for the tool he was going to use. "Fortunately, I carry all sorts of screw bits," Donald told Annie while pulling out a bit from the case. He sized it up with the screw on the plaque. Satisfied that he had the correct bit, he plugged it into the impact driver and pushed it up against the screw.

"Are we ready?" Donald said to the crowd of people standing nearby. The crowd murmured assent.

"Do it," Dan said.

Annie was surprised at how involved Dan seemed to be in this quest to help out the senior citizens of Bridgewater Harbor. Was he becoming fond of the Silver Sleuths? She smiled, looked at Donald and nodded. Donald took a deep breath and began removing the ten screws holding the brass plaque to the base wall of the fountain. After removing each screw, Donald handed them to Annie to keep safe. Once the tenth screw was in Annie's hands, Donald set down the impact driver and removed the brass plate.

"This is it, everyone!" Donald said as he removed the plate and set it up against the fountain.

Annie moved the flashlight closer to view the inside of the newly discovered nook. A flash of light indicted someone was taking a photo. Annie turned to see Marie with her cell phone, taking pictures.

"Can you get a picture up close, Marie?" Annie asked. She and Donald parted so Marie could take a few photos.

"Enough photos, Marie," shouted LaVerne impatiently. "Did you find the gold ingot?"

"Keep taking photos as we find out what's in here," Annie said quietly to Marie.

Donald and Annie noticed what appeared to be a built-in safe with a key lock. Examining the lock, Donald turned to Annie and asked, "Did you happen to bring your special equipment with you?"

Annie reached into her purse and pulled out a small case containing lockpicking tools.

"I don't even want to know why you are carrying burglar tools around with you, Annie," Dan said. He turned to see a patrol vehicle approaching with its overhead blue lights flashing. It parked on the street next to Annie's SUV.

Dan leaned down to Annie's ear, "Hurry up. I'll go talk to the officer." With that, Dan walked off and met with the patrol officer on the street.

Noticing what Annie was doing, Lorraine came to her side. LaVerne began moving people further back, as the crowd had pushed their way forward to see what was in the nook of the fountain.

"You can do this, Annie," Lorraine said, giving Annie the confidence, she so badly needed.

Annie's hands were shaking at this point. She was not sure if it was due to the cold air at night or fear that she would not be able to open the lock on the safe. She felt Lorraine's hand on her shoulder for support. She pushed the lock picks into the mechanism. To her surprise, moments later the lock released!

Annie tugged on Donald's shirt, as his attention was on the discussion Dan was having with the police officer. Donald noticed the door of the safe was ajar. He signaled Dan that the lock was open. Dan excused himself and walked quickly through the crowd to Donald's side.

"Go ahead, Donald," Annie urged. "Robert Harper was your uncle. I think you should have the honor of opening the safe."

"Actually," Donald said, "if you don't mind, I would like to turn the honor over to one of the Silver Sleuths. Uncle Robert made it their job to solve the mystery and save the apartment complex."

"Who would like to do the honors?" Annie asked the Silver Sleuths.

"Let LaVerne do it," yelled Morty, sitting comfortably in his motorized chair in the front of the crowd. "She's the bossy one."

"Let the bossy one open it," came shouts from the crowd.

LaVerne, taking the cries from the group as a compliment, walked forward and stood next to Annie. Marie took pictures while LaVerne reached in and opened the door of the safe. Inside was a black metal box. She attempted to lift the box, but it was too heavy. LaVerne looked to Donald and said, "I think I am going to need help getting this box out, Donald."

Donald reached in and carefully slid the weighted box out, placing it on the edge of the fountain.

"That's one heavy box," Donald pronounced. "Go ahead and open it, LaVerne."

"It's locked," stated LaVerne, after having attempted to lift the lid.

"Oh!" Annie shouted, remembering the key that she was to give to the Silver Sleuths. Helen had mentioned that Annie would know when to use the key. "I think I have the key." She pulled out her cell phone. Removing the cover, she produced the key and inserted it in the lock. It turned and opened the mechanism. To LaVerne, Annie said, "Now open it."

Inside the box was an envelope. LaVerne pulled the envelope out and opened it. She read it aloud:

"*Congratulations to the Silver Sleuths for solving yet another mystery which I have offered. I knew you could do it.*

As a reward, I am giving you a gold ingot with my stamped initials to present to the owner, Felix Bankford, of the senior apartment complex. As per the conditional contract, safely secured in the office of Charles Conklin, Attorney at Law, this gold ingot lays claim of payment in full to Felix Bankford of the senior apartment complex. Charles Conklin will have all the necessary documents. Yours truly, Robert Harper."

"Well," LaVerne said, "Robert would certainly be disappointed to know that the Silver Sleuths did not solve the mystery."

"Of course you solved the mystery," Annie said. "You just recruited a few extra people to help."

"I am happy I got to help," Marie stated.

"You really would have solved the mystery if Annie and I hadn't removed the papercuts from the frames," Lizzy said.

"Can we all be a Silver Sleuth?" Marie asked LaVerne.

"Marie," LaVerne said, placing her hand on Marie's shoulder, "you, Annie, and Lizzy are now honorary Silver Sleuths."

"She's just saying that because she thinks we'll need your help again on another case," remarked Morty. "Now let's get back to the box. What's in the box?"

"Pipe down, Morty," Lorraine said. "We are getting to that."

"I don't have that many years left, woman," Morty said.

LaVerne looked to Annie and motioned toward the box, "Annie, you solved the mystery. You should have the pleasure of discovering the gold ingot."

Annie took a deep breath and pulled on the black velvet case inside. It was heavy for such a small bag. She looked to Donald, who instinctively reached in for Annie and pulled the heavy velvet bag out of the box.

While Donald held the object, Annie untied the cording and exposed a golden ingot. On it were the initials "R.H."

"Oh my!" exclaimed Millie.

"It's true!" followed Elsie.

People in the crowd moved in closer. Many were asking to see the ingot. Donald, had held it up for all to see, before setting the treasure into the metal box. Gasps and comments of joy rippled through the group of senior citizens. A person clapping in the back caused more and more people to clap. Soon the entire mass of seniors was cheering and whistling. There was no longer a threat to their housing dilemma.

"Annie and Donald," LaVerne asked, "would you escort us to Felix's apartment to present this gold ingot to his son as payment in full for the senior apartment complex?"

"He ain't there," Morty spoke up. "He took off after that developer fellow this afternoon. Haven't seen him come back."

"I heard he was coming back on Friday," stated an elderly woman standing next to Morty.

"Well, I don't feel comfortable keeping this gold overnight," LaVerne said to Annie. "Would you and Donald keep it for us tonight?"

"We would be happy to keep it in the safe at home," Donald said, closing the lid of the metal box containing the ingot.

"Rest assured he will be escorted by a police officer all the way home," Lizzy offered.

"I'll make sure it gets to the house safely," Dan stated. "Donald, do you need any help getting this mess cleaned up?"

Donald shook his head no, and began the task of putting the panel back onto the base of the fountain. After cleaning up the tools and taking them to Annie's SUV, he heard Dan, who was guarding the ingot, shouting out orders for the people to head back home.

"We'll talk to you tomorrow at your shop, Annie," Elsie said, as she and the Silver Sleuths made their way to the car at the curb.

"Thank you so much," stated Millie.

"We really don't know what we would have done without you," Lorraine said, turning to head to the car.

"Like Lizzy said, you would have solved the mystery if we hadn't taken the framed art from the shops," Annie said.

LaVerne gave Annie a hug and said, "You keep saving us, Annie. I'm so glad we're friends. We'll bring the donuts and coffee to the shop tomorrow morning."

Annie laughed and wiped the tears forming in her eyes. Donald, with the metal box in his arms, walked to the car with Annie where they found Stella and Marie waiting inside.

CHAPTER 25

Friday

Annie walked from her office at Ocean Loads of Paper to see LaVerne holding open the door for Lorraine, Mille, and Elsie. The latter two were carrying a box full of donuts and a tray of coffees. They walked directly to the counter where Annie and Lizzy stood. Lizzy stopped what she was working on, and closed the lid to her laptop.

"Good morning, ladies," Annie said. "Let me help you with the coffee." She cleared a spot on the counter and took the tray of drinks from Elsie.

"This is an exciting day for you," Lizzy stated. She picked up a coffee from the tray and opened the lid to take a sip.

"You don't know the half of it," LaVerne said. "Once we pay Felix's son, the seniors can rest easy."

"Charles Conklin is on his way and plans to meet us at the senior apartments in the main lobby," Annie announced. "Donald is driving my mom and Marie here to watch the shop while we are gone. Daisy should be here any time now."

"Dan is meeting us at the apartments," Lizzy added, taking a donut from the box. "He wants to make sure the gold ingot is delivered without any trouble."

"I believe Dan was concerned that the seniors might lose their homes," Millie stated. She opened the lid of the donut box and pondered the contents before selecting a glazed cake donut.

"I think Detective Weston is getting soft," LaVerne exclaimed. "Hand me that bear claw, please, Millie." Millie picked up a napkin and used it to pull the bear claw from the box. She handed the pastry to LaVerne.

"Lizzy certainly has a positive influence on that man," Elsie said. She waved off the offer of a donut.

"The rough edge of the big city may be wearing off," Annie remarked. "But Dan is still his same old self."

The door chimed and Daisy walked up to the counter, removing her jacket. "I hope I'm not too late," Daisy said, as she breezed past the counter and into the office to hang up her coat and purse.

"Just in time," Annie said.

"Donald, Stella, and Marie were just pulling up to the curb when I walked in," Daisy commented, as she joined to the group. "Are there any donuts left?"

"Help yourself," Lorraine offered. "We brought plenty."

Marie entered the shop, holding the door for Stella, who was right behind her. Donald entered last and shivered as he took his coat off.

"I think it's going to rain today," Donald said. He looked out the window and up at the clouds in the sky.

"You still have a bit of that California boy in you, Donald," LaVerne said. "Those are the morning clouds. The sun will be out soon and the clouds will have moved on."

Annie heard her phone chime. She pulled it out of her pocket and viewed the message.

"Grab sandwiches for everyone and meet me at the senior apartment complex," Dan texted. "I just arrested the person impersonating Felix's son."

"What?" Annie shouted out. She read the text to the group standing before her.

"Oh, no," Millie cried. "Does that mean the seniors are still going to lose everything?"

"You go to the senior apartments," ordered Stella. "I can get the sandwiches and bring them to you."

"We have our own car right out front," LaVerne announced, heading for the street-side door of the shop. "Come on, ladies!"

Donald and Annie, followed by Lizzy, left the shop and headed up to the senior apartment complex in Donald's truck. Donald parked in the lot and the group met the Silver Sleuths at the front door.

Dan waved everyone to a multi-purpose room past the dining room. Seated at a large table was Charles Conklin. When he saw the assemblage of people around the table, he quickly removed his briefcase and straightened up the papers in front of him.

"Please sit down," Dan asked the people standing. "We have a lot to cover." Dan closed the door and locked it so they would not be disturbed.

Dan began by introducing Charles Conklin to everyone. Next, he explained that he called Mr. Conklin to ask about the conditional contract and what he knew of Felix Bankford's son.

"After some extensive investigating last week, I finally received answers early this morning," Dan related. "It seems that Felix's son, Todd Bankford, also known as Todd Banks, died in prison six months ago."

The sound of surprised voices emanated throughout the room. Dan signaled for everyone to quiet down.

"What does that mean for the seniors who live here?" asked Millie.

"I can answer that question for you," announced Charles Conklin. "If I may at this time, Detective Weston?"

"Please proceed, Mr. Conklin." Dan agreed.

Mr. Conklin opened a file in front of him. "Robert Harper approached me some months ago and requested I assist Felix Bankford in preparing a Will. At the time, I was just about to go on vacation, but I referred Mr. Bankford to an estate attorney in town. I have since contacted that attorney, who gave me permission to read the Will to the heirs of Felix Bankford's estate."

"If his son is deceased," Annie asked, "who is the next-of-kin?"

"After Felix discovered that his son was in prison for a fraud conviction, he decided to make a new Will and leave his estate to who he believed were the most responsible people he knew...the Silver Sleuths. More specifically, LaVerne, Lorraine, Millie, and Elsie."

"Oh, my word!" exclaimed Lorraine. "Why that dear man."

"The Will specifies that you must form a board of directors to manage the apartments. I have copies of the Will for each of you," Mr. Conklin said, as he passed out papers to the seniors.

"Well," LaVerne said, "that's one on Robert. It seems we never needed the gold ingot to save the senior apartment complex."

"I wouldn't go that far," Charles stated. "Felix ran up a great deal of debt. The gold ingot, which Dan told me was found last night, will cover the debts and leave you with plenty of money to maintain the apartments for now. You will need a good business manager to help you out."

"Ladies, we must discuss this immediately," Elsie said. The others agreed with her.

♦ ♦ ♦

An hour later, Stella entered the room with sandwiches. Marie followed, carrying two bags with small bottled waters. Annie was about to offer her sandwich to Charles Conklin, when Stella pulled two more sandwiches from the bag. Leave it to her mother to provide more than enough to feed everyone, Annie thought to herself, as she took a drink from her water bottle.

When lunch was completed, LaVerne approached Annie and asked if she and Dan would join the ladies in Felix's apartment. Annie called Dan over to her side and asked if he had a few minutes to go to the apartment.

"LaVerne wanted you to check the apartment," Annie told Dan.

"I can go with you, but the apartment was already checked when I got here this morning and arrested Todd Bankford's imposter," Dan offered. "It seems he had an outstanding warrant for parole violation in California."

"At one time he was cell mates with Todd Bankford in a California prison," Dan informed Annie. "He decided to take Todd's identity after Todd's father died. Apparently, he and Todd were very similar in appearance."

"Similar enough to pass for Todd Bankford and inherit an estate after the sudden death of Felix Bankford?" Annie asked.

"Let's go now. I'll explain it all later. I still have some calls to make today," Dan said, moving Annie along down the hallway to the manager's apartment.

Dan opened the door and stood aside as Annie, the seniors, and Lizzy walked into the manager's apartment. The first impression Annie got when she stood in the middle of the room was the smell of lemons. Not just lemons, but the same lemon furniture polish she smelled in the house on the hill.

"The apartment is so clean," Elsie remarked. "Felix never kept a clean apartment."

"Good observation, Elsie," LaVerne stated. "Felix was the biggest slob in the world."

"Who was the person pretending to be Felix's son?" Lorraine asked.

"His name is Colton Barber," Dan replied.

"Did you say Colton Barber?" Stella asked as she walked into the apartment and stood next to Dan.

"Yes," Dan said. "Does his name sound familiar?"

"He's the person listed on the permit to do the remodeling of the house behind Annie and Donald's house." Stella reported.

"That's it!" Annie shouted. "I smelled lemon furniture polish in the house on the hill and Marie and I found the furniture polish under the sink. It is the same lemon furniture polish that I smell now."

"I took that can in for prints," Dan said. "I'll call the crime lab and see what they found on the can."

"He may have been the person camping out in the basement of the house," Donald said.

"Could he be responsible for Felix's fall down the stairs?" Annie asked Dan.

"I need to go," Dan said, looking at a text message on his phone. "It seems that Mr. Barber wants to talk to me after all." Dan kissed Lizzy on the cheek and headed out the door.

"I need to get back to work too," Donald said. Annie gave him a quick kiss and walked him to the door of the apartment.

Stepping out into the hallway, Annie looked to see if anyone was in earshot. Then she asked Donald, "Do you think it would be wise to board up the hidden stairways in the basement of the house on the hill?"

"I'll see if Dad and Dan can give me a hand this weekend," Donald said. "We can't sell the house without some type of disclosure about the tunnels at this point."

"So, what you're saying is, if we close up the tunnels, we are okay to sell the house without a disclosure?" Annie asked.

"Let's talk more later, when we are alone," Donald said. "Are you okay to walk back to the shop?"

Annie nodded and watched as Donald walked down the hallway. Her scattered thoughts were all tied to the house on the hill. Was

Felix's death caused by the fall down the stairs or did Colton Barber push him down the stairs, which caused the death? Was Colton Barber planning on inheriting the senior apartments to profit on the sale to a developer from California?

Annie realized she still had the gold ingot in her tote bag. The heavy bag was practically dragging on the floor as she carried it. Even though she felt the weight of the twenty-seven plus pounds of gold, she reached inside the bag anyway to make sure it was still there. She felt the hard rectangular bar concealed in the velvet bag. This ingot belonged to the Silver Sleuths. She suddenly realized she needed to get the ingot to LaVerne and the other ladies.

Annie approached the Silver Sleuths, who were standing in the middle of the manager's apartment talking to Lizzy. She set the tote bag on a table and pulled out the velvet bag containing the gold ingot.

"Here," Annie said, placing the velvet bag containing the ingot on the table. "This belongs to the Silver Sleuths."

"Good gracious, ladies," LaVerne exclaimed. "What are we supposed to do with this?"

"I'd say we need our new business partner to help us set up an account at the bank," Lorraine said.

"Annie," Millie said. "We have decided to have R&H Enterprises handle the apartment complex business."

"Just as soon as we talk to all of the residents," Elsie added. "And Lizzy is going to help us."

"So, you just take the gold bar back to your safe until we can decide what to do with it," LaVerne instructed.

Lizzy excused herself and pulled Annie aside. "I hope you don't mind me making the decision to manage the apartment complex business transactions, Annie," Lizzy said. "I think I can help them straighten out all of Felix's apartment files and get them back on track to manage the apartments by themselves. It may take me away from the shop from time to time, but now that we have Robert Harper's office, we can do so much more for the seniors of this town."

"I put you in charge of R&H Enterprises for a good reason...I know you will do the right thing," Annie said. "I was going to talk to Daisy about taking on more responsibility in the shop while she is on break from college. Now is a good time."

Charles Conklin entered the apartment to advise Annie and the ladies that he wanted to head back to Newport. There were still papers to sign and he needed the Silver Sleuths to make a few decisions before he left. The ladies followed Charles back to the conference room.

Annie and Lizzy said their good byes, suggesting that the ladies join them for an afternoon barbecue on Saturday. LaVerne accepted for the women and turned to follow Charles Conklin into the conference room. After the door was closed, Annie and Lizzy left the senior apartment complex.

"Wow!" Lizzy commented as she and Annie made their way down the street to Ocean Loads of Paper, taking turns carrying the heavy tote bag. Marie and Stella were following behind them. "This has been one crazy week. We found a house under your house, secret passageways under the house on the hill, not to mention that you own the house on the hill."

"And your stalker," Annie added.

"Who wasn't really a stalker," Lizzy laughed. "But I did get some nice jewelry out of it. I think Dan is okay with it since the jewelry came from my father."

"And we found the gold ingot," Annie stated.

"Which really did not matter whether we found it at all, since the senior apartment complex was left to the Silver Sleuths."

"Yes, but they need the money to pay off all of the debts left by Felix," Annie reminded Lizzy.

Annie and Lizzy walked in silence until they reached the shop. While walking, Annie thought about the drawers of gold ingots in the vault room. She was wondering if she and Donald might use the money from the ingots to build additional senior apartments on the property she now owned between the senior center and the senior apartment complex. She made a mental note to talk to Donald as soon as she got home.

CHAPTER 26

Saturday

Hearing a knock, Annie walked to the front door of her house and pulled it open. She greeted John and Jacquie Spencer and invited them inside. Annie had invited the Spencers for the late afternoon barbecue. Jacquie had earlier requested another viewing of the house on the hill, but was now having second thoughts.

"Annie, I think the house is just about perfect," Jacquie said. "But there is something eerie about the basement." Jacquie and John followed Annie through the kitchen to the back yard. "Maybe it is just leftover feelings from being shut up in there."

Annie looked to Donald, who was walking up to greet John and Jacquie. Donald gave her a knowing look back. He sensed the Spencers were no longer interested in the house on the hill.

"Please be seated," Donald said, pointing to the grouping of outdoor sofas and chairs surrounding a firepit in the yard. "What can I get you to drink?'

"Iced tea, if you already have some made," Jacquie answered. She sat down on a sofa and motioned John to sit next to her.

"I'll have a beer if you have that," John said.

"I can accommodate both of you," Donald said with a smile. Donald walked to the back yard bar set up specifically for this barbecue gathering. He pulled a bottle out of the ice chest, and popped the top. Next, Donald placed ice cubes in a glass and poured tea from a large glass container on the bar. He placed the iced tea and beer on a tray with packets of sugar, a lemon wedge, and stir sticks.

Donald approached the grouping of occupied seats and walked in on a lively conversation in progress.

"Donald," his mother, Patty, requested, "please sit down and listen to what Millie is saying."

"Please, Millie, start from the beginning for Donald," Annie asked.

"I was just saying that since LaVerne and Lorraine plan to move into the Manager's two-bedroom apartment at the senior apartment complex, Elsie and I were talking of doing the same. We want to move to the Assistant Manager's two-bedroom apartment."

"But what will you do with that lovely house across the street, Millie?" Jacquie quickly asked.

"Sell it, of course," Millie stated. "I talked to my daughter last night, as soon as I knew I wanted to move. She has no interest in the house and was glad that I was moving to the senior apartment complex. The house has been just too much for me to handle lately. I'm not getting any younger. I want to be around people my age and have fun. With Lorraine and LaVerne moving, well, Elsie was thinking of moving too. It would just be too lonely for me to stay."

"I understand completely," Stella said. "I wanted to move to the apartment over the garage, because I feel closer to Annie, Donald, and Marie. And yet, I have a good-sized place of my own."

"Would you mind if John and I take a tour of your house, Millie?" Jacquie said after whispering briefly to John.

"Yes, please tell us about the house," John added.

While Millie was describing the house with its three bedrooms, office, and workshop out back, Annie leaned over to Donald and said, "I guess we'll have time to figure out what to do with the house on the hill now."

Rand stood behind Donald and Annie's sofa and leaned in between them. "Do you mind if Patty and I go look at the house on the hill after dinner?"

"Be our guest," Annie said. "Donald can get you a key."

Annie and Donald's attentions were brought back to the group when LaVerne raised her glass to make a toast to Annie and Donald for saving the senior apartment complex.

Lorraine then told the group that the Silver Sleuths had called an emergency meeting of the residents of the apartments. There was a unanimous vote that the apartments be given a new name.

"We are naming the apartments *Harper Village*," LaVerne said.

"Why, that's wonderful," Annie exclaimed. "Robert Harper would be so honored."

"Robert Harper!" Lorraine said. "Oh, poo on Robert. He could have just given us the apartment complex. Instead, the seniors nearly lost their homes, because he wanted to play games."

"No, dear," Elsie said. "We are naming the complex after you and Donald."

"If it wasn't for the two of you," Millie said, "we would have lost it all."

"Even with the inheritance, we couldn't pay those debts on our own," Millie said. "Not unless I sold my house, but my house is my retirement."

The senior ladies all nodded in agreement.

"I think Harper Village is a lovely name for the senior apartments," Stella stated. "Now, let's eat."

Dan and Lizzy joined the group just as they were sitting down at various tables on the patio. Annie, Donald, and Marie served plates of hamburgers with all the toppings, and choices of potato salad, potato chips, a green salad, baked beans, and ice cream and strawberries for dessert. Small trays of raw vegetables with a dip were placed on the tables. The conversation was lively and happy.

Annie was going to miss the Silver Sleuths across the street from her house, but knew that she would see them almost daily as they loved to walk around town and talk with everyone. Or, get into everyone's business, Annie chuckled to herself.

Lorraine turned to Donald and in a quiet voice said, "I would like you to have my husband's inventory of locks and keys, including the key making machine. I have no use for it now."

"Lorraine, I am overwhelmed by the offer," Donald said. "I promise you I will take good care of it. And, if you ever need a lock or key made, you know where to find me."

"That I do, young man. That I do," Lorraine said.

Annie smiled at Donald, knowing that this was a huge gesture of trust coming from the Silver Sleuths. Donald was now one of them. Oh, how his life has changed in the last few months.

After dinner, Jacquie and John walked the Silver Sleuths home and were given the grand tour of Millie's house. Jacquie later sent a text to Annie stating that she loved the house and it even had a workshop for John, which he loved. She felt bad about not making an offer for the house on the hill, but Millie's house had no basement and that suited her just fine after what she had been through. Annie understood completely.

"Donald," Stella asked, "where are your folks?"

"They took a walk to the house on the hill. Mom and Dad wanted to take a look around. I guess they wanted something to do this evening. I gave them the key and some flashlights."

Stella sat down next to Marie in the firepit seating area. Annie was sitting next to Donald and had brought out a blanket as the air was becoming chilly. Lizzy was sitting across from Annie and Donald. She, too, was wrapped in a blanket.

Dan added another log to the fire and sat back down next to Lizzy. Lizzy offered part of her blanket to Dan, but he said he was fine. He took a drink from a beer bottle.

"Dan," Stella asked, "can you tell us if the guy posing as Felix's son said anything about why he did it?"

Dan took another long drink from his bottle and set the bottle down on the table next to him. He sat up and leaned over toward the fire. The light of the fire danced upon his face as he began speaking.

"Todd Bankford, Felix's son, was a cell mate of Colton Barber in a prison in California. Colton told me that Todd mentioned his father had a gambling problem and that a man was paying off his debts for a price. The price was that the ownership of the apartments his father owned be given to some old ladies if his father died or wanted to sell the property to pay his debts. The ladies were given fourteen days to come up with a gold piece with the man's initials. They had to search for the gold. If they found it, they would give the gold to Felix and Felix would in turn give the apartments to the ladies," Dan told the group around the fire pit.

Dan stood and walked to the bar to get a bottle of water. He asked if anyone else would like one. Annie raised her hand. Dan walked back to the firepit circle and handed Annie the water.

Continuing, Dan said that Colton found Todd Bankford dead in their cell. With an alibi, he was not suspected, and he was not willing to say who might have killed Todd. After being released from prison, Colton was placed on probation for a period of time. Remembering what Todd had told him about Felix wanting to sell to a developer, he decided it would be easy for him to get rid of Felix, pretend to be Todd Bankford as they look very similar, and take possession of the apartments.

"It seems like Robert found out about the developer Felix wanted to sell the property to and intervened by paying off Felix's gambling debt," Annie surmised.

"Which is why Felix had never sold the property." Lizzy added.

Colton came to town and found out that that owner of the house on the hill was looking for a contractor to remodel the house. He had remodeling experience before prison, so he conned Robert Harper into letting him stay in the house and remodel it. It seems that Mr. Barber was obsessive about cleaning. His favorite go-to product was lemon scented furniture polish.

"How did Felix come to falling down the stairs?" Stella asked.

Dan continued to explain that Felix saw Colton in town one day at Ione's Bakery & Coffee Shop. Since Colton and Felix's son looked a great deal alike, Felix struck up a conversation with Colton. Once Colton realized who Felix was, he invited him over to the house on the hill with the intention of killing him. But, during a fight in the basement, Felix was slammed on the wall, causing the doorway to the staircase heading to the sump pump room to open. Felix then tripped, according to Colton, and fell down the stairs. Colton left him there and closed the door.

"Later that day," Dan said, "it seems that three older ladies somehow unlocked a door and entered the house."

"That was LaVerne, Lorraine, and Jacquie," Marie added. "Annie and I came in after they did. The front door was locked and Annie was not able to pick the lock, but I found the patio door open, and went inside to unlock the front door."

"Annie," Dan said in an authoritative tone of voice, "did you know that you owned the house at this point or were you breaking and entering?"

"Of course, I knew," is all Annie could say at the moment. Donald squeezed her shoulder. Annie was thinking back to when she first found out she owned the house. Yes, of course she knew she owned the house at the time. Didn't she?

"And Marie, we'll be having a talk about what you did." Dan said sharply.

Marie moved closer to Stella. Stella patted her hand to calm her.

"Anyway," Dan said, "Colton decided to get rid of the old ladies, but two more women showed up, so the only thing he could do at the moment was lock them in the basement in the dark."

Dan continued his story by saying when word got out that Felix was dead, Colton saw the opportunity to make money, since he wasn't getting paid for the remodeling due to Robert's death. He decided to try and scam the seniors and take inheritance of the apartment complex posing as Felix's heir. Having found a developer interested in the property, he made contact, and the buyer came to Bridgewater Harbor to look the property over. He was hoping to have either the gold or the money from the sale of the property. He did not know about the major debt on the apartment complex.

"That was when Bruce Trendle made contact with me," Annie added to the story. "He knew I owned the property next to the senior center, and the building down by the main street. Then he found out that I owned the senior community center too, and he wasn't happy when I had no desire to sell any of it."

"No, and Colton was not happy at all," Dan said. "Trendle left town immediately and Colton was without a buyer to sell the property. He tried to follow Trendle to Portland, but ended up coming back when Trendle told Colton the deal was off."

Dan said that Colton told him that he had heard of the gold ingot while staying at the senior apartments posing as Todd Bankford. He was hoping the seniors would find the gold and he would just leave with that. He didn't care what happened to the seniors at that point.

"But he wasn't expecting me to show up on his doorstep before Annie and the seniors made their way to turn over the gold ingot," Dan said. "I had done some extensive investigation into Todd Bankford and his cell mate who by chance absconded from parole and left the state a few months ago. After getting photos and fingerprints, I asked the crime lab to compare Barber's fingerprints to the can of polish I placed into evidence. Unfortunately, the crime lab did not get back to me in time, but I still have the report coming."

Dan said that when he questioned the man purporting to be Todd Bankford, Dan showed him Todd Bankford's death certificate and photo. Although Todd and Colton were very similar in appearance, Todd had a scar above his left eye. Colton did not have that scar. Dan said he arrested Colton and interviewed him later on Friday.

"So, now we are here," Annie said. "The seniors have their homes back."

"And they can pay off Felix's debt on the apartments with the money from the gold ingot," Lizzy said. "I have a meeting with the Silver Sleuths on Monday."

"I understand Millie is selling her house and the Silver Sleuths will be moving to the apartments," Dan said happily.

"From the text I received from Jacquie," Annie said, looking at her cell phone to see if she received any further texts from her, "Jacquie and John will be making an offer on the house across the street and next door to you and Lizzy."

"I will welcome them with open arms," Dan said jokingly. Lizzy nudged Dan in the ribs.

The sounds of fire crackling filled the air as the group sat almost quiet for the next half hour. The air was slightly chilled, but the heat from the fire made it all worthwhile being outside at night.

Annie watched the bats flying about the yard catching insects in their path. She looked up and noticed the stars appearing in the patches of dark sky not occupied by clouds. The frogs could be heard in the distance. All was good at the moment.

"Oh, dear me," Stella exclaimed as she looked up to the house on the hill.

"Well, I think Dad is sending me a signal that he and mom want the house on the hill," Donald said.

Annie looked up and noticed in the floor to ceiling windows, sitting on a tall bar stool, looking out over the ocean with a big smile on his face...was Oscar.

Coming next...

THE CRAFTY ELVES

OF

CHRISTMAS

Die-Cut Mystery Series

Book 4

Thank you for reading MYSTERIOUS PAPERCUTS.

Also watch for:

There's a Chicken in My Bedroom

By Judith Dickenson Ackaret

And

Jerry Ackaret

Made in the USA
Columbia, SC
01 June 2021